PRAISE FOR B

"With *Bessie*, her third work of historical fiction, Linda Kass creatively melds deep research with the breath of life from her own rich imagination. Here is a deft and touching portrait of a shy, nerdy, nearly six-foot tall young girl—one Bessie Myerson—who rides the waves of her arresting beauty to become the first Jewish woman to win the Miss America title. Kass offers a careful understanding of what made this female pioneer in broadcasting, advocacy, and government tick, and how she navigated the lifetime of compromises and opportunities her stunning good looks afforded her in an antisemitic and misogynistic world."

—HELEN SCHULMAN, *New York Times* best-selling author of
Lucky Dogs and *This Beautiful Life*

"I loved Linda Kass's *Bessie*, which brought to vivid life the coming-of-age of the remarkable Bess Myerson, who may be known for being Miss America, but who truly was so much more: a brilliant young scholar, a musical prodigy, and a woman who stood tall against the antisemitism, sexism, and injustice of her era. Kass is a superbly talented writer, and in her hands, Bess Myerson becomes every woman, and the amazing story of her time becomes the story of our time, too. Brava!"

—LISA SCOTTOLINE, *New York Times* best-selling author
of *Loyalty* and *Eternal*

"Linda Kass imagines the early life of the five-foot-ten beauty from the Bronx who became the first—and so far only—Jewish woman to win the crown, a feat made all the more fascinating by the fact that her victory came just six days after the end of World War II, at a time when antisemitism was so rampant. . . . Kass gives a detailed look at Myerson's young adulthood, the runup to winning the coveted crown, and the aftermath, when, cutting short her Miss America tour, she decides to instead tour on behalf of the Anti-Defamation League to combat prejudice. *Bessie* is a tender, sensitive, and well-researched exploration of the inner life of a legendary beauty who was fighting personal battles the world never saw."

—KRISTIN HARMEL, *New York Times* best-selling author of
The Paris Daughter and *The Book of Lost Names*

"Coming into Bessie, I foolishly assumed I knew everything I needed to know about Bess Myerson. Boy, was I wrong. Linda Kass's deeply researched novel is a poignant origin story, a fascinating window into mid-century American life, and a compelling case for Bess Myerson as an authentic American heroine."

—Louis Bayard, *Washington Post* best-selling author of
Jackie & Me and *The Pale Blue Eye*

"Kass has written a detailed, fascinating profile of the early years of the former Miss America that explores the themes of prejudice, beauty, and self-worth. Insightful and eye-opening."

—Fiona Davis, *New York Times* best-selling author of *The Spectacular*
and *The Magnolia Palace*

"Abundant in graceful storytelling and vivid historical detail, *Bessie* is a fascinating portrait of a woman who was so much more than a beauty queen. Bess Myerson's persistence against antisemitism and her determination to use her fame to speak out against prejudice resonate strongly in our own challenging times."

—Jennifer Chiaverini, *New York Times* best-selling author
of *Canary Girls* and *Switchboard Soldiers*

"*Bessie* makes the first and only Jewish woman to become Miss America, Bess Myerson, come alive in a way her celebrity status never fully allowed. Linda Kass builds the character of Bessie through the complicated layers of all Bess Myerson carried with her—her dreams of being a composer, her longing to be loved by her joyless and demanding mother, the pain she felt over racial inequality, and everything she had to tolerate in order to find the platform for her voice, a voice she was determined to use to make a difference in the world. The true beauty of this novel is Linda Kass's artistry. She's created a loving and honest portrait of a woman who meant so much to so many."

—Lee Martin, author of the Pulitzer Prize Finalist, *The Bright Forever*

"Incredibly well-researched, *Bessie* is an engaging historical novel that examines the bigotry and biases experienced by Bess Myerson, the first Jewish woman to become Miss America—with parallels to the incessant prejudices present in our contemporary life. Inspiring and thought-provoking!"

—Patrick Losinski, CEO, Columbus Metropolitan Library

"Like all celebrities, Bess Myerson seemed to come from out of nowhere—a bright meteor suddenly streaking across the night sky. But in this evocative new book by Linda Kass, we learn the backstory of Myerson, the first Jewish woman to be crowned Miss America, whose looks and talent captivated the mid-20th-century world. *Bessie* reveals the passions that propelled her and the insecurities that haunted her. Along the way, it puts this complex woman where she belongs: back in the spotlight, with all eyes upon her."

—JULIA KELLER, Pulitzer Prize–winning journalist and author of *A Killing in the Hills*

"Readers are fortunate to have novelist Linda Kass bring forth the hidden stories of American women. Bess Myerson was the first Jewish woman to win the Miss America title, but she was so much more than a beauty queen. . . . Myerson was an inspiration for women in the post WWII years and her story needs to be remembered. *Bessie* deserves a crown."

—PAMELA KLINGER-HORN, Valley Booksellers

PAST PRAISE FOR THE AUTHOR FOR *A RITCHIE BOY*

Independent Publisher Book Awards 2021:
Gold Medal Winner—Historical Fiction

". . . [a] lovely novel in stories...Kass doesn't shy away from the horrors of exile, anti-Semitism, genocide, and war. But she also presents a strong case for stubbornly opposing that darkness with tolerance, decency, friendship, love, and hope."

—*HISTORICAL NOVELS REVIEW*

"Told as a series of interconnected stories, Linda Kass's captivating, based-in-truth novel *A Ritchie Boy* is about assimilation, hope, and perseverance."

—*FOREWORD REVIEWS*

"I devoured *A Ritchie Boy* over a single weekend. What a rich, beautiful book Linda Kass has written. I found such poignancy and delight in every facet of these characters' lives. This is first-rate historical fiction."
—ALEX GEORGE, national and international best-selling author of *A Good American* and *The Paris Hours*, owner of Skylark Books

"From Vienna during the *Anschluss* to booming post-war Columbus, Linda Kass has done her homework. Half historical novel, half family saga, *A Ritchie Boy* will charm readers who loved *All the Light We Cannot See*."
—STEWART O'NAN, author of *City of Secrets*

FOR *TASA'S SONG*

Independent Publisher Book Awards 2016:
Bronze Medal Winner—Historical Fiction

"Kass's novel is a moving tribute, inspired by her mother's survival of the Holocaust, to the endurance of family, faith, and culture set in eastern Poland during WWII, when both German and Russian forces ravaged the region . . . a memorable tale of unflinching courage in the face of war—and the power of love and beauty to flourish amid its horrors."
—*PUBLISHERS WEEKLY*

"Across decades and continents, Tasa follows a song of hope that is uplifting even in the face of great adversity, proving that an indomitable spirit can transcend the greatest hardships. Kass depicts a heartbreaking time with great sensitivity and detail in this beautifully rendered historical drama."
—*BOOKLIST*

"*Tasa's Song* is a beautiful ode to all of the light and darkness history has to offer her children. Linda Kass has written a lasting tribute to life during wartime, including the hardships and triumphs that define the true nature of grace and resilience."
—AMBER DERMONT, author of *The New York Times* best-seller, *The Starboard Sea*

". . . Kass's fictional story is compelling and emotionally satisfying for reasons other than the deep relieving trauma so often retold . . . Tasa does not ponder a world where the enemy walks past every window, hides in every shadow, a foe whose wintry breath has the power to ice the heart. Rather, *Tasa's Song* is a celebration of the fullness of the human spirit, of the ties of friendship and love, of duty and sacrifice, of trust and conscience, that bind us even when the world around us unravels."
—*The Apalachicola Times*

"Linda Kass's moving debut novel brings vividly to life a Jewish family's struggle to survive World War II in eastern Poland, caught between the Nazi threat to the west and the Soviets to the east. Tasa, a gifted violinist, comes of age in the shadow of encroaching war, finding redemption in her music and through deep love despite the horrors that steadily draw near. Meticulously researched, *Tasa's Song* illuminates the day-to-day experience of war—the uncertainty and dawning horror, the devastating losses and the small acts of grace."
—Margot Singer, author of *The Pale of Settlement*, winner of the 2007 Flannery O'Connor Award for Short Fiction

BESSIE

ALSO BY LINDA KASS

A Ritchie Boy
Tasa's Song

Bessie

A NOVEL

LINDA KASS

SHE WRITES PRESS

Published 2023
Printed in the United States of America
Print ISBN: 978-1-64742-540-1
Hardcover ISBN: 978-1-64742-595-1
E-ISBN: 978-1-64742-539-5
Library of Congress Control Number: 2023902901

She Writes Press is a division of SparkPoint Studio, LLC. For information, address:
She Writes Press, 1569 Solano Ave #546, Berkeley, CA 94707

Interior Design by Tabitha Lahr

To the inspiration of Bess Myerson,
a woman who used her beauty and talents to fight
for tolerance and social justice

Beauty awakens the soul to act.
—Dante Alighieri

WARNER THEATRE, ATLANTIC CITY

Saturday evening, September 8, 1945

B ess scans the darkened auditorium. Someone told her there would be three thousand people in the Warner Theatre tonight. A photographer's flashbulb lights up the hall, and she can now see that it's packed. She stands tall, takes in a deep breath to calm herself, and waits for the announcement. She and the other semifinalists named earlier in the evening have to do it all over again—the swimsuit, evening gown, talent—to advance to the final five. It's late, but her adrenaline keeps her alert, her heartbeat pounding in her ears. She hears emcee Bob Russell smooth-talking the audience. The muscles around her mouth ache from all the smiling.

What a week this has been. On Wednesday, when she played the Grieg concerto on the piano and Gershwin's "Summertime" on the flute in the talent competition, the burst of applause at the end of her performance filled her with irrepressible joy. *They like me! Maybe I have a chance.*

Bess thinks about all the times that she stood beside Arlene Anderson or had to follow her onstage. It was always "Miss Minnesota" with "Miss New York City" walking behind her. At first, Bess would slouch—anything to keep from towering over Arlene's petite frame and feeling awkward again, like she did in grade school and every year since she reached her adult height, just two inches shy of six feet.

Now, she is pretending, isn't she? There is confidence and control in each of her movements, yet she barely knows who she is anymore: masquerading across stages in swimsuits; competing against thirty-nine contenders representing cities and states for their true American allegiance. She wasn't brought up to be a beauty queen. "Practice!" "Homework!" How Mama had drilled into Bessie and her sisters the importance of education and achievement. Hadn't she entered the contest for the $5,000 scholarship? And for the extra sponsorship money to buy things for her family?

Bessie had—still has—ambitions: to be a solo pianist, maybe even a composer. She spies Sylvia's face in the crowd, then Helen's. She scours the seats around them knowing Papa stayed home with Mama, feeling a heaviness in her chest at their absence.

Suddenly, the desperate years of war flash through her mind without warning. The bombs dropped on Japan just weeks ago. All the charred bodies in the newspaper photographs. The Nazi death camps finally liberated. Six days since the war officially ended. Millions dead.

She watches as one of the nine judges, Conrad Thibault, reaches toward Russell and hands him an envelope containing the names of five finalists. Bess expects Russell to break out in song, given his reputation as *the* singing master of ceremonies. Instead, without hesitation, he begins to tear at the flap.

As if in a dream, she's watching from the outside. All around her, silence. Russell's lips are moving, but, over the sudden roar in her ears, she can't hear him.

CHAPTER ONE

OLIVE OYL

December 1936

B essie only has to look in the mirror to see that she is built like a tall, skinny boy, all gangly legs and arms. At twelve, she's already taller than all her classmates, even her teachers, at P.S. 95. As her plaid school skirts have risen up her thighs with no more hem to be let down, she worries about exposing her underpants. She wears shorts underneath, happy they also give her some hips. But she's sure she will always be thought of as ugly.

Today's disastrous school announcement only adds to that certainty. She's been assigned to play Olive Oyl, Popeye's homely string bean of a girlfriend, in the school's winter festival of fairy tales and comic-strip characters.

Bessie is mulling over all sorts of humiliations as she sits at the kitchen table eating dinner with her sisters. Smaller girls at school, like her best friend Ruthie Singer, get hugged by their teachers, while Bessie is asked to serve as room monitor or to fetch something from the school office. Sure, there are times when she likes being seen as responsible, as the student most capable—except when she just wants to be that little girl who's embraced. The taunts about her height are especially demeaning, although she pastes on a smile when mean-spirited kids call out, "Hey, Stretch, how's the air up there?" It doesn't help to know that her most beloved Gramma Besseleh, after whom she was named, is where her height came from. Bessie broods about all the days after school when she's stuck at home studying or practicing piano while her classmates are off to the movies or spending time gossiping among themselves. Mama insists on that. Yet, as much as Bessie often acts merely dutiful, like she's only trying to please her mother, she also feels something stirring inside when she completes an advanced worksheet on prime and composite numbers or masters the preludes and fugues in Bach's *The Well-Tempered Clavier*. She, in fact, savors a secret pleasure from these accomplishments.

Bessie looks over at Sylvia, already nineteen, who obviously never had to endure the same kind of embarrassments. Sylvia is a normal height and she's pretty and feminine, a swimmer who now earns money as a lifesaving instructor *and* sports a gorgeous tan. She actually tells hilarious stories. Best of all is how Sylvia treats Bessie when she's hurting.

Helen's asthmatic wheezing cuts the silence. At ten, Helen is delicate and slight, and her condition gives her skin a pallor. Bessie immediately feels less sorry for herself and silently pledges to be more attentive to her younger sister.

Mama stomps into the kitchen, tosses her wool duffle coat over the one empty chair, and drops some change on the table. "See that? It's what I earned today scrubbing the floor of Giorgio's Ristorante." She stares straight at Bessie. "If you don't go to college, if you don't turn out to be something, that's what's going to happen to you."

Bessie tries not to take Mama's harsh tone personally, although these pronouncements can make her feel wretched. She tells herself this is about Joseph, the brother she never knew—Joseph who died of whooping cough almost two years before Bessie was born, when Sylvia was five. He was just a toddler. Privately, Papa confided that Mama's sorrow over this loss never left her. Papa, always trying to affirm where Mama criticizes, added that Bessie's arrival had helped. He told Bessie she was such a pretty baby that her mother would tie a red ribbon around her full head of black curls to ward off the evil eye, an old Jewish superstition that warned of bad luck for anyone too rich, too successful, or too beautiful. Bessie can't imagine herself as beautiful, though she knows Papa meant well.

If she really were beautiful, she wouldn't have been picked to play someone as unsightly as Olive Oyl. The shorter girls have been assigned dainty roles like Bo Peep and Snow White. Bessie will loom above them, her hair pulled back tight and knotted in a bun on the top of her head, her only semi-acceptable feature essentially hidden. Bessie is positive that playing Olive Oyl will be her final downfall.

She decides to break her mother's rule of not talking while eating supper. "I don't want to be Olive Oyl," she declares. "That's the part they gave me for the festival."

Bella fixes her stern gaze at Bessie, furrowing her brow before answering. "What? A lead role? Why wouldn't you want that?" She dismissively waves her hand through the air. "This is acting, Bess. You can make believe you're someone else."

Bessie doesn't see it that way. She wouldn't have to pretend she was unattractive. And the other students will only taunt her more. But there is no way to argue with her mother or get any sympathy. Sylvia offers an affirming nod her way and squeezes Bessie's hand under the table.

After she takes her dishes to the sink, washes and dries them, and returns them to their proper cabinet shelf, Bessie crosses from the kitchen to the living room in just a few strides. Her father is sitting on the fold-out couch that doubles as her parents' bed so she and her sisters can share the only bedroom.

She snuggles against him, laying her head into the crook of his neck. He sets down the *Bronx Press-Review* and puts his arm around her shoulder. "Ah, Besseleh, how was your day today?"

"Terrible, Papa. Did you hear? I'm supposed to be Olive Oyl in the school play. Mama doesn't care that my teachers want me to wear some ugly black dress and a pair of oversized black shoes. She doesn't understand anything." Bessie begins to cry. "They're going to squash my hair into a bun!"

Papa kisses her forehead. "Your mother just wants you to do your best, Besseleh. She knows you're beautiful no matter what part they gave you . . . in whatever it is." He pats her gently as he returns to reading his newspaper.

Whenever she feels like weeping, Bessie turns to her father. Even when he comes home worn out from painting a house or fixing cabinetry—everyone calls Louis Myerson the best handyman around, a real "craftsman"—he always makes time for her, and she feels like his favorite. When she wants to escape her own reality, she asks about his childhood in Russia. He tells her about the local gangs who would get drunk and attack Jewish boys like him. Of his many stories, the one he recounts most often is about when he was a small child and another pogrom had swept through his village. Hiding under the floorboards, he says he could hear boots pound, dishes crash, his mother screaming, and the baby cousin buried beside him gasping for air. By the time the Cossacks left, little Louis Myerson had nearly suffocated, and his cousin was dead. Bessie holds back tears every time Papa shares this horror of his past. But he always adds that when he arrived in New York at the age of eighteen, he saw that Americans were different, less filled with hate.

Bessie would ask how her parents met, and her father would always say that he fell in love with her mother the first time he saw her toiling without complaint in a Lower East Side shirt factory. He'd describe a woman Bessie didn't know: a woman filled with laughter, who loved to flirt and dance; a vivacious, pretty, and affectionate woman. Emigrating with her own father from Odessa, Russia when she was only ten, Bella received very little formal education, which explains why she can only read English and Yiddish with difficulty. Bessie figures her mother's obsessive focus on education must stem from this limitation.

Her parents married in 1915, when Bella was twenty-three and Louis was twenty-six. Like many working-class Jews, they left their inner-city New York neighborhood just before the Depression hit. Her father says they were drawn to the trees, parks, and fresh air of the Bronx. They'd thought the multibuilding complex known as the Sholem Aleichem Cooperative Houses would be perfect for raising their family. He liked the uniformity, with identical four-story walkups surrounding a central courtyard with gardens. Her parents prefer the security of living among mostly Eastern European Jews, people like them. Papa says it reminds them of the close-knit shtetls where they were raised. Bessie knows from all the stories Papa has told her that Jews weren't accepted in many places. He says they found signs and flyers in many neighborhoods dictating "no Catholics, no Jews, no dogs."

●—●——●—●—●

It is the Sholem Aleichem community that Bessie now seeks for comfort. She puts on her wool coat and walks down the stairway, acknowledging the Dorfman sisters chatting on the second-floor landing. She continues down into the maze of cellars where the cooperative's performance auditorium is located, hoping to find a musical ensemble or drama group practicing for the upcoming neighborhood festival. As she nears, she hears voices inside and carefully opens the door, edging into one of the theater seats to watch the rehearsal of *Waiting for Lefty*. She applauds at the end of the scene where the cab drivers finalize their plan for a labor strike.

"Shalom, Bessie!" Malcolm Fried, a burly neighbor from her building, calls out from the stage. "What brings you here tonight?"

"Bored, I guess. Wanting some inspiration."

Malcolm, a butcher by day, motions his fellow actors to go on without him. "Ah, you've come to the right place. I'm at your service." He steps down from the stage to approach Bessie. "What's new, sweet *meydl*?"

"I was assigned a role in my school play."

"Mazel tov, Bessie!" Malcolm smiles as he locks eyes with her. "Why the glum *punim* then?"

"It's a character I don't like." Bessie pauses as she considers how much she wants to share. "I mean, someone I don't want to be. My mother thinks I'm being silly, that I just need to pretend to be someone else."

"She's not entirely wrong." Malcolm takes a seat next to her. "Acting is not about you onstage. It's about becoming invisible, inhabiting that character so only she can be seen."

"But I don't want this role. It's a stupid character." Bessie feels her cheeks redden, knowing how trite she must sound to Malcolm.

"Maybe you find some shtick, some trick to make this character more interesting or appealing to you." Malcolm closes his eyes and strokes his scruffy beard for a moment before he continues. "Actors are often asked to play roles we initially can't identify with. Look, I know how to schmooze with my customers, not how to be a taxi driver and deal with labor unrest, yes? But, as actors, we find a way. We try to learn something about our character." He stands and turns back to face her. "Maybe I expand the idea of schmoozing into how I need to relate to my fellow cabbies. Turn a friendly schmooze into a persuasive schmooze. You see?"

❦

The drama teacher, Mrs. Bloom, puts Bessie in men's laced black shoes and some grown-up's black crepe dress to accommodate her height. She presses Bessie's curly black hair tightly into a bun on the top of her head. In rehearsals, Bessie pretends she is wearing pretty clothes. She recalls her father telling her, "You don't need fancy dresses, Besseleh. You would look beautiful in a potato sack." When she feels like a clown while pretending to be Olive Oyl, she also pretends not to be humiliated by the role or the costume.

Bessie also goes to the school library to find out more about Olive, just as Malcolm suggested. First, she learns that Olive was a character before Popeye had been created for the comic series. Then she discovers that Olive and Popeye actually hated each other when they first met. Olive's first words to Popeye were: "Take your hooks offa me or I'll lay ya in a scupper." In the rehearsal scenes with Popeye, Bessie applies this to her character and fights bitterly—and her classmates think hilariously—until the place in the script where they begin to have feelings for each other.

"Cut; let's take a break here!" Mrs. Bloom places the script down on a nearby chair in the school's multipurpose room. "Bess, I'd like to have a word with you."

Bessie wonders if she's done something wrong as she steps off the stage and walks toward her teacher. Only Mama calls her by her more grown-up name.

"I'm quite taken with your performance, Bess. I hadn't thought of Olive in the way you're playing her."

"What do you mean, Mrs. Bloom?"

"Well, I only thought of Olive as foolish, short-tempered, demanding, and fickle. But, in your hands, she is also full of energy and enthusiasm. I like her better that way." Mrs. Bloom smiles up at Bess. Even at five feet five, she barely reaches Bessie's shoulders. "You're playing Olive Oyl as a tough broad with backbone. All I'm saying is that you may have a future in acting, Bess."

CHAPTER TWO

TAR BEACH

Early June 1937

essie crosses her favorite tree-lined street on her way home from P.S. 95. The branches are so full of leaves, they create a bright-green canopy above her, filtering the sun's rays against the pavement. Walking through Fort Independence Park, she counts the days—just four more—until school lets out for summer. As she nears her apartment building, she pauses to watch a young mother push a curly-haired toddler on the swing.

Bessie sees this park and the reservoir beside it from her bedroom window. She doesn't know what she'd do without that view, given how cramped it is with both her sisters sharing the closet-sized space with her. "No room for an apple to fall," Papa likes to say.

She thinks about the many times she found her mother staring out that window, unresponsive to Bessie, tears filling her eyes. Bessie now wonders if it is a scene like this that Mama observed: a mother lovingly tending to her toddler. Or happy children skipping in the park. Little boys competing at baseball and punch ball, their cherubic faces lighting up. The crack of bat to ball. The cheering. Bessie wonders if Mama thought, *It could've been my Yosseleh out there.*

Bessie still remembers the many days—she might've been six or seven—when she would return from this playground, her playsuit stained with dry mud. She'd prod her mother to fix her something to eat. Mama would tell her to find Papa, that he would get her a snack or lunch. But Bessie's father was usually out working. Bella Myerson would then turn her back to Bessie, her attention returning to what she saw out that window.

Pangs of remorse leave Bessie feeling hollow inside, as they have so often since then. Why isn't she able to comfort her mother, to please her? Practicing her piano. Completing all her homework. Getting high scores in school. All she wants is to make everything okay. To earn Mama's affection. *What about me?* she wonders day after day. *Joseph is dead, but I'm here.*

Bessie shakes off the emotions sweeping over her now as she climbs the steep hill along Sedgwick Avenue. When she gets to her building stairwell, she takes the steps two at a time—easy to do with her long legs. She passes the Stoff twins playing marbles on the concrete landing and gives them both a shoulder squeeze, looking forward to her time babysitting the girls this weekend and to the extra spending money she pockets to buy clothes— anything to avoid hand-me-downs. She smiles to herself recalling her father's explanation about why she didn't get an allowance like some of her peers: "We're not poor, Besseleh. It's just that we don't have money."

She breathes in the melodies seeping from inside neighboring apartments. This is one of the things Bessie loves about their community, where every floor of every building is full of musicians and artists. But, over the resounding piano chords and violin sonatas, Bessie can hear Mama's shrill voice and strident tone even before she reaches her third-floor apartment.

"You work and work. Home late, night after night. All the other painters earn more gelt while you get nice letters."

"Please, Bella, no more kvetching. I'm taking care of our family."

"Of course you are. Lending Yetta and Lena money that we don't have. When will your sisters pay us back?"

Bessie pushes the door open, intent on interrupting a quarrel her parents have often. "Mama, no screaming." She walks over to her mother and gives her a kiss.

The corners of Bella's mouth turn up a bit. "What are you doing home from school this early?" Bella is slicing an apple and adds it to a plate covered with cheeses, breads, and hard-boiled eggs.

Bessie picks up an apple slice and takes a bite before she answers, trying to hide her elation at the prospect of unstructured time. "Early dismissal. An all-staff meeting." She turns to her father. "Papa, I'm surprised to see you home."

Louis holds out his arms for Bessie to fold herself into. "I was working at Sam and Pearl Pochoda's house, off Giles Place. Letting that first coat of paint dry. Thought I'd have your mother fix me some lunch." He smiles sheepishly. "I guess she has other things on her mind."

Bessie finds it odd how her parents can have such mutual devotion, despite her mother's frequent complaints. She knows they love each other because she's also barged in on moments of affection between them. Hoping to distract her mother, Bessie pulls out her exam.

"What's this, Bess?" Mama asks.

"My final math test for the school year. A ninety-eight."

"What's ninety-eight? What happened to the other two points?"

"Mama, it's the highest grade in the class." Bessie knows that even her taskmaster of a mother would appreciate her daughter getting the top score. "Ruthie asked me to sun with her on Tar Beach this afternoon. I know Sylvia and Helen will want to join us."

"Why waste your time with that when you could practice or study?"

"I promise to practice the piano for two hours after dinner. And there's no homework assigned this week. I'm practically in high school!"

＊—＊—＊—＊—＊

It was after Bessie turned in her math final to Mr. Schirmer, after she observed her classmates at their desks nervously reviewing their answers, after one student and then another walked to the front to deposit their papers, that the teacher cleared his throat and announced that school would be dismissed early for an all-staff meeting. It was then that she looked over to the adjacent desk behind her to find Ruthie Singer's gleeful smile matching her own. Ruthie had held up her index finger toward the sky on this perfect June day. Bessie nodded and gave her a thumbs-up confirmation.

Now, she gazes at the cerulean sky above Tar Beach, how its openness gives Sholem Aleichem's building roof a touch of allure. It's just a black gravel surface, after all—nothing like the grit of sand between her toes or the long stretches of beach, the expanse of ocean, the rhythmic movement of waves she imagines. But Bessie sees the rooftop getaway as an escape from demanding parents, grueling schoolwork, and an insular life attending Yiddish *schules*. They all do.

"Did you bring an extra reflector?" Bessie asks Ruthie. She lays her towel on the asphalt between Ruth and Sylvia. Pulling a bottle of baby oil out of her bag, she slathers some over her arms and legs.

"I don't think you need a reflector with that grease, Bess. You'll get sunburned, and then Mama will throw one of her usual fits. Why don't you use the Bronze I brought? That'll protect you some."

Bessie inwardly smiles, appreciative of the affection underlying Sylvia's motherly concern. "I'm okay, Syl. I won't burn with my dark complexion. Anyway, my hands will now be free for reading through the stash Ruthie brought."

"Which do you want first?" Ruthie holds out *Vogue*, *Harper's Bazaar*, and *Collier's*. "Check out the tans and the two-piece suits. Hey, Sylvia, you can't wear those when you're on lifeguard duty, can you?"

"Our mother would never go for those. But yours wouldn't either, Ruth."

Bessie nods her agreement with Sylvia as she reaches for *Harper's Bazaar* and rifles through bathing suit ads. "Wow. Look at these beach scenes." She holds up the double spread of glamorous models lounging on the sand, some with parasols shielding them from the sun, others racing into the ocean against a long coastline backdrop.

She looks over at Helen who, at eleven, seems pleased to be hanging out with the older girls. Helen annoys her at times, causing Bessie to lose her temper, but Bessie is making an effort to include her younger sister more often, trying to be more solicitous.

"I know *I'll* burn. But Mama says the sun's heat and fresh air is good for my asthma." Helen dips her fingers in the Bronze jar and begins applying it to her face.

Bessie is tired of Mama's focus on Helen's condition and wants to change that subject. "Listen to these articles. Enough to turn your brain to mush." She scans the table of contents. "'Proper Technique for Achieving a Good Tan,' 'Fashionable Attire for Tanning,' 'It's Fashionable to Be Brown in a Light Evening Gown.' And for some caution, 'Dangers of Too Much Sunshine.'"

"Why don't you read them, Bessie, and just give us the take-away?" Ruthie stretches her arms above her head, then flips onto her stomach. "Helen, can you put some Bronze on my back?"

Bessie pauses to watch Helen rub the salve on Ruthie's shoulders before she answers. She loves how Ruthie treats Helen like a sister. "Tans are the rage of the moment, according to *Vogue*. One article talks about the fashion, makeup, and accessories to show off tanned skin. Geez, can you hear Mama screaming at us if we wore makeup? You don't count, Syl; you're already an adult."

"As long as I remain under her roof, she treats me as if I'm Helen," Sylvia says. "No offense, Helen."

Closing the jar of suntan lotion, Helen raises her head quizzically.

Bessie lays back on her towel and shuts her eyes. She thinks about the three of them, their bond, all affected in different ways by Mama's ire and gloom, all a result of the loss of the brother Bessie never knew, as Papa repeatedly shares with her. *Yosseleh.* The ghost who continues to cast a pall over their young lives. Sylvia probably took the brunt of their mother's despair. Bessie is the one Mama expects so much from. Poor Helen was the last attempt to fill a hole of sorrow. Bessie is thankful Ruthie is around so often, the unofficial fourth sister, as a buffer against too much talk about this shared family tragedy.

She pushes away these uncomfortable musings and pictures herself at a real beach, like Orchard Beach, just a dozen miles to the east. She read how they're fixing it up through the WPA, sand-filling and landscaping. She conjures up all the other places they might visit if they could afford to, maybe the south shore of Long Island. Or Coney Island, where she heard about game stands, roller coasters, and restaurants. But here they are on Tar Beach, the neighbors' laundry hanging on a clothesline stretched across the roof, enclosing them atop several buildings where everyone knows one another. It's the only home Bessie remembers, but she knows they haven't always lived at Sholem Aleichem.

"What was it like with Mama and Papa before they moved here, Syl? Were you living in Harlem?"

Helen turns her face from the sun's glare, suddenly all ears.

"I only remember the apartment on Prospect Avenue in South Bronx. I was ten, you were three, and Helen was just one when we came here. The park and Jerome Reservoir were a major appeal, and Mama seemed a little more . . . contented, I think. For the first few years, anyway."

"Until people started losing their jobs and getting evicted." Bessie could still hear the crying children around the courtyard entrance trying to get their parents' attention, but the parents were in a state of shock. "Ruthie and I'd be walking home from school, and the contents from someone's apartment would be on the sidewalk."

Ruthie raises her head and pushes a lock of hair out of her face. "Remember how scared we were, Bessie?"

"Yeah. Our first thought was that our belongings were out there." Bessie tosses the magazine toward her feet, tired of the shallow messages inside. She wipes her oily hands and carefully pulls out a book she took out from the school library, *National Velvet* by Enid Bagnold. She identifies with fourteen-year-old Velvet Brown, growing up in the late 1920s in a small English coastal village, dreaming of one day owning many horses. She has a horse named Piebald. A high-strung, shy, nervous child, Velvet manages to train and ride him to victory in the Grand National Steeplechase. Just an ordinary family, yet Velvet clearly is a person to whom great things happen.

As dusk nears, the girls pack up their things. To save time getting home, they cross the rooftops that connect the buildings at Sholem Aleichem. Bessie and her sisters hug Ruth when they reach her section and continue to theirs. Bessie wonders if tonight they might light the *Shabbos* candles, maybe say a blessing over challah . . . or not. She's always aware that everyone who lives at Sholem Aleichem is Jewish, but it has less to do with religious traditions and is more about so much else: an overriding belief in education; a love of Yiddishkeit, the language of Yiddish and the wit and wisdom of its literature; a dedication to culture and the arts; a social conscience. Bessie breathes this air, yet at the same time within her resides a fierce desire, an expectation of reaching beyond this sanctuary.

The door to their apartment is ajar, and she catches the savory whiff of brisket, which must have been cooking much of the afternoon, mixed with the smell of apricots in a sweet noodle kugel, the only two dishes her mother manages to capably prepare. After the girls clean up for dinner, the family crowds around the kitchen table. Usually, it's Mama serving Bessie and her sisters early so they can get to their homework and practice, Papa getting home late from work and eating by himself. But tonight, it's like a *Shabbos* dinner with all five of them, absent the rituals.

———————

After Bessie helps clean up, she walks to the living room, pulls out the piano stool, and sits down to practice. She would have done it anyway, as she promised. But while the last bite of kugel was still in her mouth, Mama couldn't help herself and reminded her.

Bessie scans the eighty-eight keys, black and white, all of which had been so intimidating at first as she had to learn what all the notes are called. It seemed overwhelming until she realized there were only twelve keys that mattered, and those twelve-note patterns repeated themselves across the entire keyboard. If she learned the twelve—those seven white keys and five black keys— she would know all eighty-eight. She liked that about the piano.

She begins with scales, getting her fingers warmed up, admiring the simplicity of the instrument's alphabet, the notes that are in all music, starting with C, then D, E, F, G, A, B. Her favorite classical songs remind her of the beauty and diversity of the music. She begins with the gentle, flowing melody of "Für Elise" by Beethoven, with its repeating pattern. Running through this piece until she plays it perfectly, she moves to the detached staccato notes of Minuet in G Major by Bach. Its more challenging finger movements require her intense focus. She plays one hand, then the other, each hand independent of the other, before she plays the piece in its entirety. It takes longer to perfect, and she finds herself slowing the pace to get it right.

She becomes fidgety and decides to walk to the kitchen. She finds some sliced apple on a plate and bites into it, savoring its tart flavor. She checks the wood clock on the living room dresser, its Roman numeral gold letters set around the cream enamel. Seven thirty. She's only played for half an hour. Mama won't be pleased if she finds her idle, and the current silence will trigger a frequent command: "Practice!"

Sitting back on the stool, she begins fussing with the height, which feels low; she adjusts it several times before she gets comfortable. She finds the sheet music for "Gymnopédie no. 1" by Eric Satie, a slow, dreamy song. She adores this piece because she can bring her own emotions to it, add a dramatic interpretation depending on where the music takes her. It's this emotional journey that keeps her playing, not Mama's nagging.

⋅—⋅—⋅—⋅—⋅

The next evening, Bessie climbs back to the rooftops to get to her Aunt Fanny and Uncle Samuel's apartment. Bessie's entire extended family lives among the more than two hundred dwellings that fill the fifteen-building complex, where tenderness and affection abound. There's Mama's other sister, Aunt Ethyl, and her two brothers, Uncle Pete and Uncle Jack. Papa's four siblings also live here: Aunt Yetta, Aunt Lena, Uncle Sam, and Uncle Alter. But Aunt Fanny's is the central gathering place on Saturday nights for tea and sweets, card games and kibitz.

Bessie's uncles are trade unionists, members of the Workmen's Circle. Papa explained to her that the WC promotes social and economic justice. She understands the politics of Sholem Aleichem because it's simple. A small group of people are the so-called Communists, known as *der Linke*, the Left. They read the *Daily Worker* and often belong to the International Workers Order. All of Bessie's extended family, and most of the families at Sholem Aleichem, are *der Rechte*, the Right, since they're socialists. Papa insists the cooperative's communists aren't true Communists; they're only slightly left of the socialists.

Bessie knocks gently on Aunt Fanny's door, then pushes it

open. The foyer connects to a cozy parlor on one side and the living room on the other. The kitchen comes off the parlor, the dining room off the living room, and the private quarters are in the back. It is easily twice as large as Bessie's apartment.

Uncle Samuel leans over the card table in the parlor, shuffling several decks as Uncle Pete and Uncle Jack watch. "Shalom, Bessie! We're waiting for your papa to be our fourth."

Aunt Fanny appears with a plate of raspberry rugelach and smiles at Bessie. "Will your parents be joining us?"

Bessie shrugs. "I'm not sure." She's not interested in sharing that her father is still out working and that her mother is in one of her moods.

"Harold's in the living room," says Aunt Fanny. "I know he'd love you to accompany his arias on the piano."

Aunt Ethyl enters the parlor with a pot of tea and several cups on a tray that she lowers onto a sideboard. "We'd all love to hear some music tonight!"

The talk among the men is about what they read that morning in the *Jewish Daily Forward*, and the conversation, as it does so often, turns to justice for workers. The familiar banter over socialism versus communism begins anew, then between fascism and communism and the war in Spain, with Uncle Jack suggesting Spain's class struggle could lead the world into another war. Bessie considers how to politely leave the room as Uncle Pete changes the subject to the Yankees' winning streak and whether the renovation of Yankee Stadium would increase Joltin' Joe's home runs or lower Lefty Gomez's ERAs.

Over the chatter, Bessie hears Harold begin his vocal-range warm-up in the next room, his voice deep and rich. She grabs a rugelach on her way out of the parlor, lifting the buttery pastry to her mouth, relishing the burst of raspberry flavor and chewiness of the chopped walnut.

"Boy, your mother really got all the baking talent in the family, Hal," she says to Harold while sitting down at the Baldwin upright, spreading her fingers apart, and rotating her wrists. As she plays a few scales, she asks, "So, what are you singing tonight?"

"Can you play 'Deh! Vieni alla finestra' from *Don Giovanni*?"

"With the sheet music in front of me I can."

Bessie adores the sprightly piano accompaniment to Mozart's greatest operatic composition. By the time she plays the first sequence of notes, her aunts and uncles are standing in the back of the living room. Harold's vibrant baritone and antics transform him into Giovanni serenading a beautiful maid. When he finishes to applause and cries of "Bravo!" he bends down to Bessie, asks her to play from Mozart's *Die Zauberflöte:* "Der Vogelfänger bin ich ja." Now he portrays the lonely bird catcher Papageno, who wants to find a wife—or at least a girlfriend. Bessie observes how easily Hal inhabits the characters in the arias he sings, something she had to learn the hard way playing Olive Oyl last winter. There's something so carefree about him and about how Bessie feels at Aunt Fanny's. Sure, she enjoys her role as piano accompanist and appreciates how much she's learned about the tragedies and comedies in all these operas. But here she is at ease. Here, she feels a sense of pride at her growing talent.

She thinks back to when she was nine and Mama managed to install a battered secondhand baby grand piano in their tiny apartment. The instrument had to be hoisted up three flights and wheeled into their crowded living room. All the tumult! Frugal Mama willing to spend the little money they'd saved for this treasure. Papa doing whatever Mama wanted. He even found old carpet samples from different jobs and stitched them together with an enormous needle, transforming it into the patchwork rug where the piano now sits so the downstairs neighbors wouldn't complain of the constant sound of her practicing.

That was when Bessie's life began to revolve around music. And, just two years later, she started lessons with Mrs. Dorothea LaFollette, the nurturing mentor who ever since has been teaching Bessie that musical expression can be her friend and companion.

CHAPTER THREE

ESCAPE THROUGH MUSIC

July 1937

I t feels like a long time ago, although just two years have passed, since Bessie first made the pilgrimage to Dorothea LaFollette's apartment overlooking Central Park. Back then, Mama accompanied Bessie on the forty-minute subway ride from their Bronx enclave. Sometimes Helen came along since she studied violin with Mrs. LaFollette's husband, Chester.

Bessie still recalls her exhilaration at the cacophony of urban noises and flurry of people that greeted her as she emerged from the station at West Eighty-Sixth Street and Broadway. Her body trembled, as if chilled, goosebumps tingling the hair on her arms even though it was a hot July day like this one. Their brisk walk covered two short city blocks south and one avenue east to Mrs. LaFollette's imposing building, passing many such grand structures in limestone and brick, adorned with sculpted figures that might befit palaces.

That heady anticipation fills Bessie today as she lifts the ring of the brass door knocker. Mrs. LaFollette greets Bessie with her usual affirming smile, and instantly Bessie feels her muscles loosen. As she follows Mrs. LaFollette's graceful strides across the marble front hall and up the spiral staircase, she notices her teacher's honey-colored hair is wrapped around her head, adding to her statuesque appearance. Then, upon entering the magnificent salon, Bessie's eyes land on the two Steinway baby grand pianos, and her stomach flutters in eagerness, just as it does for every lesson.

"I'm going to take care of a few things in the kitchen while you warm up." Mrs. LaFollette waits for Bessie to get comfortable. She lingers as Bessie settles in and pulls the bench closer to the keyboard. Then she nods for Bessie to start and turns and walks out of the room, the sound of her heels fading with each step.

Bessie pauses long enough to consider how far she's advanced with Mrs. LaFollette, who replaced Bessie's first music teacher, the one she started with when she was nine. Mama had to march Bessie across the rooftop of their cooperative complex to the section where the teacher lived, wait for her to be finished, then hurry her back across the rooftop to their little flat, with five people squeezed into a living room, kitchen, and single bedroom. Now, thirteen-year-old Bessie sits amid a room with an ornate fireplace, plush draperies, fresh flowers, and graceful antiques, and she can't wait to begin making music. She inhales deeply, a calming satisfied breath. She bends her neck from one shoulder to the other, places her hands on the black and white keys, and starts off with the Hanon exercises—the movements she repeats daily to strengthen her hands and fingers. Mrs. LaFollette gave her Charles Louis Hanon's *The Virtuoso Pianist* at that unforgettable first lesson.

It was also Mrs. LaFollette who suggested that Bessie apply to the High School of Music and Art, opened just a year ago near City College in Manhattan. Bessie's mother was skeptical. "She thinks *you* can get in? What a schlep it would be to that school!" Bessie's elementary school principal at P.S. 95 was more encouraging, sending in grades from all her school subjects by the early June deadline. Under Mrs. LaFollette's guidance, Bessie perfected the standard piano pieces she'd be asked to play for the performance exam: Beethoven's "Für Elise" and Bach's Minuet in D Minor, the alla turca movement of Mozart's Piano Sonata no. 11, Chopin's Prelude in C Minor and *Military Polonaise*. And they'd practiced everything she'd be tested on, from sight-reading to her knowledge of musical symbols and terminology.

As Bessie reflexively runs through her exercises, Mama's constant command, "Practice!" bellows in her mind. Mama has been so determined that all three sisters should become musicians—music teachers who could earn their own living, she repeatedly told them. "Don't count on being supported by a husband. He could lose his job, and where would that leave you?" Sylvia, being the oldest, began piano at nine when Bessie was only two, so that same drilling and nagging was inflicted first on Sylvia, later on Bessie, and then on Helen, with Mama insisting they practice for hours every single day. Bessie knew that Sylvia couldn't hear the tune on the piano like she did, couldn't appreciate the harmonies. For Sylvia, it was work; when she recently turned twenty and began studying to be a speech therapist, Mama finally moved her full attention to Bessie and Helen.

Bessie knows how Mama has sacrificed to be able to pay for all these lessons—how Mama wants them to succeed, to get out of their insular ghetto. And that ambition dominates her mother's relationship with all of them. To her, music is like food, Bessie thinks. A necessary and integral sustenance for their well-being.

She switches to playing scales, changing up the routine by experimenting with different rhythms. Mrs. LaFollette returns and sits at the adjacent piano. Her milky pink-and-white complexion gives her an exquisite beauty, a bit like the Swedish actress Greta Garbo. Bessie suddenly regrets all the tanning she's been doing on Tar Beach and becomes especially aware of her teacher's watchful eyes, her perfect posture. How composed and controlled she is. Her steady, unflustered manner and inner calm. There is no doubt about it. Dorothea LaFollette is the person Bessie wants to be when she grows up.

Mrs. LaFollette suggests Bessie take out Mozart's Concerto no. 23 in A Major. "I'd like this to be your piece for next month's recital, Bess." She shares that Mozart finished his concerto just two months prior to the premiere of *The Marriage of Figaro*. "There are three movements we need to perfect, but today let's work on the second adagio, the only movement by Mozart in F-sharp minor."

Bessie loves learning about the pieces, the scholarly part of being a striving musician. And then there's the expressive part. As she begins to play the notes, her rhythm is lilting, resembling a slow jig. She plays it softly as it is marked, accentuating its deep and painful expression of longing, a hunger she feels within her own being. For affection. For acceptance. To feel happy. To belong to something. To achieve. She pours all of this into the second movement.

"This is excellent sight-reading, Bess! You're not just playing the notes; you're feeling the notes. *I* can feel them." Mrs. LaFollette's eyes are gleaming. "Your playing has been advancing to an entirely new level these last few months. I'm proud of you.

"I'm proud of you." How many times has Bessie wanted Mama to say those words to her? But, instead, from her there is only constant criticism. Mama would stand in the kitchen while Bessie practiced and, at regular intervals, she'd shout "Wrong!" even if Bessie played the piece flawlessly. Her mother knows little about music; Bessie sees that as a liability in the LaFollette studio, where the other children are from wealthier families with parents who are much more learned than Bella Myerson. It is another reason for Bessie to feel insecure and self-conscious, yet her piano teacher's supportive manner soothes her like a healing

balm. Bessie beams at Mrs. LaFollette, soaking up the praise as if parched.

After playing several more sequences of this somber second movement, Bessie absorbs its pathos, releasing the weight of guilt and inadequacy that she carries with her. The playing feels cathartic. Mrs. LaFollette suggests they spend some time practicing her approach to the piano as if it were an actual recital—by entering the room, acknowledging the audience, then settling on the bench before beginning the composition. Bessie pushes herself away from the keyboard and positions herself at the living room entrance. When her teacher gives her the cue, she saunters back over, her steps echoing across the parquet floor. She's ill at ease somehow, feeling inhibited, slouching as she often does because of her height.

"It's not the altitude, Bess; it's the attitude. You must stand tall when you're walking to the piano." At that, Mrs. LaFollette rises from the bench, and Bessie finds herself directly eye-to-eye with her teacher. "Pretend that God is watching you from above the ceiling over the stage, and he is reaching down through the ceiling and straightening your back by pulling the hair on the crown of your head straight up."

Bessie giggles. "That's quite an image, Mrs. LaFollette."

"It's the composure you need to project to your audience, and to the world. You are impressive, Bess. You need to accept the gifts you have. Appreciate your talent."

Bessie feels a flush creeping over her face. She's not practiced in responding to compliments and not used to someone speaking so forthrightly, especially someone she idealizes like Dorothea LaFollette.

"You have mastered enough repertoire that I want you to give a solo recital at my next Steinway Hall concert program."

Bessie is dumbstruck. Mrs. LaFollette invites only her top students to perform at Steinway Hall. She can't imagine playing alongside that level of talent, having just become comfortable with the monthly recitals here at the studio. And what on earth would she wear? She wants a pretty new dress for such an occasion, but there is no money for that.

As if reading her mind, Dorothea adds, "And, Bess, you must wear that red dress you have. It's exquisite on you."

The wine-colored print, with its dirndl skirt and puckered smocking across the midriff, is the only nice outfit Bess possesses. "Are you sure? I've already worn it to three recitals."

"No matter. In that dress, you're radiant."

⚬——⚬——⚬

As the lesson ends, the ticking of the mahogany grandfather clock gets Bessie's attention. Mrs. LaFollette catches her glancing at the regal timepiece. "Are you hungry?"

Bessie nods, curious as to why Mrs. LaFollette asked. Her teacher walks to the telephone and dials what Bessie realizes must be the Myerson apartment. "Bella? Dorothea . . . Yes, we had a very productive lesson today. I wondered if Bess could stay for dinner. We could review important takeaways from today's session since Chester is out tonight." Another pause. "Wonderful. I'll send her on her way while it's still light outside."

Bessie can't believe her ears. "That's so kind of you to have me for dinner, Mrs. LaFollette."

"It's about time we got to spend some informal time together, don't you think?"

As she follows her teacher to the kitchen, Bessie tries to hold herself straight, her shoulders back. Just that stance gives her a dose of confidence. "Can I help you prepare anything?"

"How about if you chop some tomatoes, carrots, and radishes for a salad? I'll wash a head of lettuce." Mrs. LaFollette pulls on an apron over her dress and opens the Frigidaire. "I have a chicken, noodle, and vegetable casserole that I just need to heat on the stove, unless you'd like that Kraft Macaroni and Cheese everyone says is wonderful. I bought a box to try."

"Whatever you're having is fine." Bessie regards the capacious kitchen. A butler's pantry. A lengthy preparation surface. Appliances positioned so two people don't collide if one is at the sink and the other is cooking at the stove. It is easily five times the size of the kitchen in her apartment, and the ceiling height makes it seem even grander.

They eat in the dining room, the table large enough to seat a party of twelve. Bessie sits adjacent to Mrs. LaFollette, quick to put her napkin on her lap as she waits for her teacher to start eating before she helps herself. For a second, the image of her first music teacher pops into her mind, a dour and didactic woman who would trim Bessie's nails at the start of each lesson.

"I've told your mother I'm pleased with your progress, Bess. I know she is proud of you and how hard you work."

"You think so?" Bessie remembers what her father told her, that in the Russia of her mother's childhood, Jews were barred from attending universities, but they could leave their shtetls to study at the great music conservatories of Moscow. Scholarship is what matters to Bella Myerson, Papa said, even though she wasn't educated herself. "My mother sometimes acts like I don't practice enough. If I am with my friends, she waits for me at the door and . . . well, she demands that I sit at that piano bench right then and there. She makes sure I understand there's nothing more important."

Mrs. LaFollette listens intently, her blue eyes wide as she nods empathetically. Not for the first time, Bessie feels a bond with her teacher, someone she can talk to like a friend. "You may not like her taking you to task, Bess, but you will thank your mother later for her steady hand and for the discipline she's teaching you."

Bessie takes another bite of the noodle casserole, chewing slowly while reflecting on those days leading up to recitals, how Mama shared in the high level of tension, especially when Sylvia was still playing. Their mother always tried to help them. The

three girls struggled to memorize their pieces because the LaFol-
lettes didn't allow their students to use musical scores. Mama
would get all stirred up, then send the three of them outside and
order them to take a brisk walk, just to unwind. She'd tell them,
"It's good for you. Walk fast, and don't forget to breathe."

"My mother has a different way of teaching me than you do."
Bessie wipes her mouth with the napkin, grinning with a vivid
memory. "On the day of our recitals, Papa has our old Chrysler
sedan ready. You know how we always arrive with several guests?"

Mrs. LaFollette nods, smiling.

"Well, we crisscross the Bronx to pick up some woman
Mama's bragged about us to. My friend, Ruthie, joins us, squeezing
into the back seat with Helen and me. Sylvia's in front with Mama."

Bessie explains how she visualizes her lap as a piano keyboard,
how Helen silently fingers the strings on the violin that rests across
her thighs. How Bessie always feels a tightness in her chest during
these drives, this pressure to do well mixed with a terror of being
late as Papa shouts at Mama for taking them out of their way. "And
as if that weren't enough, Mama's friend is full-bodied, cramming
into the back seat and nearly breaking Helen's violin."

Mrs. LaFollette's eyes twinkle, her smile so wide that Bessie
sees her perfectly straight teeth for the first time. "And isn't the
distress you endure worth it, Bessie?"

Of course it is. When they finally arrive at the LaFollette
apartment, a uniformed maid answers the door, takes everyone to the salon, and makes sure they are seated comfortably.
Bessie recalls how the fragrant aroma of red roses permeates
the room, how the chandeliers shimmer as the afternoon sun
streams through the windows. If Bessie plays a piano concerto,
Mrs. LaFollette takes the role of the orchestral accompaniment
on the other Steinway. Bessie's mother always turns her head to
hear any compliments. Bessie looks over at Mama at the end of
her performances and sees that the applause makes her mother
happy. At these moments, Bessie feels valued.

Recalling all this as she finishes dinner, Bessie realizes she, too, takes pleasure in the accolades and recognition. Under Mrs. LaFollette's tutelage, she now dreams about great things for her future, just like Velvet Brown. But instead of riding a horse to victory, Bessie contemplates being a composer. Or a conductor. Especially after last week's golden opportunity.

"I almost forgot to tell you, Mrs. LaFollette." Bessie begins to blush slightly and takes a gulp of water. "I completed the seven-day testing and audition for the arts high school. Their feedback was very . . . encouraging. But my stomach is in knots now. There are so many applicants."

"Oh, Bess. I feel confident you'll be accepted."

"My mother doesn't think so. She doesn't think I'm ready for that level of rigor."

Mrs. LaFollette purses her lips. She pushes away from the table and takes her plate and Bessie's to the kitchen. "Which piece did they ask you to play?"

Bessie gathers the glasses and follows. "They gave me a choice, so I played the *Military Polonaise*. I felt like playing something a bit dramatic, you know?"

"Good choice. And what kinds of questions did they ask?"

"Some of the ones you predicted. What concerts I've heard lately, what music records or broadcasts I've listened to, how long I've taken lessons. Why I'm applying to the school. They asked about various composers and they had me sight-read some newer compositions."

"I keep reading how the school has been Mayor LaGuardia's pride and joy. Without his devotion to music and the arts, it would never have happened. It will be his legacy, as it should." Her teacher takes in a deep breath. "When will you find out, Bess?"

"As early as next week. School starts right after Labor Day."

CHAPTER FOUR

A SPECIAL HIGH SCHOOL

September 1937 – May 1938

The morning is clear and cool for early September as Bessie walks past Jerome Reservoir along the shady streets and quiet houses of Sedgwick Avenue. She soon picks up her pace to catch the train that will take her to Harlem for her first day of high school. She clutches her five-cent fare, with the rest of her weekend babysitting earnings—two dimes—safely tucked in her pocket.

Students with book bags and commuters with lunch pails dot the passenger car when Bessie enters the train, the babble of voices blurring into a hum. She sinks into an open seat facing the aisle, closes her eyes, and concentrates on the train's vibration. She relaxes, enjoying this time to herself after the whirlwind events of the last month. First, her acceptance from the school selection committee, indicating flawless scores on her exams and the highest accolades about her performance. Then an unprecedented celebration held in her honor at Sholem Aleichem with family and neighbors, even her mother acknowledging Bessie's hard work and musical talent. Finally, a personal letter from Principal Benjamin Steigman congratulating her on her admission. He specifically noted that she rose to the top of the nearly two thousand applicants, half of them music students. She pinches herself to make sure all of this is actually happening to her.

Bessie exits at 137th and Broadway. A couple of girls wearing knapsacks bound up the stairs ahead of her. Apartment buildings, brownstones, and row houses line the leafy street. As Bessie walks several blocks toward 135th Street and Convent Avenue, she passes a Russian Orthodox church, a bakery, and a delicatessen before noticing a slight, dark-haired boy about her age across the street, ambling in the same direction. As they intersect at the next corner, she's not surprised to find herself nearly a foot taller than he is. An unexpected light rain begins to fall, and she instinctively raises her book bag above her head, expecting her hair to frizz as it always does from moisture, wishing she'd worn pigtails.

The boy gazes up at her.

Bessie smiles shyly and lowers her book bag. "Are you headed to the High School of Music and Art?"

"Yeah. I won a cartooning contest and got a scholarship." The boy pauses as if considering his next comment. "I'm just thirteen, but I skipped a grade."

"I'm thirteen too." Bessie catches his look of surprise. "I know. I'm tall for my age."

The boy nods, a reaction she gratefully interprets as matter-of-fact. "What'd you get in for?"

"I'm a music major. I play the piano." The two are now standing side by side, craning their necks to get a good look at the massive five-story building of limestone and mottled-brown brick in front of them. "I was so overwhelmed coming here for the exams that I counted all these steps."

The boy starts climbing. "And?"

"There's 137!" Bessie restrains herself from taking two steps at a time. "Jeez, it does look like an ancient castle, doesn't it? By the way, I'm Bessie Myerson."

"Harvey Katz." He begins wheezing as they get to the third landing, and she wonders if he's asthmatic like Helen. "What borough'd you come from?" he asks.

"The Bronx. You?"

"Same."

As they approach the top of the hill, Bessie counts off the seven stories for the double Gothic towers and notices they're adorned with quirky-looking gargoyles, almost in the shape of creatures bearing shields.

"I'm not far from the Zoo," Harvey says. "On Clinton Avenue. Took me an hour to get here."

Bessie turns around when they reach the final landing. "Look how this building stands over all the treetops."

"That's St. Nicholas Park. It's huge—someone told me twenty acres." Harvey pulls open the entrance door, and Bessie slips inside. "Did you know that part of this building is still a high school for girls?"

"I suppose they need to fill all this space." Bessie scans the entrance hall. She feels the same astonishment now as when she first saw the bronze bust of Toscanini during her exams.

Dozens of students carrying book bags scurry around the lobby. Bessie's heart begins beating fast, and she hopes Harvey can't tell how she's panicking. But when she glances down at him, he looks as nervous as she feels. "Well, um, I guess we need to check in." She pulls the straps of her shoulder bag tighter.

"Yeah, sure. See you around, Bessie."

◆ — ◆ — ◆

Once Harvey leaves and students continue to file into the lobby, Bessie stands motionless, taking in the grandness of it all. The long and wide halls and high ceilings make her feel small. The waxed linoleum floors sparkle under the natural light coming through all the large bay windows. Not wanting to be late, she follows the flow of students and quickly finds her designated homeroom, whose door, like each classroom's, is oak with frosted glass panels. She takes a seat among about twenty classmates. When everyone is settled, a teacher introduces himself as Mr. Pincus and outlines the school schedule: heavy in music theory and orchestra, but including all the basic courses—classic literature, civics, world history, biology, and algebra.

Next, Bessie finds herself among thirty freshmen in orchestra class, each seated in front of an empty music stand in the gymnasium. Large arch-shaped windows on two sides stream in the light. Bessie recognizes the teacher as one of the examiners who observed entrance auditions, a petite, middle-aged woman who introduces herself as Mrs. Siegal.

"I'm a violinist and play in a local chamber orchestra when I'm not teaching." She surveys the faces in front of her, nodding in recognition to some. "Because it's essential to understand all parts of any ensemble, music majors at M&A are expected to play a second instrument." Amid some chatter, Mrs. Siegal weaves her way around the metal stands, taking student attendance and making individual assignments. Bessie overhears the teacher assign the tympani to a boy in the row behind her and then the trumpet to the girl next to him, although the girl insists the instrument might ruin her lips. Mrs. Siegal kindly responds that she's never met a trumpet player whose lips were disfigured, male or female.

As she steps in front of where Bessie is seated, Mrs. Siegal smiles broadly. "You're Bess Myerson, aren't you?"

Bessie nods.

"I so enjoyed your rendition of Chopin's *Military Polonaise*. Bess, I'd like you to play the double bass as your second instrument."

At first Bessie tries not to reveal her uneasiness at this request. She knows it's about her height but resents the implication. She feels a flush creep into her face and neck.

"Bess, is something wrong?"

Bessie searches for the right words. "I'm commuting an hour each way from northwest Bronx, Mrs. Siegal. It would be hard for me to carry such a bulky instrument back and forth on the train."

"Ah. You have a point. What would you like to play instead?"

Bessie remembers what Mrs. LaFollette tells her about maintaining good posture and finger dexterity, and her decision becomes clear. "The flute?"

"That's a wonderful choice, Bess. There aren't enough wood-wind players. Everyone seems to go for strings or brass."

Bessie is surprised how agreeable her teacher is—sort of like her elementary drama teacher, Mrs. Bloom, although everything here feels a lot different from her previous school, where students had no say in anything.

Later, all 250 first-year music and art students gather for a school assembly in the auditorium, directly below the gymnasium, and she finally gets a first glimpse of Principal Benjamin Steigman, a slight man with a graying mustache and a pleasant smile. He addresses the students from a lectern on the stage, flanked on each side by prominent photographs of President Roosevelt and Vice President Garner.

"Here we have gathered art and music students from every borough." He moves from his podium and walks toward the front of the platform, closer to the seated students below. "You are the best and brightest young talent our city has to offer."

An excited murmur spreads throughout the hall. A dainty girl with short brown hair next to Bessie mumbles under her breath, "I can't believe I was accepted."

"We are just in the second year of this important experiment: a public high school dedicated to music and art—the most hopeful accomplishment of Mayor Fiorello LaGuardia's administration—where students like all of you can hone your prodigious talents."

Bessie looks around at her classmates and sees she is not the only one struck by his comment. She turns the word over in her mind. *Prodigious.*

The diamond-shaped amber windows cast a warm glow on

the dark wood interior of this spacious hall. That same warmth stays with Bessie as she leaves the assembly and moves through her remaining periods of instruction. At her lunch table, she meets several students and learns that many travel from the far reaches of the city to come to this high school. Bernie Garfield, a fellow pianist in her orchestra class who'd been assigned the bassoon by Mrs. Siegal, says his commute is ninety minutes from Brooklyn. He tells her that a boy in his math class comes from Staten Island. "He rides the ferry and several trains, and it takes him two hours door to door." In her ninth-period literature class, she is happy to see a familiar face: Harvey Katz.

Lying in bed that night, Bessie listens to Helen's raspy breathing. She's used to her sister's nocturnal noise and finds it almost soothing. Since Sylvia moved out last month after marrying Bill Grace, the bedroom feels spacious. She misses having Sylvia around all the time, but not at this moment, as she stretches out in bed under her cool sheets and replays her first day of high school. If she had to boil the day down to one word, it would be *special*. The High School of Music and Art is a special place that she is privileged to attend. The teachers and students there are exceptional, and she, Bess Myerson, is one of them.

◦—◦—◦—◦—◦

Bessie finds the weeks and months of her first year at M&A filled with creative thought, interesting friends, and her own energized attitude. The study and performance of music arouses her greatest inspiration, but she thrives on the exposure she has to all forms of art. One afternoon in the spring, Bessie is overwhelmed by the smell of chalk dust when she enters her literature classroom. A lengthy quote from E. M. Forster's *A Room with a View*, their reading assignment due today, fills the blackboard:

> *We cast a shadow on something wherever we stand, and*
> *it is no good moving from place to place to save things;*

because the shadow always follows. Choose a place where you won't do harm—yes, choose a place where you won't do very much harm, and stand in it for all you are worth, facing the sunshine.

Classmates pass on each side of her as Bessie slows to take in the words. She dimly remembers the passage from the book but seeing them now on their own leaves her baffled and curious and hopeful all at once. Someone bumps her elbow, and like a stream of hot air on water, her thoughts evaporate. She quickly takes her seat in time for Mrs. Volpe's first question.

"What do you think Forster is attempting to say here, students?"

Bessie watches the sunlight from the window cast a beam across the floor. She hesitantly raises her hand, which Mrs. Volpe acknowledges with a nod. "In the novel, the character George compares kindness to sunlight." She hesitates, sensing some vague longing she carries deep down inside herself. "Maybe it's a fancy way of saying: once you find that place in the world where you are doing good, hold on to it. And . . . and don't let anyone or anything push you out of that place of sunshine, of goodness."

Mrs. Volpe smiles. "I think Miss Myerson's suggestion makes a lot of sense. Anyone else?"

Harvey raises his hand. "Maybe the writer is also trying to say that wherever you are, you affect your surroundings." He looks down at his desk, fumbling with a pencil. "What I mean to say is—what you do influences the things and people around you . . . for better or worse."

Mrs. Volpe affirms Harvey's opinion and listens as several other students also comment. She then emphasizes that the deeper understanding of fine literary works can hold personal truths for the reader. She ends the class by asking them to consider their own talent and how each of them might use it to create good, to impact others. "And how you might remain in that place of sunshine," she adds.

At the end of the school day, Bessie bumps into Harvey as they approach the main entrance.

"What'd you think of lit class, Bessie?"

She pauses to consider her answer. "It got me thinking. I want to be a concert pianist . . . or a composer. I mean, how can a concert pianist create good?" She wonders if it is merely in giving pleasure to audiences or if her performance could make them feel like she does when she inhabits the music of the masters. Rapturous. Transported. "A composer at least creates art, and that could have impact . . . if the composition is really good." Bessie feels unsettled and fumbles to secure the buckle of her book bag as Harvey pushes the door open.

"Do you want company? I can walk you to your subway stop."

"Sure." She likes Harvey and finds him easy to talk to. At one of their several lunches together, he told her that his mother, just like her own, had encouraged his artistic development. So, while Bessie took piano lessons with Mrs. LaFollette on the Upper West Side, Harvey had been riding the subway every Saturday to Manhattan for formal art instruction. "What about being a comic artist, Harvey?"

"Well, storytelling is pretty important. Geez, look at Forster's novel. When did he write that—like early in this century, and we're talking about it in class. Comics aren't literature, but they tell a story." Harvey shifts his satchel to his other shoulder. "I'd someday like to illustrate and write for comic magazines or books. Maybe like the adventure and humor comics I follow. You know, *Dick Tracy* or *Alley Oop*."

"I don't read comics. But I see what you're saying." Working toward social good makes perfect sense to Bessie. She just isn't sure what that looks like. "It's pretty neat that our teachers here are helping us try to figure out how to use our talent to improve society."

The two keep walking in silence until they reach the subway entrance. Bessie turns to Harvey and smiles. "I guess it's something we'll figure out when we're older."

CHAPTER FIVE

SOPHOMORE YEAR

September 1938 – May 1939

Throughout introductory orchestra freshman year, Bessie sits next to a funny, self-assured boy named Murray Panitz. She quickly masters the flute, aided by Murray's tutelage. At the end of that year, she and Murray learn they will both advance to senior orchestra, the school's premiere ensemble, whose members have the good fortune of working under some of the world's finest guest musicians, composers, and conductors.

On a Monday in early September of their sophomore year, the famed Walter Damrosch stands before them. All the students sit straighter in their seats. Bessie clasps her hands tightly on her lap as he begins to speak, his deep voice familiar from the many Thursdays she and her orchestra group have listened to his popular NBC radio lecture on classical music.

"Students, I have the privilege of leading you in George Gershwin's Piano Concerto in F Major. Over the next six weeks of intense practice, you will become proficient in this great piece. At the end of that time, we shall perform in front of a public audience."

Murray almost falls out of his chair as he leans toward Bessie and the section's third flute, Sam Morris. "Incredible. That's the piece he commissioned Gershwin to compose for the New York Symphony Orchestra. He conducted its world premiere too."

A few students in the woodwind section overhear Murray's pronouncement, and a rustling of sheet music and whispers follow. Bessie relishes her common heritage with Gershwin, who was also the offspring of Russian Jewish immigrants.

Damrosch clears his throat as he surveys the orchestra from woodwinds to strings to brass. "Since the concerto requires a piano solo, I would like Miss Myerson to play this, as I understand her primary instrument is the piano. Mr. Garfield, I know you also arrived with piano as your primary instrument, but I hear your talent on the bassoon has quickly surpassed your ability at the keyboard."

Bessie's jaw drops. She turns to Murray, flustered. "My God! He must know who each of us is. What am I supposed to do now?"

"He came prepared, that's for sure. Just do what he tells you, Bessie."

"Concerto in F calls for two flutes, so Mr. Panitz and Mr. Morris are sufficient to handle the flute sections. Let's get started. Please take your place at the piano bench, Miss Myerson."

⊶ ── • ── • ── ⊷

Bessie and Murray spend several hours of their school days together and become good friends. She finds his skill with the flute extraordinary, his timing flawless. Along with Conductor Damrosch, Murray's feedback during their many weeks of practice proves invaluable. The Piano Concerto in F begins with blasts from the timpani in a Charleston rhythm reflective of the young enthusiastic spirit of American life. During final rehearsals, Bessie perfects the timing of her initial solo entry, a single key and glissando that follow the quick and pulsating orchestral introduction. She is especially careful to modulate between that first movement's majestic and delicate sections. After the elegant melody of a trumpet solo, she perfectly enters the bluesy second movement. Since piano and flute play a variant of the blues theme together later in that movement, Murray helps guide her, so her tempo is just right. But nothing is as challenging as the vigorous third movement, with its rat-a-tat rhythm and energy of ragtime. As Bessie fingers the fast-paced notes, the orchestra plays a countermelody. Her fingers glide across the keys to return to the sultry theme from the beginning. The pace never lets up. By the time this thirty-five-minute concerto reaches its final chord, she is breathless.

On the day of the public performance, the newspapers come to take pictures of the orchestra. The photographer spends most of his time snapping several shots of Bessie.

"I wish he would find someone else to point his lens at," Bessie later tells Murray under her breath.

"Maybe he should be more interested in my pretty face in the first flutist seat." Murray chuckles as Bessie lightly punches his arm.

"Oh really, Murray. This is an orchestra performance."

Murray eyes Bessie incredulously. "How often do you think they see an attractive high school sophomore playing a piano solo the way you do?"

"You think I'm good, Murray? Really good?" She is bothered by his calling her *attractive*. It's her talent she cares about.

"Don't you hear yourself play, Bessie? Or ever look in a mirror?"

She shakes her head in denial. Beauty is not in her vocabulary. It has no value to her. Scholarship and musical skill are all that matter, are what she's judged by at home. And any form of compliment still makes her uncomfortable, even coming from Murray. She's more conditioned to her mother's lackluster feedback despite her hours of practice on both piano and flute. Bessie often finds herself stuck in the mindset of her gangly, awkward twelve-year-old self, even though she's since filled out and blossomed. Whether she will admit it out loud or not, it's as if she went to school one morning and found that boys were following her around and the girls were strangely hostile.

———————

A week after the concert, Bessie receives a scholarship to study flute privately with a teacher named Ralph Freundlich, a tall man with curly red hair and one of the younger members of M&A's faculty. She is thrilled because he is a revered musician, yet she finds him easily approachable. She wastes no time before she asks if they can work on "Summertime" by George Gershwin.

"I love everything Gershwin composes, how he combines classical and jazz and blues." She tells Mr. Freundlich that when she was nearly twelve, she went with her mother, her Aunt Fanny, and her cousin Hal to see *Porgy and Bess* at the Alvin Theatre. "I'd never been to a Broadway theater before and got to go because my cousin is training to be an opera singer. His mother wanted him see the production." Bessie loves that her name is in the featured title but doesn't share this with her new flute instructor, recognizing it as a silly and even childish notion. She recalls that her mother had commented that the girl playing the part of her namesake was not much older than Sylvia, just twenty, and that she studied at Juilliard, where Hal had applied for a scholarship. These things impress her mother, who was very pleased to learn of Bessie's scholarship to study with an esteemed flutist.

Mr. Freundlich keeps smiling at Bessie as she describes the folk opera, shares how sad she finds the story, and expresses how much she loves the evocative melody of "Summertime." "Of course we'll work on learning this piece, Bess. I very much look forward to our time together."

———————

A few days later, Bessie is the washroom when two girls approach, talking loudly. She thinks she hears her name, so she quickly steps inside a stall and closes the door just as the girls enter.

"It's her looks, not her talent. Why else would she have been bumped into senior orchestra after freshman year and now get a scholarship to study flute under Freundlich, who only takes the most promising students?"

"Sandra, you have to admit, she had an amazing piano solo last month. I mean, Concerto in F is a *hard* piece!"

"Okay, but piano is how she got into M&A, Rachel. Flute was an afterthought. Why all the attention with her flute playing if not for *other* reasons?"

Bessie silently repositions herself in the tight compartment, wishing she could disappear. The girls are sophomores, still in introductory orchestra. Sandra Pirwitz plays piccolo; Rachel Gerstein plays clarinet. They're both in Bessie's music theory class but rarely talk to her. She hates Rachel just then, wondering if there's truth to this gossip. She flashes on how Freundlich looks at her when she talks or plays her flute. He's always smiling and has this look in his eyes that does make her squirm, sort of that flirty look she sees some boys give her. Like that photographer at the concert. *Could it be I received the scholarship not because of the way I play but because of the way I look while I'm playing?*

She feels hollow inside. She recalls the previous summer's family music contest put on by the Bronx Parks Department. She entered with her sisters—she played flute, with Sylvia on piano and Helen at violin. They only received an honorable mention. As she crouches inside the bathroom stall, beads of sweat forming on her brow, she isn't considering what Murray tells her or what Mrs. LaFollette tells her. Just what Mama keeps drilling into her: "Practice! Work harder!"

Within two weeks, the slight becomes a distant memory. Panic erupts throughout her Sholem Aleichem neighborhood as word spreads about the terror brought against the Jews of Germany and Austria. Gathered around their wooden radio box on the night of November 9, Bessie listens with her family to a frightful news broadcast. The announcer calls the smashing and burning of Jewish shops and synagogues *Kristallnacht*—the "Night of Broken Glass."

In school the next day, Bessie sits solemnly in her civics class as her teacher, Daniel Rosenthal, holds up a copy of that morning's *New York Times*. "JEWS ARE ORDERED TO LEAVE MUNICH," its headline blares.

"This is what we are going to talk through today, students. *Nothing*—I want to emphasize—*nothing* could be more important to civics education than exploring this massive act of brutality against a religion and a people. This violent act will illuminate your understanding of our American democracy in comparison to the devastation wrought by a foreign government." Mr. Rosenthal, visibly agitated, begins to pace the room's perimeter. No one says a word. Bessie finally gulps in air, realizing she's been holding her breath.

"I brought several copies of this edition. I want all of you to take several minutes in small groups to read this." Mr. Rosenthal places a copy of the paper on the first desk of each of the classroom's four rows. "When you are done, return to your seats, and we can begin our discussion."

Bessie finds herself in the second group and moves with several students near the back window. One of her classmates, Ava Cohen, a refugee from Germany, begins to cry uncontrollably. Bessie, unsettled, awkwardly puts her arm around Ava's shoulder, the way Sylvia would when Bessie got upset. Bessie has heard about stories of antisemitism that Ava shared with others over the past months. Yet it seems like something happening so far away. Bessie suddenly realizes she's been living in her own bubble, between her insular Jewish neighborhood and a school where nearly half the students are Jewish. She just hasn't paid much attention. Until now.

When the movement of students and scraping of chairs subsides, Mr. Rosenthal addresses the class, his voice barely above a whisper. "Can anyone begin to share accounts you've read or heard that might have predicted these horrific events in Europe?"

Joshua Stone raises his hand and stands to speak. Bessie knows he's a friend of Harvey's, an illustrator who works on *Overtone*, M&A's school paper. "Yorkville is home to one of the largest German communities outside Europe. There's a group there that calls themselves the German American Bund, and they've been conducting lots of pro-Hitler activities." He pauses until Mr. Rosenthal nods for him to continue. "Just last month, nearly a thousand of these Bundists marched in a parade across Eighty-Sixth and Lexington. It was reported in the *Herald Tribune*. They marched behind American and swastika flags with thousands of spectators lifting their arms in the Nazi salute."

As Bessie watches Joshua lower his slight frame into his chair, she wonders how she didn't hear about these fascists right here in the city. But she did. She just didn't know the context. Her heart beats faster. She suddenly remembers Papa showing Uncle Samuel a series of photographs he saw in the *Daily Worker*, not a paper he usually reads. He said "even *der Rechte*" at Sholem Aleichem were getting copies of the Communist-leaning paper and talking about it. The pictures appeared under a headline: "Inside a Nazi Summer Camp." The conversation caught her attention because Papa said the photos were taken by a Brooklyn high school student who used an assumed name and snuck a camera into this Long Island camp. She'd stolen a glance at some of the pictures. Boys and girls were uniformed. There were swastikas inlaid in stone over the front doors of the camp's cottages. She didn't think to ask questions about it then. She now considers the implications of what she learned in World History freshman year and raises her hand.

"Germany forcefully annexed Austria last March. So Germany is acting as an imperialistic regime. Does this connect to the violent anti-Jewish acts that happened last night?" Bessie asks.

Ava Cohen stands up and speaks haltingly. "It is connected. The violence and hatred against Jews have been going on for years all over Germany, ever since Hitler became chancellor. I have relatives still there. They don't have passports to emigrate but are being forced to give up their homes to the Nazi government. How is this allowed?"

Mr. Rosenthal stops pacing. "So last night's wreckage of synagogues and Jewish businesses parallels rising tension over time. Last night's horror might even have been predictable, at least by those living within these countries. You read about important banks being taken over. I think the article described that a prominent banking business was in the process of being 'Aryanized.' Have you heard that term before?"

Murray raises his hand. "I heard it during *the* sports event of last summer, last June's rematch between Joe Louis and Max Schmeling, the hero to the Nazis. A perfect Aryan, they'd called him." Murray scans the room, his eyes settling for an instant on Bessie before he continues. "Thousands of his German fans arrived here on ocean liners, swastikas flapping from their masts. I would have loved to join all the New Yorkers who packed Yankee Stadium, but I got to listen on the radio—didn't most of you as well? I mean, our streets were deserted that night—I remember it was sweltering."

Bessie clearly remembers the scene Murray describes—how everyone in Sholem Aleichem was listening to Clem McCarthy's gravelly voice spilling out of all the open windows.

"We know that Hitler hates Negroes. He's all about the superior Aryan race." Murray nods toward Gerald Smith, an African American trumpet player in senior orchestra who's one of his best friends. "But that night, a Negro man ended up pummeling the Nazi in two minutes."

Bessie is heartened by Murray's directness. She wants to cheer him on but instead waits for someone else to do so. She looks around the room and notices some disquiet among her classmates. Gerald is staring at his hands, and Bessie suddenly recalls a conversation at home about how badly Negroes are treated, especially in the South, how they are separated in schools and other places. As she thinks about it, she realizes Gerald is the first Negro she's ever met—her Bronx neighborhood is all white—and she's grateful M&A isn't segregated. All these thoughts are swirling in her head as Mr. Rosenthal steps toward the front of the classroom and turns to face the students.

"Yes, we are hearing more about Germany's talk of their 'superior' race." He pauses before continuing. "What is especially troubling is that there is nothing in this article that reports any public outcry against the rioting and looting. The article describes a main street in Munich that looked as if it had been raided by a bombing plane, yet it indicates the crowd filled the streets to *gaze* at the destruction." He gathers the newspapers as he eyes the wall clock. "All of your comments reveal that we have much, much more to discuss. For next class, think about the responsibilities of citizenship. And the checks and balances in the American democracy that wouldn't tolerate this kind of attack."

Bessie remains in her seat trying to process these last shocking comments, the image of a community observing the destruction of their neighbors' businesses and houses of worship frozen in her mind. She's vaguely aware of several students walking up to the teacher and others hovering near the door. But she's in a sort of stunned shock, wondering if such barbarity could ever happen here.

◆――――――◆

In the ensuing months, Bessie becomes more aware of all kinds of social injustice. She pays greater attention to current news, an obvious result of her civics class and the growing tension in Europe.

Rumors of war are circulating at Sholem Aleichem, with most New York Jews anxiously following Hitler's rise in Germany yet the rest of America seemingly detached. When a large Nazi rally takes place at Madison Square Garden in February, she reads about these Bundists and how Mayor LaGuardia finally has enough of them, calling in the police and FBI. She's aware of the controversies during the weeks preceding the opening of the world's fair in April, with hundreds of Negro New Yorkers picketing outside the Empire State Building where City Commissioner Grover Whalen's office is located. They rightly charge that the fair hired few Negroes and that the fair's theme, "The World of Tomorrow," depicts a world almost completely devoid of their race or their achievements. Bessie can't help but consider the treatment of Negroes and Jews together, two sides of one coin somehow.

By late May, she's ready for the school year to be over. She finds comfort in the routine of her weekday afternoons, filled mostly with practice, rehearsals, and part-time jobs like babysitting and giving private piano lessons. She takes pride in her earnings, always placing them on the kitchen table for her mother to retrieve. Now that she's in high school, she is expected to contribute to the household. She continues to enjoy her weekend time with Ruthie up on Tar Beach on warm days and her Saturday nights with her extended family at Aunt Fanny's, accompanying Hal's blossoming baritone now that he's enrolled at Juilliard. Her closest M&A friends continue to be Harvey and Murray. She really doesn't have the time to develop many close friendships, and when she does, she rarely reveals much about herself.

One Sunday, when she's at the piano, playing the slow, dramatic introduction of Beethoven's *Pathétique Sonata*, she hears a familiar voice call from outside, "Bessie! How about some Gershwin!"

She pushes away from the keyboard and walks over to the open window, surprised to find Harvey Katz standing in the courtyard squinting up at her. She breaks into a wide smile. "What are you doing here, Harvey? And what's that you're carrying?"

"I was over at Will Eisen's working on some illustrations. You know him; he's a year ahead of us. Doesn't live far from here." Harvey raises a large black leather booklet. "I have my sketchbook with me. Hey, sorry I didn't ring first."

"Come on up, Harvey. I'll play your Gershwin while you sketch me!"

Half joking, Bessie wouldn't mind seeing a sketch of herself by Harvey. She is excited about this happy break in her afternoon and quickly introduces Harvey to Helen, who is doing homework at the kitchen table, and to her mother, who couldn't be more welcoming, offering Harvey cookies and milk. Bessie knows only too well what is going through her mother's mind. The fact that Harvey is at M&A marks him as an achiever, Mama's top criteria when judging Bessie's friends. And that he is encouraging her to play Gershwin, Mama's favorite composer, makes him even better.

Harvey takes Bessie at her word and sketches her as she plays *Rhapsody in Blue*. The opening wail of a clarinet rises in her head as her fingers stretch across the keys in rapid rhythm, the jazzy melody painting for her a kaleidoscope of the melting pot of America, and she loses any sense of her surroundings until Harvey pauses to yell "Brava!" and "Encore!" and he shows her his drawing. Her heart quickens when she sees the lovely image. Even seated, she appears willowy, her raven hair falling past her shoulders, her expression intent. A striking silhouette.

CHAPTER SIX

A GIRL CAN DO; A GIRL CAN BE

Fall 1939 – Spring 1941

Bessie whips through her algebra midterm, taking advantage of her break to stroll the school halls, pausing at the sunlit window to admire the red, orange, and yellow hues of autumn. She passes a classroom, its door half-open to the lilting voice of music theory teacher Helen Ross discussing the fine points of keyboard harmony. She approaches a studio class with several string players beginning their rehearsal. As she gets closer, she can make out the graceful singing notes of Mozart's Quartet in F Major, a favorite of hers, with its starring role of the cello in dialogue with viola and violins. This is one of the composer's "Prussian" quartets because Mozart dedicated them to the then king of Prussia, who happened to be a cello player.

Across the hall, she peeks into the repair shop where classmates were being taught how to restore and rebuild damaged instruments. She wanders through a wing with displays of student art covering the walls, admiring several oil and ink-wash paintings and pen-and-ink sketches, amazed at the variety of sculptures in alabaster, wood and clay, and ceramic sitting on pedestals. She stops in front of a wood carving of abolitionist John Brown in motion, one leg bent and stepping forward, his lengthy beard looking windswept. She smiles at the realism of an oil piece called *Lunchroom Scene*, with its blurred background of classmates lined up at the food counter and, in the foreground, a solemn boy intent on a book, his sandwich and a full glass of milk untouched beside him.

She silently blushes as her eyes rest on the charcoal drawing entitled *Portrait of a Classmate* that Harvey had apparently worked on all summer, rendering depth to it, filling it out, refining and perfecting it to a point that his teachers submitted it for the national Scholastic Art Award. Music students are welcome models for art students, so Bessie knows she shouldn't feel so self-conscious, except that the portrayal's likeness is so flattering. She finds the attention of the entire student body uncomfortable.

"That's almost as pretty as you are."

Bessie pulls back, startled, unaware of anyone near her, and turns to find Frenchie Wolf—tall, blond-haired, quick-witted, and nicknamed for the French horn he plays.

"Says a lot about the artist but more about the subject," he continues.

Bessie first met Frenchie sophomore year—he, too, was a rising star in senior orchestra. It wasn't long before he began joining her, Harvey, and Murray for lunch. Now, her eyes are drawn to his, so piercing and blue. "What are you doing here during class time?"

"Same thing as you. Getting some air." Matching her in height, his eyes directly meet hers and, flustered, she looks away. "It's hard for me to sit through a full period of chemistry," he says.

"I think it's just hard for you to sit, period." This time she meets his gaze.

She thinks back just a couple months to the first time they had lunch together, alone. Classes started in late August for junior year, and by early September papers were ablaze with the news that Nazi Germany invaded Poland, officially starting World War II. Bessie had gone to the cafeteria in a daze, her European history period totally taken over by the headlines—history being made that day. She was in an emotionally charged state like most of her classmates. Some were refugees or children of refugees from Nazi rule, like Ava Cohen, immigrants who M&A students learned about at assemblies or in articles in *Overtone*. After Frenchie sat down beside her, she ate her cheese sandwich in silence, comforted somehow by his presence during that disorienting day. She recalls how he squeezed her shoulder, how it felt like they were the only ones in the dining hall.

But just as they were finishing, a bunch of other juniors plopped down with their food trays next to them—Harvey, Murray, Joshua Stone, Ava Cohen, Gerald Smith. She doesn't remember who first made the suggestion, but someone asked what they could do to help. Frenchie thought they should organize a protest. Joshua proposed bringing in political speakers; he could publish their talks in *Overtone* with a distribution beyond the parent community. Many ideas seemed vague, naive, or idealistic. Quite a few were quickly discarded. The next day after school, their conversations moved to an open-air assembly in St. Nicholas Park, the school's "front yard" and for many their one daily contact with nature. They agreed on the immediate need for fully equipped ambulances to be used overseas and began devising ways to raise money for the Red Cross. This was the moment Bessie began to feel a sense of community with her classmates.

⚬—⚬—✦—⚬—⚬

The same week after having bumped into Frenchie in the hall, Bessie and her friends attend the High School of Music and Art parents' association meeting. Her heart beats faster when she sees

Frenchie arrive, watching as he easily chats with someone in the back of the room, where he remains standing. While several are still finding seats, a dour workman in overalls stands up and says he's come straight from the Brooklyn Navy Yard, where they're working three shifts around the clock "to keep our country safe from the submarines and all that mess in Europe." He tells the assembly of parents he has a good mind to take his boy out of the school, talent or no talent, if he has to listen to any talk about getting more pianos or filling out art-contest submission forms. In listening to the back-and-forth argument, Bessie starts to worry that music and arts are being considered "soft education," pitted against the realities of an emerging war. She can't believe the school could be regarded as having lax standards, given its lengthened school day, lack of study hall periods, and emphasis on history and civic education. She sneaks a look toward the back of the room, catching Frenchie's pensive expression.

During that fall of 1939, the mood is somber. Like so many M&A students, Bessie is angered by the isolationist stance of the US government toward the war in Europe. Soon after their fundraising effort, Frenchie invites her to her first meeting of community organizers. She tells her parents she has orchestra practice. She sees this as no different from the small tactical fibs she offers her overprotective mother, whether it has to do with wearing lipstick or smoking the occasional cigarette.

At the meeting, Bessie listens to impassioned activists as they organize letter-writing campaigns and demonstrations intended to shake the government out of its inaction. Frenchie volunteers to assemble a group of M&A student protestors and promises to take them downtown to city hall to get the attention of the press.

On the way back home, she and Frenchie find leaflets strewn on the street. Bessie picks one up and begins to read a stream of conspiracy theories. "They're blaming the deteriorating world situation on 'the Jews, the Freemasons, the Communists, the British Empire, and FDR'!" She can barely catch her breath, a rage pulsing throughout her veins as she reads the hateful words out loud.

"We can fight these lies beginning with our M&A classmates." Frenchie quickly details the work ahead of them—identifying who they'll ask to participate, the posters they'll create, the newspapers they'll call. Bessie feels alive and, for the first time, like she has some weighty purpose. She knows it's the activist fervor that makes her feel this way, although there's something more too—the chemistry she has with Frenchie.

But she knows deep down that Frenchie is off limits for her, despite his liberalism and his support for the Jewish cause, because he isn't himself Jewish. There's an unspoken rule among her family—and everyone at Sholem Aleichem—against dating outside of their religion, even though they aren't religious per se. She's aware that Frenchie's mother would also be deeply disturbed to find her son dating a Jewish girl. Yet, Bessie remains undeterred, seeing her involvement at these meetings with Frenchie as important, telling herself that they aren't *actually* going on dates. Besides, she likes being around him. She likes how he makes her feel warm inside.

They arrange to see each other before the next meeting at a nearby café. Bessie tells herself the encounter is innocent. They're just sipping tea, talking about the war in Europe, planning protests. But, tonight, as their knees touch under the table, she feels sparks. As he gazes into her eyes, her heart quickens. After the meeting, they ride the subway together shoulder to shoulder. When Frenchie turns her head toward him, he tenderly kisses her for the first time, and she feels his heart beating as if it were her own for that brief instant. They secretly arrange to see each other a few days later in an empty coffee shop where their kisses won't be noticed. And then the next night. Yet, to each rendezvous, Bessie carries a nagging burden of guilt.

"We can't do this," she tells him. "I don't want to get in trouble, sneaking around with you." Bessie twists the cloth napkin on her lap. She wants more than anything to be with Frenchie and thinks about him constantly. She's never felt a desire like this before. But she knows their time together must remain hidden from others, from her parents especially.

"We're not doing anything wrong, Bessie. We care about each other." Frenchie takes her hand in his. "Let's just enjoy this time together."

Bessie tells herself that he's right, but deep down she feels she has crossed some perilous line.

⋅—⋅—◆—⋅—◆—⋅—⋅

On a cold night in December, Bessie lies to her mother so she can attend another community meeting to see Frenchie, returning home late enough that she hopes to find her parents asleep. Instead, they are waiting for her, seated solemnly across from each other at the kitchen table.

"Where have you been? Orchestra practice doesn't go on this late." Her father's words burst from him, his eyes glaring.

"She was with that boy, that organizer she spends time with!" her mother yells.

Bessie is startled to hear her mother bring up Frenchie. *Did she overhear me tell Helen about him?* "He's just a friend," she retorts. "And he's working hard to persuade our government to do the right thing in terms of this war." Part of her believes she's getting chastised for doing good. She doesn't want to think about the late hour or the fact that she lied to her parents. Or how she truly feels about Frenchie.

"I don't believe you. You spend too much time with this boy, sneaking around. Enough is enough." Bella turns to Louis, urging him on. "Do something!"

Bessie is dumbfounded. She thought she had solid alibis. She watches her father roll up a newspaper. Her eyes widen when, quick as lightning, he raises his arm and smacks it across her face.

"No more lying!" he shouts. "No more boyfriend! Go to your room!"

In a state of shock, Bessie runs to her room, her cheek stinging from the blow, her self-worth wounded. Papa has never hit her before. Her joy in being with Frenchie has been shattered by her limited and narrow-minded parents. And yet she knew they would disapprove, despite Frenchie's assurances, as they are laden with all their immigrant customs and rules. How she wishes at this moment that she had normal parents, born in America. Parents who understood her. Lying in her bed in this tiny apartment in the dark of night, she is left simmering with resentment and no one to talk to.

⋅—◦—◦—◦—◦—⋅

The alarming events in Europe, as England and France declare war on Germany, heat up the debate between the isolationists and interventionists. In February of 1940, *Overtone* reports on this growing isolationist movement featuring the National League of Mothers of America, formed by several prominent New York women and dedicated to keeping American boys out of foreign squabbles. The student paper discloses that the New York chapter alone now claims one hundred thousand members. Strong sentiment prevails against the United States entering the war. Bessie continues to find ways to stay involved but, along with many M&A students, she begins to feel her voice is not being heard, and their activist efforts lose steam. She stops attending community-organizing meetings where she'd spent so much of her time with Frenchie.

She tells herself she isn't avoiding him. Rather, she's bowing to the pressure she feels from her parents, their unspoken but vehement order forbidding her to see "that boy."

One day, as spring approaches, he follows her as they're leaving senior orchestra. He almost corners her near the drinking fountain in a hall alcove, away from the crowd of students rushing to their next class. "Bessie, what's the matter with us? I try to reach out, and you act like I'm some kind of alien."

She hesitates at first, suddenly feeling exhausted. "It's me, not you, Frenchie. It's just . . . complicated. It's . . . we can't . . . it's better if we stop seeing each other." Bessie looks down as she speaks, afraid to make eye contact, telling herself this is the best decision. That she's keeping the peace. "I'm sorry."

"Did I do something? What changed?" His eyes are pleading, his face drawn.

"No, you didn't do anything." She fumbles with her books, searching for her next words. "I need to keep my focus on school, on my music. And my family." She feels a tightness in her chest, a churning in her gut. Her life has been prescribed, insular. She always knew what was expected of her, and she followed the rules, even when she didn't like or agree with her parents' wishes. Continuing to see Frenchie would mean lying and sneaking around. She doesn't think she is strong enough to handle that. "Don't you see? It wouldn't work between us. You deserve better, Frenchie."

The bell beginning the next period rings. Bessie lifts her head; her eyes fill as she takes in Frenchie's crestfallen face, the ache in her chest unbearable.

He reaches his hand toward her and squeezes her shoulder. Then he turns and walks away.

"Sylvia!" After spending much of the past week moping around the apartment, Bessie looks up from her notations for Grieg's Piano Concerto in A Minor, excited to see her older sister.

Sylvia's face is flushed, and she looks around quickly. "Where's Mama? And Helen?"

"Mama took Helen to her violin lesson. What are you doing here?"

"I came to ask if you'd like to see *Gone with the Wind*. It's playing at the Loew's Paradise."

"Even if Mama put you up to this, I'd love to go! I'll get my sweater. It gets chilly in the theater." Bessie is thrilled to do anything with Sylvia, whom she's seen so infrequently in the two years since her sister got married—to a nice Jewish boy Mama and Papa found acceptable. What a contrast to Bessie's sacrifice to honor the family values. Sylvia never had to navigate any explosive terrain when she brought Bill Grace home.

On the bus ride to the theater, Bessie is quiet, Frenchie very much in her thoughts. Finally, Sylvia remarks, "You're awful pensive today, Bess."

"It just isn't so easy with Mom and Dad, especially with you gone." Bessie purposely leaves out any details. The whole situation with Frenchie has left her emotionally spent.

After they arrive and walk through the theater lobby, an usher gapes at Bessie as he takes her ticket. She blushes and, turning to Sylvia when they are past him, grimaces.

"Oh, Bessie, he probably doesn't see many good-looking teenage girls like you." Sylvia chuckles softly.

Bessie shrugs off the comment and bounds for the front of the theater, grabbing two seats just as the room darkens and the screen lights up with the opening scenes of *Gone with the Wind*. She stretches her neck back and gazes at the faces of the actors she idolizes: Vivien Leigh as the strong-willed Scarlett O'Hara, Clark Gable as the dashing Rhett Butler, Olivia de Havilland as the kind and wise Melanie Hamilton. The lengthy film is a perfect escape for Bessie. She imagines living in the sprawling cotton plantation in Georgia, experiencing the tide of war and Scarlett's fight for survival.

The sisters decide to walk home. Bessie replays the story in her head: the romance and drama, the setting during a key period in history. The only thing she doesn't like is its depiction of Negroes.

As they stand at a corner waiting for traffic to pass, Bessie says, "I don't get why the slaves are looked down on just because they want their freedom. And worse, how Pork, Big Sam, and especially Prissy are made to seem stupid."

Sylvia's facial expression is inscrutable and somewhat quizzical.

"What? What's that look for?"

"You're really quite perceptive, Bessie. Good for you."

Bessie pauses as Sylvia's affirmation sinks in. She smiles with satisfaction.

—————

Bessie's dream at this point is to become a symphonic conductor. Thanks to her conducting class senior year, she gets to lead the school orchestra in the first movement of Beethoven's famous Fifth Symphony. When the day arrives, her heart pounds as she mounts the conductor's podium and looks out at the players. She's studied every possible recording made of this influential composition. She knows every detail associated with the work and the composer, including the facts that Beethoven was in his mid-thirties when he wrote this piece; that his personal life was then troubled by increasing deafness; that the premiere in 1808 at Vienna's Theatre an der Wien wasn't immediately well received. But it is a creation that later inspired the work of Brahms, Tchaikovsky, Berlioz, and so many others. Bessie has soaked up the deluge of information about Beethoven's oeuvre, and she is now completely prepared to conduct the first movement.

Raising her arm for the downbeat, she has chills as the four-note opening motif, *ta-ta-ta-taa*, resounds in an outburst of wild energy, followed by the pithy imitations tumbling over each other with such rhythmic regularity that they seem to form a single, flowing melody. She can't help but feel giddy at the sound of the violins throbbing and pleading, of the trumpets stirring, of the full orchestra bursting forth, and she is uplifted by this oneness she feels with all the instruments, with all her fellow musicians. For days she continues to play records on her home Victrola, waving an imagined baton and pretending to be a conductor, reliving that visceral feat.

It seems serendipitous that not long afterward, the famous guest conductor visiting her class is none other than a woman named Antonia Brico, who is forming a youth symphony and recruiting members. Their conducting teacher, David Ratner, is effusive in his introduction. "Antonia Brico is one of the most extraordinary women in the history of music!" Miss Brico nods graciously as Mr. Ratner shares that she is the founder and conductor of the Women's Symphony Orchestra and, just two years earlier, became the first woman to conduct the New York Philharmonic. He tells of her lively career as conductor of many European orchestras, including the Berlin Philharmonic. Bessie wasn't aware that there are women conductors or that any major symphony orchestra even employs a female player. She sits at the edge of her seat in anticipation of what else she will learn today.

Miss Brico shares that she is from Colorado, that her early conducting work took place there, and that she was willing to move where an opportunity presented itself. She gives the students a vivid account of her time with the Wagner festivals in the town of Bayreuth in northern Bavaria. And she encourages the girls in particular to perfect their skills. "A woman musician must seek professional equality with men."

No wonder she is wearing a prim, unwomanly plain black dress, Bessie thinks.

"When it comes to music, there is no difference in ability between men and women. It is about your knowledge and competence."

Bessie's rapt focus on Miss Brico's words is momentarily broken as she hears several boys snicker in response, but Miss Brico ignores them.

"Challenge the boys for all available positions, and may the best musicians win, regardless of sex, race, or color."

For the rest of that day, it is as if Bessie has fallen under a spell. *A girl can do; a girl can be.*

—————

Bessie stands behind the glass in the control room of NBC's Studio 8-H in Rockefeller Center and presses up against the partition to get as close as possible. She is among a handful of her orchestra classmates selected to observe the eminent Arturo Toscanini conduct rehearsals of the NBC Radio Symphony Orchestra. The fact that she is there to witness and learn from this legendary musician is almost inconceivable to her, but what she also finds astonishing is that Toscanini is conducting without a score.

The orchestra is playing the first movement of Franz Schubert's "Unfinished" Symphony no. 8 in B Minor. Just as the horns reach a crescendo, Toscanini taps his stick on the podium and the music comes to an immediate halt. "French horns, turn back to page four. Second horn, you hit a B-flat on bar three."

Bessie's mouth falls open. She's dumbstruck at how thoroughly he holds the music in his head. Someday it could be her at the podium, inspiring everyone to play so beautifully.

Soon after this outing, Murray Panitz secures an audition for Bessie with the Columbia University Symphonic Band at the Morningside Heights campus, walking distance from M&A. She is excited at the possibility of joining Murray in this extracurricular activity. She plays "Summertime" for the tryout and is immediately accepted. The band performs classical and pop music rearranged for brass, woodwind, and percussion instruments. At times, she becomes so moved by the sound of the music they are making together, so thrilled by the experience, that she starts to salivate and can't play her flute. She is more convinced than ever that she wants to be a conductor.

Bessie quickly learns that while she and the other female players are allowed to rehearse with the boys and play with them at concerts in Columbia's town hall, they can't march with them when the band plays at football games. At halftime, Bessie sits with the girls in the stands and watches the boys play, the music drowning out Antonia Brico's voice in her head. Her dream begins to look fanciful and senseless. The reality of what's possible for her, or any woman, is as transparent as a stream of clear water.

— — —•— — —

As Bessie's final year at M&A draws to a close, the school council sponsors its traditional senior dinner, recognizing the "winners" of the designated awards voted on by the entire student body—the tributes ringing both true and in jest. Murray Panitz receives "Most Likely to Succeed in Music" and Harvey Katz "Most Likely to Succeed in Art." Frenchie Wolf is named "Most Likely to Turn Heads," and Joshua Stone is awarded "Most Likely to Work for the *New York Times*." Bessie is voted by her classmates as "Prettiest Girl" and "Girl with the Most Charming Smile." What will her mother say to this?

Bessie tries to act gracious and take the accolade in stride as she walks up to gather her two certificates, but she bristles inside at the notion that she is just a pretty face with a charming smile. It is the piano that she cares about. The flute. Her future in music. *What about what is inside of me, what I feel, what I understand to be true? "Pretty" can't define me during these four years*, she thinks.

As she leaves the dinner with Harvey, he assures her that while others see her as very beautiful, with *magnificent raven hair*—and he emphasizes this for effect, dodging her immediate punch to his arm—he adds, "Everyone knows you're not conceited or self-centered, Bessie." He goes even further. "All of us think you're down-to-earth, smart . . . and talented."

All Bessie can do is roll her eyes. She knows Harvey means well, but his reaction only adds to her own prickling discomfort.

— — —•— — —

The class of 1941 welcomes Mayor Fiorello H. LaGuardia as its commencement speaker. Adored by M&A students, the doughy, roly-poly mayor and school's founding father receives rousing applause. The auditorium finally becomes still as the graduating students await his address.

It is well known that Mayor LaGuardia has loved music ever since his childhood, and his remarks begin with his immigrant father. "As a boy, I was thrilled by the army band my father conducted." LaGuardia adds in his rasping voice, "Our favorite numbers were the melodies of the Italian operas."

Bessie marvels at the thought that an army bandmaster, a refugee, taught his son to play the cornet and his daughter the violin. The two would perform duets in their high school auditorium in Prescott, Arizona, with their father at times accompanying them on the piano. Bessie imagines the cherubic boy delighting in these family trios.

"'My baby' is here to stay!" he says in his speech.

Everyone knows LaGuardia is referring to the High School of Music and Art, that he is paternal about the school and enthusiastic about all the honors its students win. The mayor's plump face rounds, and he wags his pudgy finger at them to make his point.

"The Maestro"—his nickname for the bronze sculpture he commissioned of Toscanini for the school's entrance hall—"has reminded you of what is meant by excellence and the tireless work to achieve excellence. Thanks to your accomplishments, this pride and joy of New York City is making its mark. I am proud of you, Class of 1941!"

Bessie finds herself emotional at his words, already nostalgic that this remarkable period of her life is ending. She looks around at her fellow graduates, holding on to this moment and to all the moments and memories that came before. She still feels the gentle touch of hope on her shoulder from her teachers. She can hear those wonderful affirmations that she never heard at home: *You did well, Bessie. Good for you.* At M&A, she's experienced a democratic anti-elitist spirit and ethos. During her four years, she's learned that her aim is not a selfish one: that of not only becoming a great artist but sharing the beauty she finds in music with others.

"We can't be completely happy in a world that is torn with war. We can't rest in peace when millions of children are hungry and in danger. You creators of beauty rebel against any such conditions. Class of 1941, I want you to shout out to the whole world." LaGuardia's voice turns shrill. "Yes, shout out to all who will listen: 'We insist that the ingenuity of man and the progress of science must and can be utilized for the enjoyment and welfare of humanity the world over!' Say to the dictators, 'Your end is coming, and we will continue to create beauty!'" His vehement gestures rouse the students into a standing ovation.

As the cheering dies down, his message reverberates for Bessie. When she plays her music, she steps into an ethereal space. Whatever is in her mind—anxiety, fear, even terror—the music takes over as she enters the tone world. It is like walking through a corridor of light and reaching toward a glimpse of eternal grace. Music is her solace, her healing, her love, her voice. Listening to Mayor Fiorello LaGuardia's eloquent remarks, she hears the ringing of hope and joy as she takes her next step forward.

CHAPTER SEVEN

THE WAR BEGINS; HUNTER COLLEGE AND THE 68 CLUB

Summer 1941 – May 1942

essie hears from M&A friends almost daily as their plans materialize. Harvey gets a scholarship to Cooper Union to continue his art study. Murray calls to share his good news: he's been accepted at the Curtis Institute of Music. She tells him how happy she is for him, then hangs up and laments her own state of limbo.

"Besseleh, why the long face?"

Bessie didn't know her father had been standing in the hallway, likely listening to her side of the conversation. "I feel lost, Papa. All my friends have futures. They're taking steps to bring their talent to the next level."

"And you're not? What about those piano lessons with Mrs. LaFollette?"

"I want to do more, Papa. I'd love to go to Curtis, like Murray, or to Juilliard."

"You think you can just strut into conservatory?" Mama was obviously eavesdropping from the kitchen. "Everything requires money. Your clothes, your piano lessons, and now, as a high school graduate, your room and board."

"Of course we want you to continue your schooling and growing your gift, Besseleh. But something affordable. A four-year liberal arts school." Her father gives Mama a stern look before he turns back to Bessie. "Education is more important than food."

"I don't disagree, Louis," Bella retorts, shaking her forefinger at Bessie. "But we have rules here. You contribute to the household while you live under our roof. You pay for your education or get yourself a scholarship. What you do next is your responsibility, Bess. And your choice."

Bessie knows these things, but hearing her mother put it out there so bluntly feels like a punch to her gut. She glances at her father but sees only acquiescence. She turns away from her parents and retreats to her room.

—————

Bessie knows that Mama only wants her and her sisters to earn their own living—and, of course, to get married, but not to count on being supported by a husband. Being a music teacher fits neatly into her mother's plan but this is not as much an aspiration for Bessie. She knows money is tight. It's why, for now, she works several jobs. Her dozen young piano students pay her fifty cents an hour for her services. An aspiring opera singer pays her a dollar a session to be his rehearsal accompanist. She babysits for everyone who asks her.

And every day, Bessie takes the train to Eighty-Fourth Street, wrestling with her desires versus her reality. Three hours teaching piano pays for one lesson with Dorothea LaFollette, time she yearns to spend with her beloved teacher for much-needed psychic nourishment. She feels loose—completely unrestrained—in Mrs. LaFollette's presence. She can engage fully in the music she adores: the physical aspect of playing piano like a sport, the intellectual part of memorizing that challenges her, and the emotional part when she can give voice to the notes. Bessie is aware of the sacrifices she makes to perfect her craft as a pianist—time away from her friends, time she might be doing something different—and tells herself it is the same for anyone who wants to excel at something. The loneliness is there, though, something she's become more aware of as she's gotten older, and what she feels now as the M&A camaraderie is but a memory. She's torn by her own ambivalence about her future. What does she want? What is she willing to give up to have it? *It's just you and the piano, just you on the stage.*

But as she sits beside her friend and mentor, that loneliness disappears. Mrs. LaFollette places the sheet music of Edvard Grieg's Piano Concerto in A Minor on the rack, telling her this is the only concerto Edvard Grieg completed and that it's one of his most popular works for good reason. "I know you've had a chance to practice this at home. Let's hear what you've got."

When she begins to play, Bessie immediately gets caught up in the music's passion, and she escapes into a whole range of places. Her mind journeys into faraway towns and villages. She sees steep mountains, verdant meadows, and winding waterways. She feels her heart racing while her fingers rapidly explore the landscape of the composition, aroused as she transforms the notes on the page into a vivid expression of sounds. She finds an imagery and beauty in Grieg's concerto that is impressionistic in the gentle second movement, but it is also filled with a roughness and wildness in the folksy dancing of the last movement, the notes tumbling over one another. When she strikes the final chords, she's exhilarated and exhausted at the same time.

She looks up to find Mrs. LaFollette's face lit up, her eyes glistening.

"You've made Grieg's love letter to Norway your own," her

teacher says. "It was all there—the fantastic dances, the beautiful colors, all that history and folklore."

"I adore this piece! So lyrical, so unique . . . and very real. Playing it today was just what I needed."

"Yes? Something bothering you, Bess?"

Bessie leans back uneasily, her mouth forming a pensive frown. "I'm not sure what I want. Or what I'm capable of. I know you'd like me to work toward being a concert pianist and to enroll in a conservatory like Juilliard or Curtis." Suddenly her face rearranges itself as a pleasant thought arrives to lighten her disquiet. "By the way, did I tell you about my friend from M&A orchestra, the flute player Murray Panitz? He got into Curtis for the fall."

Her teacher nods, listening. "That's wonderful for Murray. And you?"

"My parents would rather I go to Hunter. It's free, and money is an issue. I'd need a full scholarship for conservatory."

"And what do *you* want, Bess? Your talent is developing beautifully. Your skills are exceptional."

Bessie shares her memories of Walter Damrosch visiting her high school, how special she felt when he singled her out to play the piano solo for Gershwin's Piano Concerto in F, how she was amazed to learn that he conducted the world-premiere performances of that piece and of *An American in Paris.* "And I've finally perfected 'Summertime' on the flute," she adds with pride.

Bessie pauses as a flood of thoughts fill her head. "Damrosch was also instrumental in founding Carnegie Hall. What a dream it would be to play as a solo pianist with the orchestra there someday. Or to become a conductor." Discouraged, she looks down at her hands. "But I don't know if I have the kind of genius to be a concert soloist. Even if I did, how could I sustain a performing career when major orchestras don't even offer a woman an audition?"

"What kind of a musician do you want to be?"

Bessie doesn't know how to answer. She explains that some days she sees herself as a concert soloist. Some days she thinks she doesn't have the talent. Some days she wonders if a career is what she really wants for herself.

Her teacher doesn't respond right away. "A woman has to give up a great deal to do serious music, Bess."

She used to believe a girl could do anything, be anyone—and have everything: a profession, a husband, a family. But she's slowly discovering that it's not that simple.

———•—•—•———

In September, feeling pressure to make a decision as she watches all her peers move on, Bessie enrolls as a music major at the Bronx campus of Hunter College, an all-women's school. Still holding on to her bigger dream, she chooses to attend night classes so she can leave her days free to study piano with Mrs. LaFollette. The worst-case outcome, Bessie thinks, is that she would make a good accompanist or music teacher, perversely following her mother's prescription. She keeps the idea of a scholarship at some later date in the back of her mind and reminds herself that Hunter's music department is renowned for excellence, even though it is her only affordable option. The entire college has the reputation as the school with the smartest, and poorest, girls in the city. She finds it ideal to live at home yet have the campus so near, since she can conveniently enjoy the spaciousness of Hunter's sixteen acres, attend classes in ivy-covered Gothic buildings, and socialize in its large, cozy lounges.

Standing in a long line to register for classes, she finds herself behind a young woman wearing a large felt-brimmed hat. To make conversation, Bessie introduces herself and compliments her fellow student on her fashion statement. Margie Wallis tells Bessie she doesn't usually wear hats but had a "catastrophe" with a bottle of peroxide. She removes her head covering to reveal a big streak of platinum. "I tried to cover it with mascara." Bessie tries to keep a neutral expression while noticing the black stains on Margie's forehead. Oblivious, Margie calls out to another woman. "Lenny! Over here. Stand in line with us and meet my new friend."

While Bessie stands several inches above Margie, the friend is taller than Bessie. "So nice to meet you. I'm Lenny Miller, a fellow freakishly tall Hunter student and now, officially, a sophomore."

Bessie can't stifle her laugh or swift retort. "And you slouch like me when you walk."

"You'll be happy to know, there's a club for you to join here. Some tall, brilliant woman came up with the idea. The 68 Club." Responding to Bessie's puzzled look, Lenny adds, "Inches! Sixty-eight inches minimum. That's five feet eight inches tall. Margie's only five six, but we let her in as our mascot."

A club for tall girls only? Bessie is speechless and a bit incredulous. "Are there actually that many women at Hunter tall enough to make up a club?"

"Oh, yes, indeed! It's famous here. A real social club. Last semester we discussed making a certain height requisite for young men who attend our parties. Considered a six-foot marker on the door, although a few members thought that would be unfair discrimination."

◦—◦—◦—◦

Bessie feels on steadier ground through the fall months. On Friday nights, members of The 68 Club gather at each other's houses. They gossip and laugh and bond with one another while their mothers bake and their fathers read the newspaper, often Yiddish news since most club parents are Jewish immigrants like Bessie's own. And on Sundays, she spends the day and evening with her family.

On the first Sunday in December, it is too cold to go outside, so the whole family is in the Myerson apartment trying to stay out of one another's hair. Bessie's mother fixes a late lunch of cheese sandwiches. Helen, now in her senior year of high school, is reviewing math homework. Bessie is studying for a test in

Ethics, with one ear on the Giants-Dodgers game her father is listening to on the radio.

"This is the last NFL game of the regular season. I'd really like to be watching at the Polo Grounds, Besseleh, wouldn't you?"

"I'm happy to be inside in this chill, Papa. And football isn't really my favorite spectator sport." She buries her head back into her Ethics notes, tuning out the play-by-play commentary.

"But it's the New York Giants and the Brooklyn Dodgers. Nothing like it!"

Suddenly, announcer Len Sterling cuts into the broadcast: "*Flash*: Washington—White House says Japs attack Pearl Harbor."

"What? Did you hear that?" Bessie's father spins the radio dial and turns up the sound. The apartment fills with CBS newsman John Daly making the same report. Louis changes the radio dial again, and the voice of NBC's Robert Eisenbach announces a nearly verbatim message.

"Now this country will finally have to act!" Bessie is gleeful about the news, her interventionist stance validated, but immediately feels guilty as she realizes lives must have been lost in the attack. Conversation erupts among Louis, Bella, Bessie, and Helen. Bessie calls Sylvia and Bill, then Ruthie Singer as soon as the phone line is free. The remainder of the afternoon is spent on the phone and out in the courtyard as the neighbors of Sholem Aleichem exchange predictions of what might come, understanding that this moment is history in the making.

That night, the entire family heads to Aunt Fanny and Uncle Samuel's apartment to listen together to Eleanor Roosevelt's weekly Sunday-evening program on NBC: "We must go about our daily business more determined than ever to do the ordinary things as well as we can," Mrs. Roosevelt urges, "and when we find a way to do anything more in our communities to help others, to build morale, to give a feeling of security, we must do it. Whatever is asked of us, I am sure we can accomplish it. We are the free and unconquerable people of the United States of America."

On Monday at noon, the president declares war. Bessie is already at Student Hall on Hunter's campus so she can be among her fellow students as further news unfolds. She finds a stack of civil-defense leaflets titled "If It Comes" giving advice to New Yorkers, under Mayor LaGuardia's signature. It notes that an air attack is unlikely but "not impossible," given the city's role as "the nerve center of the nation." It counsels citizens that in the event of an air raid, they should ". . . keep cool. Don't be alarmed. Just use common sense!"

Antiaircraft artillery is wheeled out to various points around the city, and Bessie's Bronx neighborhood is not spared. Periodically their spotlights scissor the night sky. The next afternoon the city has its first air raid alert. A frantic confusion erupts.

Bessie keeps watch as the mood around the war shifts.

Up to this point, a war without American involvement was primarily fought on the ground in Europe. Now, with the Japanese as an enemy, the United States is vested in the Pacific theater of war, requiring battleships and aircraft carriers. Naval and air power are suddenly much more important. In addition, New York immediately becomes the principal port of embarkation for the European warfront with the presence of troops, the dispatch of fleets, and the focus on war news from media outlets overshadowing the city's customary commercial and creative bustle.

Bessie and her new Hunter College friends try to make do. They try to brush aside their sense of powerlessness as they watch brothers, cousins, and young male teachers get called into service. When a war agency sends navy-blue wool to the college, Bessie remembers Mrs. Roosevelt's message and urges The 68 Club to take on a project of knitting hats, socks, and gloves for brave soldiers to wear in the North Atlantic. With rationing of virtually every type of consumer good, Bessie is left to smoke cigarette substitutes, kept secret from her mother, despite the way they smell like maple syrup. She guards her nylons with her life, since only rayon hose is now available. She's unmoored and seeks something to occupy her nervous energy.

Bessie and Lenny soon take salesgirl jobs at Saks 34th Street after impressing upon the store management that they are sturdy, tall warriors who could restrain bargain-hungry customers. On Thursday evenings and Saturdays, they meet on the subway station platform at 125th Street—Bessie comes down on the D line from the Bronx, and Lenny comes down on the A line from Washington Heights—and giggle their way to Thirty-Ninth and Sixth Avenue, passing the many Allied soldiers and sailors crowding the city. In another era, Bessie knows she would have been dating, kissing, even falling in love. Instead, she sells at Saks and does a damn good job of it.

By spring, Bessie enrolls as a daytime student, getting the hang of juggling her classes and piano lessons with the part-time work. She can't help noticing the flyers on buses and subway cars touting a thriving entertainment scene, advertising Broadway plays debuting and new films being released. An idea pops in her head as she and Lenny are eating their lunches outdoors after English class on a warm Tuesday afternoon in late April. "There's a movie I want to see at the Strand. It's called *The Male Animal*, adapted from a James Thurber play." She takes a bite of her cheese-and-tomato sandwich. "So there's an actual story."

Lenny looks up. "What's it about, and who's in it?"

"That good-looking actor, Henry Fonda, plays an English professor at this football-crazed university. The review I read in the *Times* says he finds himself in the middle of a free-speech debate on campus. And guess who plays his wife?"

Lenny throws her hands up in the air. "I give up!"

"Olivia de Havilland! She played Scarlett O'Hara's sister-in-law in *Gone with the Wind*."

LINDA KASS 87

"God, she's *gorgeous*. And speaking of gorgeous, I saw Fonda in *The Grapes of Wrath* last year. Count me in, Bessie. I don't have any more classes today. Do you want to try to see the late matinee?"

The two dispose of their lunch bags, gather their knapsacks filled with books, and race to the subway for the Seventh Avenue line to Times Square. They arrive in time to buy two five-cent bags of popcorn before rapidly walking along the darkened aisle in the theater at the start of a short film called "Fighting Fire Bombs." Bessie motions Lenny to follow her to a row of empty seats near the front. She slides down into her seat, careful not to block those behind her who groan when they realize her height. The video reel has an urgent tone while providing a basic lesson in the methods of extinguishing incendiary bombs in the case of an air attack. Bessie hears the crunching of the popped corn and the rustling of bags in an otherwise-silent theater as the credits for the Office of Civilian Defense flash across the screen.

"Geez, you can't avoid the war even in a movie theater." Lenny shoves a handful of popcorn in her mouth as the opening credits for *The Male Animal* begin rolling.

The film is everything Bessie hoped for: a charming, comical, and non-formulaic story. The rah-rah college students are properly satirized at a pregame football rally. The hero is a married young English professor uninvolved in the politics of the day who outrages his conservative trustees by innocently planning to read to his class the sentencing statement by a famous anarchist as an example of eloquent prose composition. Bessie thinks Fonda gives a moving performance.

It is dusk when the girls leave the Strand. They decide to walk around Times Square and soak in the street life. The air is thick with cigarette smoke and the sounds of music in the nearby clubs, people are streaming out onto the crowded sidewalk; the multicolored neon signs glow as darkness sets in. Suddenly, as if a giant switch has been thrown, everything goes dark. Streetlamps and traffic lights dim all at once.

Bessie screams and grabs Lenny's arm. "What the—?" Bessie's heart pounds, and she has trouble breathing as she thinks of her family.

"Let's head toward the Fiftieth Street station," Lenny says. When they arrive, the subway appears dark. "It doesn't look safe, and the trains may not be running." Lenny's hands shake as she opens her purse. "I may have almost enough to splurge for a cab. Give me whatever you have."

They try to hail a taxi, hearing echoes of "Taxi!" but only seeing headlights on the darkened street. A cab finally stops, they flop into the back seat as Lenny shouts out her address, and an hour later it drops them both off in Washington Heights. Bessie calls home, relieved to hear her mother's voice. Her father gets on the phone and tells her that the entire Eastern Seaboard is under an imposed "dimout" that went into effect that night. The girls turn on the radio, and the full news about the plan is conveyed: vehicle headlights must be painted over; outdoor floodlights are banned, so no more night games at Ebbets Field or the Polo Grounds; offices and apartment towers have to switch off their lights or hide them behind shades from the fifteenth floors up; people must keep their homes darkened; neons and marquees are prohibited.

Bessie woke up that morning expecting the day to be like the one before. But now everything is changing, and who knows what the days and weeks ahead hold for them.

⟵—◆—◆—⟶

As her freshman year draws to a close, Bessie finds herself floundering, sick of the additional blackouts, the sugar and gas rationing, and all the war work infiltrating daily life. The Associated Press regularly reports of death counts steadily rising. She suffers anxiety, grief, and boredom along with every New Yorker. But she also feels the strong sense of unity and national purpose against the Axis powers. She continues to focus on her music with weekly treks to Mrs. Lafollette's studio; she still dreams of becoming a conductor, although that dream is slipping behind what she and many of the other young women at Hunter want most of all: a husband and family.

But few men are present, just the passing sailors and soldiers on weekend leave. Through their unseemly glances, Bessie is uncomfortably aware they are responding to her looks, nothing more. Margie Wallis tells Bessie, "Use your mind, even when others may just think you're a pretty face." Her friends don't act like the girls at M&A, and for that she is grateful. She realizes the lack of jealousy may just be due to the absence of the male eye. No one is competing. The horror of war makes Bessie and her peers wise, but the manless city keeps them sexually immature and innocent.

At the end of a school week in May, Bessie reaches out to Harvey Katz. The two meet for lunch at a sidewalk café off Astor Place, near Cooper Union. She is surprised at how happy she is to see her old M&A friend.

"Lucky for me I've stopped growing, but you're starting to catch up, Harvey." Bessie can't help teasing Harvey about his height, noticing that he had a spurt during the past year.

"Hard to catch up to your altitude, Bessie. How is Hunter treating you?"

Bessie shares the highlights, touching on her courses, her progress with her music studies, the friends she's met, and the fact that she's in a club for tall girls.

"Female power. I love it." Harvey takes a bite of his hamburger. "You must know that a female superhero is the rage in the comic world now, fighting the Nazis and all."

"Seriously?" Bessie leans forward. "I thought Captain America did all our combat now that we're at war."

"I'm afraid Betty Grable has competition from Wonder Woman. She's joined Hop Harrigan and Captain America in the fight against the Axis powers." Harvey smiles at Bessie.

"Remember when we talked about our talent creating good back at M&A? Well, comic book publishers have jumped in with both feet in the fight against Nazis and fascism. I've been doing some writing and illustration on the side with Will Eisen and feel ready to start making comic books."

"Good for you, Harvey. Looks like you'll fulfill the class's prediction of your success even sooner than we expected." Bessie feels inspired by Harvey's focus and almost hopeful for her own aspirations after her time with him.

Over the weekend, she spends an afternoon sunning on Tar Beach with her oldest friend, Ruthie, who plans to begin classes at Hunter after spending a year working to save money. Bessie promises to bring her into The 68 Club fold, since Ruth makes the cut at five foot eight. Being around such tall women has helped keep Bessie from feeling like a freak. While the group hasn't really come together formally this last year, Bessie tells Ruthie, the friendships have stuck. What Bessie doesn't share are the unsettled and contradictory feelings she can't seem to shake. She wonders if she expects too much for herself, wonders if her dreams and hopes are just that—mere fantasies, like Harvey's comic books.

CHAPTER EIGHT

SUMMER CAMP AND WAVES

Spring 1942 – Early 1943

Thanks to Sylvia, who spent several years as a summer-camp counselor herself, Bessie gets an interview with Sam and Tuck DuBoff, owners of the all-girls Birchwood Camp in Brandon, Vermont. She meets them that spring in Manhattan during one of their final camper recruiting trips and is hired on the spot to be their music counselor for the summer. She is eager to cast aside her urban life, her cramped apartment, the crowded subways, and the presence of war.

On the twentieth of June, she leaves at eight in the morning from the Bronx Park East station, arriving in Brandon eight hours later. After the DuBoffs pick her up at the bus station, they walk her all around their seemingly boundless property, nestled within the dramatic Green Mountains. She takes in the clay tennis courts and the pitch-roofed red barn and stables. Sam points out that even the counselors ride horses as he waves his hand toward the expansive fields. They pass a lake with sunlight glistening off the water, and three dinghies attached by rope to a wooden dock. She notices the dense forest along the edges. There are hiking trails in the woods, Tuck adds. Bessie's tour ends at the mess hall for dinner. She's even getting to replace her mother's bad food with tasty camp cuisine. When she tells the DuBoffs the meatloaf is "delish," Sam proudly notes that the cooks use Tuck's own recipe. Bessie concludes that working as a camp counselor will be more like a vacation than a job. Campers arrive the next day, and she's excited to begin this new adventure.

—————

Every night, Bessie counts the eight heads in bed, comforting those away from home for the first time. She names her assigned cabin the "Soulful Songbirds" because all her eleven-year-olds sing out their feelings. On rainy days, it's Lena Horne's hit "Stormy Weather," or when they're bored, it's the box-office success of that summer, "Why Don't You Do Right?" by Benny Goodman and Peggy Lee. Bessie chuckles every time she hears the girls sing the bluesy chorus: "Get out of here and get me some money too."

Her campers remind her of the students she met in Mrs. LaFollette's school. The campers come from wealthy homes in Jewish suburbs: Rachel from New Rochelle, Sarah from South Orange, Leah from the South Shore of Long Island. Their mothers are sensitive, educated, kind. On visitor's day, the moms go on hikes and swim with their daughters. Observing that comradeship produces a pang of jealousy and hurt in Bessie that she struggles to shake off. She also must deal with her envy of the cashmere sweaters and stylish slacks the little girls bring with them, thanks to fathers working and prospering in the garment industry as they manufacture goods for the war effort.

Alongside her best friend at Birchwood—the blonde and buxom drama counselor Gloria Winter—Bessie adapts the lyrics of songs from the lighthearted Broadway hit *Best Foot Forward* and prepares for an all-camp musical to end the summer. She has a knack for knowing what tunes bring out the exuberance in the girls' rendition. In "The Three B's," she assigns her top Songbirds to key roles:

RACHEL: *I never wanna hear Johann Sebastian Bach.*
SARAH: *And I don't wanna listen to Ludwig Beethoven.*
LEAH: *And I don't give a hoot for all Johannes Brahms.*
ALL/CHORUS: *The b's we want are these. The b's we want are these.*
SARAH: *They're the barrelhouse, the boogie-woogie,*
RACHEL: *and the blues.*
ALL/CHORUS: *Yes, the barrelhouse, the boogie-woogie, and the blues!*

Bessie wears her raven hair in long pigtails, and within weeks, her lean legs are deeply tan against her white shorts. Counselors from their "brother camp," Green Mountain Camp for Boys, arrive each week from across the lake. Bessie and Gloria meet the boys for a soda in town on their rare time off and attend square dances the two camps cosponsor. This is Bessie's first relaxed encounter with boys, unencumbered by parental judgment. At first, she is self-conscious about the way some of them look her up and down—mostly up, since she's taller than they are—and eye Gloria almost hungrily. After several visits, she exchanges photos with a guy named Ronnie, who seems harmless and a little shy. They flirt. But their encounters are brief and infrequent, never much beyond a walk in the moonlight or a kiss good night after a dance. Her feelings for Ronnie are void of any real passion—certainly nothing near the longing she'd had for Frenchie. Sometimes, lying in bed in the cabin, she thinks of him, of the closeness they felt for each other. Her physical and emotional desire comes to the surface but so does a sense of remorse and guilt.

At night, after their charges are fast asleep, Bessie and Gloria smoke cigarettes behind the cabins and exchange stories about their days at Birchwood, the latest note or message from any of the guys from Green Mountain, and, as the summer draws to a close, their wistful farewell to camp life.

"This place is sort of a dream, isn't it?" Bessie brings the cigarette to her lips and draws in but doesn't inhale. She doesn't like smoking and isn't sure why she is doing it now.

"I know. We don't hear much about the war out here, but I will when I get back to Skidmore." Gloria swats a mosquito that lands on her knee. "I won't miss the bugs, though."

The two have been so immersed in this other world in Vermont that Bessie realizes they've never spoken about their lives back home. "Do you have any special fella?"

"Naw. You know how it is at a girls' college. And the guys are all at war anyway."

"More reason to miss all this. You coming back next summer, Glo?"

"Absolutely! And since I want to teach drama in high school, the experience here will eventually help me get a job. I'll miss you, Bessie, but we'll keep in touch."

Bessie looks off into the trees, holding tight to this moment and the magic of this escape at Birchwood.

❖—❖—❖

That idyllic sweetness of summer quickly fades to memory as fall swings into gear for Bessie. Gloria doesn't write, and Bessie understands; that other world stays tucked in its own reality. The rhythm of living at home, practicing piano, attending Hunter classes, and hanging out with her 68 Club friends once again becomes a routine. Bessie can't help noticing how void of men the city has become. In the absence of meaningful relationships, she invents passionate fantasies. All the girls in The 68 Club create their ideas of romance from fleeting rendezvous with soldiers at USO dances and from watching movie heartthrobs like Clark Gable, Cary Grant, and Humphrey Bogart. In late November, Bessie—with Lenny, Margie, and Ruth—views the world premiere of *Casablanca* at the Hollywood Theatre.

"Can you believe the sparks between Bogart and Bergman?"

Bessie says afterward. "My heart was in my throat in every scene they were together."

"What about that line, 'Here's looking at you, kid.' I would have melted right then and there." Margie sways as she places the back of her hand against her forehead.

"You've got the drama, Marge, I'll give you that." Lenny walks ahead, leading the group east on Fifty-First. "Let's find a place to sit down and have a bite to eat. We need to begin planning our New Year's Eve and 'end of 1942' celebration, girls!"

"Getting through a full year of war is definitely something to cheer about. But not so much for us." Ruthie's voice quivers. "Actually, I feel guilty that we're enjoying ourselves while so many are sacrificing their lives."

"I know what you mean, Ruthie. I never know what to say when I pass Gold Star mothers on the stairs at Sholem Aleichem. The same women who I swear used to look at me and my sisters as potential future wives for . . ." Bessie stops herself and yet knows the unspoken words are now dangling. She can't bring their sons back to life, and she can't stop this horrid war, the harsh truth filling her with hopelessness. She tries to recover, to redirect her thoughts, and blurts out, "Look, we need to put the best face on this."

"How does one put a good face on the war, Bess?"

Ruthie's question at first feels like a slap. Things are hopeless, but God knows they all need something to hold on to, so Bessie forges ahead. "Look, the good news of late is the Allied invasion of North Africa. Maybe we celebrate the Allies making headway against the bad guys."

One after another, the three absorb this information, nodding slowly at first, then breaking out in a grin. "Yeah!" they call out in unison.

The girls meet at Margie's apartment for their New Year's Eve party. The mood is somber, though, because all everyone has been talking about is Edward Murrow's December 13 radio broadcast. Rumblings began last June after a World Jewish Congress report of more than a million Jews killed. But Murrow's broadcast just weeks earlier, confirming that millions of Jews are "being gathered up with ruthless efficiency and murdered," left everyone hollow. He told his listeners that the phrase "concentration camp" is obsolete, suggesting they be called "extermination camps."

Margie's father says the girls are too young to be exposed to these images of war. He reminds them that the Allies are making progress, that they will prevail over evil. He tells them to put on some catchy music and try to enjoy themselves. He even gives them a bottle of champagne. Bessie and her 68 Club friends get drunk for the first time in their lives, escaping into the music of Glenn Miller, Artie Shaw, and Benny Goodman. "Chattanooga Choo Choo," "In the Mood," and "A String of Pearls" play on the Victrola as they finish off their second glasses. Margie decides to replay "In the Mood."

"I've only listened to this song a zillion times on *Chesterfield Moonlight Serenade*." As she unsteadily places the needle back on the vinyl, she pretends to hold a mic up to her mouth. After the introduction, with saxophone blaring and trumpet and trombones adding accent riffs, she belts out the lyrics in time with the music:

> *Mister, why'd you call up, what you doin' tonight?*
> *Hope you're in the mood because I'm feeling just right*
> *How's about a corner with a table for two?*
> *Where the music's mellow and some gay rendezvous*
> *There's no chance romancing with a blue attitude*
> *You've got to do some dancing to get in the mood.*

Lenny, Ruthie, and Bessie laugh uncontrollably. They quickly get the idea and join in.

Sister why'd you call him, that's a timely idea
Something's ringing dear, it will be good to my ear
Everybody must agree that dancing has charm
When you're in the circle with your love in your arms
Stepping out but you won't be a sweet interlude
Oh, fill the room without me, put me in the mood.

The four girls are swaying and swinging to the riff-like tune, the rival tenor sax solos egging them on. Their singing takes on an almost-hysterical edge.

"In the mood," all four chorus.

"That's it, I got it," croons Lenny at the top of her lungs.

"In the mood," they join again.

"You're in the spot when you're . . . ," solos Ruthie.

"In the mood," together they belt out and join arms.

"Oh, what a heartache, feel alive, I get the jive, you got in that hall." Bessie nails the closer as the girls begin to add spontaneous, wild dance moves, readying to join again for the final refrain:

Hep-hep-hep, head like a hepper
Pep-pep-pep, hard as a pepper
Step-step-step, step like a stepper
Muggin,' to hug him
We're in the mood now.

As the music stops, they crumble in a heap, and it is then that their tears start to flow. Is it pent-up sorrow or a shared shame for singing and dancing while people are dying? Or of being powerless females unable to do something, anything, to fight the world's darkness?

⚬—•—•—•—⚬

On a Monday morning just eleven days later, Bessie sits in Hunter's Student Hall lounge trying to enjoy the bright winter sunshine. She gazes mindlessly through the floor-length windows at her fellow students trekking across the snow-covered campus. With extra time before her first class, she picks up a *New York Times* laying on the table in front of her. She casually glances through the front-page headlines, her eyes widening as she takes in unexpected news: "HUNTER UNIT TAKEN BY NAVY AS ITS CHIEF WOMEN'S CAMP." Swelling with pride, she reads further, incredulous to discover that twenty-five hundred personnel of the Women's Reserve, part of the United States Naval Reserve, will start their "boot camp" training February 1 right there at the Bronx campus. That several thousand more WAVES and SPARs would be arriving soon after.

She scans quickly past the administrative backstory—the three-sided arrangement among the Navy, the Board of Higher Education, and the mayor, just approved on Friday—which explains how she and her classmates have remained clueless. "The two thousand girls now enrolled in the Bronx division of Hunter College will be distributed . . ." Carefully reading through the rest of the paragraph, she learns that all of them will be doubling up in classrooms on Hunter's main campus on Manhattan's Upper East Side. Hunter president George Shuster is quoted, saying plans were being worked out "for a distribution that would assure maximum efficiency and minimum impairment of normal education routine."

Bessie leans back into the leather couch and takes in a deep breath. She's thrilled that these capable women will be joining the war effort. So what if she and other Hunter students are displaced? It's for a noble cause. She notices the bright sun is no longer splaying across her legs and looks up at the shadow of the person blocking it.

"You look like you've escaped to another world, Bess. What are you reading?" Lenny leans over, squinting at the headlines.

"The *Times*. Looks like our experience at Hunter is about to change, girlfriend."

Lenny grabs the newspaper, her eyes quickly taking in what Bessie already knows. "Well, our classrooms are soon to become the 'USS *Hunter*'—training reserve women for onshore naval duty. Isn't that nifty?" She drops onto the couch next to Bessie and is quiet for a bit, then breaks into a mischievous grin. "You know, this is important for the war effort. And it might be a pretty great thing for us, heading into Manhattan for college. Where the action is."

CHAPTER NINE

MODELING

Spring 1943 – Early 1945

G iven the wartime reality, it turns out that Manhattan doesn't provide the thrill the girls were hoping for. During spring semester, Bessie and her friends often linger at the newly acquired Sara Delano Roosevelt House on East Sixty-Fifth Street, Hunter's social center for the mostly commuting students. Occasionally, the girls bring evening clothes to slip into for dances hosted at the house, as well as at USO clubhouses. Bessie finds these events wooden. The military men in the city for one-day furloughs are difficult to get to know. Conversations with them remain polite and shallow. The evening's highlight is when the girls are personally escorted to the subway by the City Patrol Corps, the affable volunteers LaGuardia assembled after Pearl Harbor to prevent muggings beneath the dimmed streetlights.

After the death of President Roosevelt in April, when Bessie and her Hunter friends staggered into Central Park weeping with thousands of other New Yorkers, she can't wait to head to Camp Birchwood for the summer, counting the days until her needed respite from life in the wartime city. The DuBoffs call to ask if she'd mind adding tennis instructor to her list of responsibilities; they'd heard about her ease learning the game the previous season and are short one coach. Bessie immediately agrees. She looks forward to her other life in Vermont, filled with campers, tennis competitions, music programs, and free evenings with Gloria.

Much of the summer is spent like the previous year, as pleasurable as Bessie remembered it. She is busy every moment—other than those late evenings with Gloria—adding horseback riding and sailing to her cornucopia of outdoor responsibilities. Nonetheless, the intensity of battle seeps into the idyllic world of Camp Birchwood with discouraging reports in newspapers and on the radio. The summer rushes by all too quickly.

— · — · — · — · —

In the fall, Bessie returns to her junior year at Hunter's East Side Manhattan campus for more of the same. The commute becomes wearying; only her weekends at home allow her to relax and pretend as if the war doesn't exist. One Sunday afternoon, she bumps into Malcolm Fried after a Sholem Aleichem community theater performance, harkening back to years earlier when he made her see that the role of Olive Oyl in a school play wasn't the end of the world.

"Ah, Besseleh. So grown-up you're becoming! Why the sad *punim*?"

"You just always find me in these miserable moods, Malcolm. I'm totally bored but have absolutely no good reason to complain." Bessie hates herself for whining and offers a half smile before she glances at the tall and broad-shouldered man standing next to Malcolm.

"I'm being rude." Malcolm takes a step to the side. "Let me introduce you to my friend, John Pape. John, this is my neighbor, Bess Myerson, who I've known since she was a girl. Now she's a young woman. Attends Hunter College, and I hear she's a wonderful musician. Bess, John's taken up photography in his retirement."

"Lovely to meet you, Bess." Pape holds out his hand, and she shakes it. Bessie assesses the man to be about fifty but realizes he must be a bit older if already retired. "You're very photogenic. Has anyone ever told you that?"

Bessie blushes. "Well, not exactly. Although I did model for a friend who sketched a portrait of me when I was in high school."

"I'm a retired steel manufacturer. Like Malcolm said, I've taken up photography as my full-time avocation. Had dabbled in it for many years." He nods as he regards her. "College students are always looking for work. You could earn some extra money modeling for my amateur photographers' club. We're a bunch of retired men who've taken our hobby more seriously. We call ourselves The Little Studio Group."

Bessie awkwardly smiles at Pape, not sure of how to answer.

"The photo club meets in an office building in downtown Manhattan. We'd love for you to come pose for us."

Bessie takes a deep breath to calm herself, uneasy by the idea of modeling, something she thinks of as undignified. "I do earn some money already, Mr. Pape. I tutor music students."

"Well, we pay five dollars an hour as our sitting fee." He writes the address on a card and hands it to her. "Just think about it. We don't bite, I promise you."

Five dollars an hour? That's a staggering sum compared to what she earns giving piano lessons. She realizes she's holding her breath, so astonished by this proposition, one that seems almost reckless. Surely it's outside of anything she's done before, unless she considers when Harvey was sketching her back in high school.

Glancing up, she does her best to seem calm. "I . . . that's quite an interesting offer. Let me think about it." And then she quickly excuses herself.

Over the next week, Bessie can't stop thinking about the prospect of modeling or about John Pape's comments and the enormous pay he proposed. Her stomach turns somersaults every time she considers saying yes. *Pape does seem like a kind man, though. Harmless, really.* She impulsively picks up the phone and makes the appointment.

She spends her subway ride to his office in a terrible sweat. *What have I gotten myself into? What if they ask me to take my clothes off?*

She arrives to find five older gentlemen waiting for her. They are fatherly looking, she thinks, and all seem very kind. They show her their prop room and tell her to use whatever she likes. It is filled with jewelry, furs, silk brocade shawls, long black gloves, corsets, feathery boas, and an array of hats, one that reminds her of the one Margie was wearing when Bessie first met her.

Her eyes are drawn to a tray of makeup. Feeling giddy, she wastes no time powdering her nose and then adding blush to her cheeks. She grabs the brocade shawl, flings it over her shoulders, and enters the room where Pape and the others await with their cameras. Eager to earn her five dollars, she does all the provocative, animated, introspective, leisurely, and smiling poses that she's seen in all the movie magazines. She pretends to be glamorous like Betty Grable and Rita Hayworth. She puts flowers in her hair like Dorothy Lamour. She paints her lips with dark lipstick and makes them twice as full to look like Hedy Lamarr.

"You're a natural, Bessie, an authentic beauty."

Pape's praise is lavish, unguarded. Bessie can hear her mother's voice in her ear: "Poo, poo, poo," Mama would say to protect her from the evil eye. Surely such superstitious fears would mean nothing to a man of Pape's worldly stature.

Modeling becomes her escape. Along with the fun of the dress-ups and the nonthreatening praise from the gentlemen,

Bessie thrives on the covert aspect of this work, so at odds with her life as an upperclassman at Hunter. She feels only small pangs of guilt hiding it from her mother, who thinks modeling a disgrace, and she squirrels away most of the earnings. She does tell Sylvia, by now the mother of two baby girls, and it becomes their private secret.

On a cold day in January, Bessie takes a bus from Pape's studio to Sylvia's West Side apartment, weighted down with a portfolio of photographs to share. After Sylvia makes them both hot tea, the two riffle through the early series, then begin to view them more slowly, one pose at a time, oohing and aahing over a suggestive tilt of Bessie's head, the pucker in her painted lips, the lure in her dark eyes. Bessie feels like she's looking at someone else, discovering nuances with each image. Modeling appears as a glamorous fantasy, part of her invented romances with dashing pilots and officers in uniform. It's as though she has become two people: one the rule follower—single-minded and diligent about her schoolwork and her preparation as a musician; the other an appealing, bewitching cosmopolitan woman with handsome men trailing her to parties and clubs. She might be that alluring figure in *Vogue* or *Glamour*.

Sylvia eggs her on. "I'd thought about suggesting modeling to you for a long time, Bess. Why not earn extra money for your appearance?"

"What do you mean? I *have* been earning money modeling for John."

"My point is that we take advantage of your good looks." Sylvia flips through more photographs. "Look at your high cheekbones and almond-shaped eyes. Your lean figure. I'm stuck with Mama's wide shoulders and large hips, but you're modeling material, Bess. Just think about the money you can save for lessons and clothes."

"Instead of worrying about earning money, I should be finding a man, getting married." Bessie frowns. "But I have no prospects. Look how lucky you are to have found Bill. I wonder if I'll ever fall in love."

"You're young, Bess. Too young to worry about marriage." Sylvia suggests Bessie have John Pape take some photographs that can be used in a modeling portfolio. "Look, let's just see what comes of this. I know a modeling career isn't the kind of profession a smart Jewish girl like you should aspire to, but everyone is entitled to earn money where they can."

Bessie wonders what nice Jewish girl *is* a model, although she's read that the modeling business has gained more respectability recently. And she is tempted by Sylvia's money argument. If Bessie expects to have options after college so she doesn't find herself at another dead end, she must make them for herself. That much has always been clear to her.

◆ — ◆ — ◆

Just months before Bessie's Hunter graduation, Sylvia sends a couple of Pape's photographs to Harry Conover and John Robert Powers, the two most powerful agents for models in New York, important men with connections to Hollywood studios, big ad agencies, and the fledgling television industry. "They'll snap you up right away," Sylvia tells her. "I'm sure of it."

Bessie thinks she might have a better chance with Powers, whose models tend to be tall and sleek, while Conover specializes in "the girl next door" type. She begins to warm to the idea, having read magazine reports of what fun it is to be a cover girl, that it often leads to television work. Improved printing processes that enhance photographic reproduction have added a fresh artistry to modeling, and she hears the industry seeks smart models able to deal with expanding technology. Part of her is attracted to a new and exciting adventure, lured by tales of salaries as high as $18,000 a year.

One Tuesday afternoon, Sylvia asks Bessie to come over after classes for tea and cookies. Bess is barely seated at the kitchen table when she notices the two envelopes in her sister's hand and shoots her a questioning glance.

"They aren't what I expected, Bess."

Bessie knew Sylvia gave her own home address for the responses—God forbid their mother might find out what they were up to. "Let me see them, Syl."

Sylvia reluctantly hands them over and looks away. Bessie reads the two letters out loud. Powers flat-out writes that he doesn't like what he sees in the photos. Conover says he wants the "All-American type," which, in his opinion, she isn't.

"Clearly, the agencies just have too many clients right now, Bess. This sounds like boilerplate language."

Bessie won't hear any of Sylvia's attempts to lighten the rejections. Her mood breaks in a snap. She feels as humiliated as she did at age twelve. *Gawky, skinny, too leggy.* She's ugly again. She looks too Jewish. She's crushed by what she sees as a shunning and ashamed of how she invested such emotional energy on an industry focused on beauty. She isn't supposed to care about her looks. How did she let this glitzy fantasy distract her?

Bessie puts modeling out of her mind, determined to find another half dozen piano students. And maybe, just maybe, one of the five million Americans soon home from war would happen to fall in love with her.

CHAPTER TEN

MISS NEW YORK CITY

Early Summer 1945

As Bessie's Hunter days end, so does the country's involvement in the European theater of war. The victory over Nazism and the liberation of concentration camps makes this a monumental moment that she recognizes when she stops thinking about her own needs. The idea of being a professional musician seems remote. Then she becomes ashamed of her self-centered concerns—petty in the face of such epic suffering, with the number of casualties rising daily.

After her June graduation, she is consumed with the same uncertainty about her future that she experienced following high school. No longer getting a paycheck from John Pape and swearing off all modeling, she has no money for graduate studies or enough savings to provide a down payment for a new piano or to open her own music school. And there are no men in her life. It feels to her like everyone is turning to the security of marriage—at least *yearning* for it after the tumult of a world war—although her close friends remain single. Still, Bessie's lack of prospects leaves her anxious. Will she ever find the kind of emotional connection she had with Frenchie? She doesn't want to think about a future filled with nothing but giving piano lessons. At least she still has the peaceful escape of Birchwood Camp for Girls to look forward to.

In late July, as Birchwood's head music conductor, Bessie is directing the girls in *H.M.S. Pinafore* with Helen at her side. She had lobbied the DuBoffs for her younger sister to be a counselor at Birchwood and her assistant music director. She finds Helen's musical training and organizational skills useful in handling a production of this size. And Bessie welcomes the comfort of her companionship. Now that Helen is in college, they have more in common.

"Bessie, Connie is trying to find you." Helen enters the rehearsal barn out of breath. "Seems Sylvia called. Message is that it's urgent. That she has news."

"Does she expect me to call her now? You don't have any details?"

Helen shakes her head. "I can take over while you call Sylvia in the office. I'm curious too."

Bessie races to the camp office, slowing as she walks through the door, and acknowledges Connie, the receptionist. "I'll make that phone call now." She dials Sylvia's number. Her sister answers after the first ring. "It's me, Syl. What's up?"

"Oh my gosh! You won't believe this, Bess! You're among 350 contestants for the Miss New York City competition!"

"What are you talking about? I didn't apply for that!" Bessie realizes she's almost shouting and looks over at Connie, who has stopped typing and is listening to the one-sided conversation.

"*We* did! John heard about the competition last month and he called me. It's being conducted by the Blue Network's WJZ. I agreed we should enter you, he sent in the photos, and I filled out the forms. They had twelve hundred applicants, and now you've been chosen!"

"Geez, Sylvia." Bessie is seething inside. "How could you do that without telling me?"

"I didn't want you to get disappointed again in case nothing came of it. Look, there's a further selection process to narrow the field. You need to come home."

"Absolutely not!" Bessie turns her back to Connie, then lowers her voice while cupping her hand around the speaker. "They'll just reject me like Powers and Conover did. I'm done with this beauty business, Syl. It's embarrassing." Bessie stands straighter and takes a deep breath to calm herself before she ends the call. "I appreciate you and John, Syl, but consider this closed. I left Helen at our rehearsal and need to get back to work. Love you."

Bessie puts down the receiver and smiles sweetly at Connie before she walks out. As she sprints back to the rehearsal barn, she bristles inside. What nice Jewish girl competes in beauty contests? It is tacky, dishonorable. In the moral scheme of things, physical beauty isn't important. Even the modeling she did with John Pape disregards that she has a brain in her head. *How could Sylvia do this to me?* she fumes.

But, by the next day, Bessie realizes that Syl is not about to take no for an answer. She'd already contacted Sam and Tuck DuBoff and secured their agreement to give Bessie time off for this.

Now, her call to Bessie is commanding. Sylvia instructs her to find a becoming bathing suit ("Yours are all unflattering," Syl tells her), return to New York immediately, and appear in the pageant. "Look, there's a talent component, and a win means cash and a future. Don't think of it as just a beauty contest."

Bessie relents, seeing there is no arguing with her sister; the talent requirement and cash prize actually pique her interest. She hands over responsibility for *Pinafore* to Helen and Bessie asks one of the tallest campers if she has a bathing suit she can borrow. It's a two-piece white suit. With that in hand, Bessie is on a train the next morning.

She appreciates the hours on the train to gather her ambivalent thoughts about what lies ahead of her. How is it that Sylvia keeps getting her involved in these exotic distractions—the modeling agency long shots, now a beauty contest? As much as she adores her sister, Bessie is exasperated.

She chooses an unoccupied compartment and sinks into its well-upholstered velvet-covered seat. The day is hot, but it's cool in the train; its rhythmic vibrations relax her. She gazes out the window, watching the dense woods and Vermont mountains disappear into lofty meadows covered with wild red clover.

She notices a *New York Times* spread across an adjacent seat, the front-page headlines so bold that she leans forward to read it. "FIRST ATOMIC BOMB DROPPED ON JAPAN." She doesn't know what an atomic bomb is, thinking at first it's just a bigger bomb than what the Germans dropped on London. She begins reading the lengthy article: "...possesses more than 20,000 tons of TNT ...one of the scientific landmarks of the century ..." She learns the bomb had been researched for years at great cost. She shudders to think of the implications of using such weapons against one's enemies. At the same time, she feels relieved, guessing this could end the war for good. She tries not to think much more about anything, the train's movement finally lulling her to sleep.

Sylvia meets her at Penn Station in the late afternoon, and they take the subway to the Ritz Theatre on Forty-Eighth Street. Bessie, quiet at first, begins to soften her resistance to the whole beauty-contest affair. "The Blue Network is the home of the NBC Symphony Orchestra broadcasts. Back when I was at M&A, I got to watch Arturo Toscanini conduct a rehearsal."

"They're running a professional competition, if that's what you're finally realizing." Sylvia folds down Bessie's turned-up shirt collar. "You need to follow exactly what they tell you to do. There's the bathing suit part and the performance part. You'll do great, honey."

A short and thickset man extends his hand to welcome Bessie, as he does each of the contestants entering the Ritz. He introduces himself as Don Rich, the public relations director of radio station WJZ, and then leads them to the stage. Bessie looks out at the large theater and trembles, fretting about how she could possibly appear before an audience this size. She spots a piano at the left side of the stage. *Thank goodness for the talent competition.* She reminds herself that she's been playing in front of audiences since she was ten. She thinks about Dorothea LaFollette's encouragement and that of her M&A teachers.

But her confidence wanes again as she observes the other girls, very blonde and curvy. Here she is, a Jewish girl from the Bronx, her parents Russian immigrants, her raven-black hair frizzing in the August humidity. She feels almost desperate. *I'm tall and dark with no hips,* she thinks. *I'm the wrong person in the wrong place. I don't have a chance.*

Rich's directions break into her self-absorption. "You are to go backstage and change into your bathing suits. You'll rehearse walking across the stage, then change into your performing clothes. You can practice your performance piece before the audience arrives, and then you'll do the entire routine over again for them. Any questions?"

Bessie feels shaky but follows the girls backstage, and almost as if by rote, she models the bathing suit, pretending she is walking in front of the five kindly gentleman photographers in their studio. She goes through the day in a kind of numb trance. When it comes to the actual contest that evening, she forgets the real audience. Then she plays a three-minute arrangement of Grieg on the piano and Gershwin's "Summertime" on the flute to tremendous applause. By the end of the evening, Don Rich reads out a list of fifteen finalists, and her name—Bess Myerson—rings out as one of them above the din in her ears.

Bessie stands frozen in disbelief, unable to respond until she hears Sylvia's scream. As if on cue, she flashes her genuine smile, lifts her chin up, and revels in the thunderous applause, giddy as she begins to realize some of this is for her.

She returns to Birchwood the next day, leaving her sister to break the news about the beauty contest to their parents. It *was* Sylvia's idea, after all, and Bessie is confident her sister will convince Bella and Louis about the opportunity this could create for her future.

At lunch that first day, a beaming Sam DuBoff calls everyone to attention. "Campers, counselors, and staff, I want to announce that our very own Bess Myerson has made the finals for Miss New York City!"

The girl campers cheer. Several whistle. Sam asks Bessie to say a few words, and she waves him off, too embarrassed at the attention. Later, Gloria Winter asks Bessie for every detail. "It's just so exotic. A real beauty contest!" Bessie flinches at Gloria's words. The cast of *H.M.S. Pinafore* begins to greet her with "Hi, Miss New York City!" and Bessie offers a silent prayer of gratitude that the finals take place at the end of camp, so she won't have to deal with all the disappointment. She keeps her mind on *Pinafore*, pleased that Helen skillfully handled the production in her absence. Still, in spite of herself, the enthusiasm at Birchwood begins to affect her.

She takes the midnight train to New York on a sultry mid-August day only to find the city teeming with jubilant New Yorkers. People are cheering and crying. Streamers and confetti are strewn over the streets and sidewalks. She, too, is exhilarated by the news. Truman has just announced the Japanese surrender. The war has ended. She heads straight for Sylvia's, collapsing until the evening for the parties. She overhears her brother-in-law expressing doubt about her chances. "You're exhausting yourself for what, Syl? She'll never win. A total waste of time." Bessie's confidence takes another nosedive.

The next day, Bill stays home with their daughters as Sylvia accompanies Bessie to the Ritz for the finals. Before they leave, Sylvia grabs a white scarf and tells Bess to tie it around her hair.

"You'll stand out, the white against your black hair and dark skin." After the afternoon rehearsals, Bessie meets Miss America pageant director Lenora Slaughter, who asks her to join her in the third row of the empty theater for a talk. Bessie has never met a Southerner before. She thinks back to the very proper, unhurried, and emotional *Gone with the Wind* stereotype she once held in her mind. That is *not* Lenora Slaughter.

Lenora wears a flashy orange silk dress and bright-red lipstick. She speaks fast and with self-assurance. "I intend to make the pageant the first major national event of the peacetime era." Lenora leans even closer to Bessie, a musk scent overpowering, her voice barely a whisper. She reminds Bessie that the winner will receive a $5,000 scholarship. "There is a very strong possibility you might become Miss New York City tonight. And then you'll have a good shot at being Miss America and winning that scholarship. If that happens, what would you like to do?"

Bessie's heartbeat quickens as she tries to process the full meaning of Lenora's words. She wonders if this forceful woman gives the same message to each finalist as a test. *What is the right answer here?*

"I would continue studying piano. Buy a new instrument—maybe a baby grand. I could start a music school. I could even go to graduate school."

"I wanted to go to college more than anything in the world, but I didn't have the money." Lenora edges back in her seat. "This scholarship gives you girls options. I had to fight the board to make this happen. Had to raise the money to fund it."

Bessie listens intently, sizing up this woman before her. "How did you go about that? Raising money, that is."

"Just convincing businesses there's a value to exposure. Catalina Swimsuits, for example. Now their suits will be Miss America's crowning uniform." Lenora shares that she handwrote letters to 230 companies who sold products a beauty queen might endorse. "I even recruited the executive director of the

Association of American Colleges and Universities to head our new scholarship program."

Bessie considers what she's just heard. Lenora Slaughter is a bright woman who knows exactly what she wants and gets things done. And she's succeeding in a man's world. Bessie thinks back to her role model, conductor Antonia Brico, and her message about women musicians, that there is no difference in ability between women and men. "It's about your knowledge and competence," she said. Yet so few women are conductors or players in major orchestras. Bessie now recalls Mrs. LaFollette's words when she matter-of-factly declared that reality: *A woman has to give up a great deal to do serious music, Bess.*

Bessie wonders what Lenora has given up, achieving all that she has. "I hope that I can attain in music what you've been able to accomplish in your field. That scholarship money is why I'm here."

"Yes, but you've got to be flexible, Bess. What if music doesn't work out for you? You might also decide to go into show business or the movies. Many girls do." Lenora smiles, exposing her big white teeth. Several seconds of silence pass as she seems to consider her next words. "And you need to consider all the things that could get in your way if you choose that path."

For an instant, Lenora turns away, and Bessie thinks their conversation is over until the pageant director suddenly blurts, "Bess Myerson is just not a very attractive name for a career in show business."

"I really have no intention of going into show business." Bessie feels her face get hot.

"Well, even for this competition, changing it couldn't hurt."

Bessie knows it is an ordinary thing to do. People with ethnic names change them. Lauren Bacall was born Betty Persky. Cary Grant was Archie Leach. Kirk Douglas understandably changed his name from Issur Danielovitch. "What would you suggest?"

Lenora doesn't reply immediately. "Maybe Betty ... Merrick, or something like that."

Bessie eases back in her seat, and then something hits her like a gut punch. Papa, having survived a pogrom as a child in Russia, told her to remember who she was—he meant being a Jew. Bessie senses something leaking from Lenora's deliberate affect, something deeper than the desire for a name change. She realizes suddenly that she is dealing with Lenora's own bigotry, her attitude about having a Jewish contestant and, potentially, a Jewish winner.

Bessie clears her throat, tightens the white scarf around her head. "No. I'm not going to change my name."

Lenora's face tenses; her brows tighten.

"If I win this contest tonight, the only people who will really care are my family and the families I've grown up with. My friends from Hunter and from high school. My campers. And if I win and my name is Betty Merrick, they won't know it's me. I want them to know it's me. So I think I have to keep my own name. I am Bess Myerson."

Lenora doesn't let up. She shares her own desire for her "girls" to succeed, to have opportunities she missed as a Southern Baptist whose family couldn't afford for her to have a college education. In the end, a name change will help Bess become who she wants to be, Lenora adds. And then the clincher for Bessie: "Bess, I just don't know if the world is ready to crown a Jew, or at least one who wears that heritage so openly."

Bessie doesn't respond, just fixes her eyes on the pageant director. Maybe it's the weight of a five-thousand-year-old history. She knows there is more at stake in her relationship with this woman and instinctively sees that how she presents herself to Lenora and to the world she comes from will be of great consequence going forward. She already feels like she's losing her sense of who she is, already in a masquerade, marching across stages in bathing suits. Whatever is left of the Bessie she knows at this moment, she has to hang on to it. She must keep her name. And she owes it to herself and to this moment in time to do everything in her power not to lose.

—•—•—•—•—

As the competition gets started, Bessie can barely register emcee Ray Knight's breezy commentary. She glances over at the judges' seats. American bandleader Paul Whiteman, at one time considered the king of jazz, is sitting next to syndicated columnist Danton Walker, known across the country for his coverage of Broadway. She can't help being starstruck. Photographers' cameras are flashing. She sees Papa in the second row, beaming with pride. Next to him is John Pape. No sign of Mama, but this isn't unexpected. Bessie knows how uncomfortable her mother is at large public events. It was enough for her to attend the intimate recitals at Mrs. LaFollette's studio.

Everything is happening so fast. Bessie goes through the motions of the bathing suit competition, then the talent portion. Everything feels strange and unfamiliar. But why would that be? She's done all this in rehearsals. She did this with a larger group of contestants to get to the finals. What is so strange? That she has a chance? That she's getting close? That she could *win*?

Just before midnight, Ray Knight announces her name as Miss New York City. *Her* name. Bess Myerson, not Betty Merrick, has won. She still has her identity. *This is happening to me.* Publicity photographer Murray Korman presents her with a watch, and she tries to recall what John Pape had told her about his own aspirations to emulate Korman's high-gloss style, but she's too shocked to think clearly now. All she knows is that she is still Bess Myerson.

Backstage she is introduced to a tall, blond, and extremely good-looking man, Bob Steen. She hears someone say that he manages the Ritz Theatre. She tries to keep her heart flutters in check, tries to keep herself from gazing too long at his handsome face.

She is whisked to the Monte Carlo nightclub, accompanied by its manager, Dick Flanagan. Sylvia is at her side as well as John, their presence the only thing familiar. She lights up when she sees Bob walking toward her, wishing she could spend the whole night with him alone, but Sylvia sticks to her side like flypaper. Lenora is also there with her. There are many toasts of champagne, calls to family and to Birchwood, more photographs.

All of it is a blur, except the call to her cousin Harold sometime during the night. Now that he lives on his own as a working musician, she doesn't worry about waking an entire household.

"You *what*?"

"I *won*! I'm Miss New York City! I'm going to compete for Miss America, Hal!" Bessie is tipsy, not sure she is making sense.

"Ma told me you were in some beauty contest. I was sorta surprised, actually."

"I know. Not what you'd expect. Parading around in a bathing suit!" She giggles self-consciously but is reeling inside. What must Hal think of her now? "I have a chance at a $5,000 scholarship if I win."

"Ah, I get it now. Conservatory could be around the corner, Bess! Hey, were there any other Jewish girls in the contest?"

Bessie mumbles through the rest of her conversation, apologizing for waking Hal, promising she'll meet up with him soon. After she hangs up the receiver, she staggers back to the festivities. All she knows is that it's the middle of the night and she's in the middle of some kind of alternate reality. There's more drinking and dancing, more people she meets whose names she forgets. At one point, the room begins to spin. Sickened from the champagne, she rushes to the bathroom not a moment too soon, her head hanging over a toilet, retching as she empties her stomach.

At dawn, after a wild night of celebration, she is driven home by a chauffeur. Just one month past her twenty-first birthday, she has been crowned Miss New York City. She wonders if her life will ever be the same.

CHAPTER ELEVEN

MEDIA WHIRLWIND; PANIC SETS IN

August 1945

B essie feels a hand shaking her shoulder.
"Bessie . . . *Bessie* . . . *Sis!*"
Helen's voice is high-pitched. Bessie tentatively opens her eyes to find her sister hovering over her, her stare piercing through her tousled mouse-brown mop of hair.

"*Ugh.* Let me sleep. I had quite the night."

"You're a celebrity, Bessie! Look at all these papers!"

Bessie jolts up in bed, grabbing the newspapers out of her sister's hands. Far below the block headline, "WORLD HAILS JAP SURRENDER," in the *Herald Tribune,* she spots the photo taken last evening of her being crowned Miss New York City. The *Daily News* features a similar portrait with a caption, "Jewish girl from Bronx is Miss New York City!" *Post* gossip columnist Earl Wilson says about last night's celebratory parties: "Bess Myerson's sister is keeping the wolves from the door!"

"This . . . this is unreal." Bessie feels slightly nauseated, her brain foggy from the champagne and lack of sleep. She does remember that gorgeous man. *What was his name again? He owned the Ritz Theatre.* And all the other men. All the flattery. It was almost six when the limousine deposited her back home.

"The phone's been ringing all morning for you, Bessie. Radio stations are calling. Reporters are asking to interview you. There's a bunch of invitations—a lunch, a cocktail party. Someone even mentioned a television program! Imagine that!"

Bessie hasn't seen Helen this animated since she won the Bronx Police Department music competition as a violin soloist three years ago. She throws off the covers, walks to the sink, and splashes her face with cold water. "Okay. Sit with me while I have some coffee and toast. Then I can deal with all this craziness."

For several days, Bessie lives in a fantasy world, meeting celebrities and being whisked around to dinners, interviews, photo shoots. She takes a train to Schenectady to appear on DuMont TV. She doesn't know anyone with a television and is very impressed with this new technology. She meets many people, including radio announcer Johnny Olson, who invites her to come on his show. She decides to keep many of the details of her new life from her mother. *The evil eye!* During her few moments alone in taxis and trains, she can't help scribbling about all her escapades in a personal diary.

She returns from a radio interview in Manhattan to find her father attempting to read through a long-form letter from Lenora Slaughter and a complicated contract that just arrived, his eyes glazed over. Bessie asks him to give her the document and gently tells her father not to open her mail.

"'We are eagerly anticipating your arrival in this resort on Monday, September 3,'" Bessie reads out loud. "I'm supposed to be in Atlantic City in just over two weeks!" Her mouth suddenly feels parched. "Helen, hand me a glass of water."

She takes a gulp and continues to read: "'We know it is going to be a grand experience for you to meet the charming and representative girls from every section of this great nation of ours, as well as Cuba and British Columbia.'" Bessie scans farther down. Her eyes freeze on a closing sentence: "'I am confident that your mothers will be just as happy with your participation in the Pageant as you will be and I am personally anticipating meeting not only you beautiful and charming girls but your mothers, for to them goes a great deal of the credit for the success you have obtained.'"

Mama will never agree to go! And, if she did, how awful would that be? Bessie imagines her mother staying locked up in the hotel room, refusing to eat what was prepared, embarrassed by her English, awkward with the other mothers. Bessie would have to take care of her. If that isn't enough to panic over, she becomes more agitated to read that "a minimum of three flattering evening gowns" are needed for several formal appearances where she will be judged. Bessie only has the one long white dress she wore during the WJZ contest.

By the time she pulls on shorts and a blouse and has her coffee, John Pape is at the door, as are Sylvia, Bill, and her nieces. Mama returns from the grocery. The tiny apartment feels suddenly overcrowded, confining.

Bessie hands over Lenora's letter to her older sister amid the low hum of conversation. Sylvia scans through the missive.

"Mom, they are expecting you to accompany Bess to Atlantic City."

"I have no intention of going. Bessie, you'll go with your sister. Sylvia, you'll send Michelle and Francine to me so they can get a decent meal."

Bessie breathes a sigh of relief. With Sylvia, she can be herself. Syl understands her and has been more of a mother to her anyway. Now Bessie only needs to fret about her lack of clothing. She gives her mother a kiss. "You can be the mother of Miss New York City without any of the hassles of this cumbersome contest, Mama."

John offers to pay for a seamstress to make her daytime clothes. Bessie catches Bill mumbling to Sylvia, "What does this old guy want with Bess, spending so much money on her?" She screws up her eyes at her brother-in-law, then reaches out to give John a hug.

"I really came over to talk about what picture you want to use for the pageant booklet, Bess." John looks over at Sylvia. "This is an important decision because you want to distinguish yourself."

"I've heard that most contestants will be submitting poses of themselves in bathing suits." Sylvia folds Lenora's letter and hands it to Bess. "Maybe you want to use something different."

"If I can share my two cents, I agree," Bill says, "You should be more clothed for the picture."

Bill has only made negative remarks. Bessie waits for what will come out of his mouth next.

"I'm just saying, there's that awful photo that's appeared in all the city papers of you up on Tar Beach in your two-piece. Why call attention to that?"

Bessie knows her parents were embarrassed about the unflattering shot of her seated, her legs extended on their rooftop, tanned from summer camp, and wearing her white two-piece bathing suit with lacing down the hips.

"How about using those photos I took of you in the academic cap and gown you wore for graduation?" John looks inquiringly at Bess, then Sylvia.

No one says anything at first. Then there is a rush of agreement. At least one thing is settled.

— — — ◆ — — —

"Hello?"

"Is this Bess Myerson?"

Bessie doesn't recognize the low gravelly voice at the other end. "This is she."

"Guess what I have in my hand for you."

Bessie slams the receiver back into the cradle and screams for her father. She is aware of the steady stream of obscene letters and crank phone calls. Her father tries to intercept them and keep her from knowing too many details. But it's hard to keep secrets in their closet-like apartment. The perverts are writing one dirty letter after another. She overhears her father telling WJZ public relations man Don Rich to call the police after he finds a condom around the doorknob. "It wasn't empty," Bessie hears her father whisper into the handset. Her father later tells her that they shouldn't call the authorities, that Don thinks it will draw attention and invite more indecent letters.

The next day Bessie receives a crank letter that includes a photo of her cut out from a newspaper with crude and suggestive comments scribbled across her face. When her mother learns that men have been badgering the superintendent of Sholem Aleichem to find where Bess is, she calls Bill. Her brother-in-law contacts the FBI. Bessie finds it difficult to brush all these attacks aside. Mama barely speaks to her now.

The next morning, Sylvia stops by to have breakfast with Bessie. The phone's shrill ring makes Bessie jump. Afraid of what she might hear on the other end, she says, "You answer it."

"Hello?" Sylvia's face relaxes. "Who?" She listens for a minute, nodding, then smiling. "That is so generous, so kind. Thank you, Mr. Knapp. We'll come downtown to meet you later today." Sylvia stares open-mouthed at the telephone as she hangs up.

"What was that all about?" Bessie is relieved it wasn't another prank.

"You're not going to believe it. This man, this Samuel Knapp, is a Seventh Avenue fashion designer. He read about you, that you're from the Bronx. This address isn't exactly a wealthy neighborhood, and he concluded you could use some dresses. Said he's doing this out of a sense of patriotic duty."

"You mean he's willing to donate dresses to me?"

"He's offered you whatever you want from his line of evening dresses. But we have to go down to his showroom on Seventh Avenue as soon as possible." Sylvia wipes sweat from her forehead. "Boy, it's sweltering today. Time to get dressed, Bess."

They arrive two hours later. The dark-haired Knapp is distinguished and impeccably dressed. Cuff links, manicured fingernails. Bessie smells his fresh lime aftershave. A number of attractive models and several seamstresses surround him and light up when Bessie and Sylvia introduce themselves.

"Miss Myerson, it is my honor to meet you and to have you showcase my designs to all of America." The designer's speech sounds to Bessie like a mix of Laurence Olivier playing Max de Winter in *Rebecca* and a Russian immigrant from Minsk. His eyes twinkle. "You and I both know that even a pretty girl like you can't make do with a burlap sack."

— ◆ — ◆ — ◆ —

Bess again boards a train for Schenectady, this time because WJZ is promoting its newly selected Miss New York State, June Jenkins. Bessie hits it off with June, the two fooling around behind television cameras pretending they are shooting scenes of each other. Bessie feels a premonition of power at the cutting edge of an infant industry. Later, she plays Chopin's *Fantaisie-Impromptu* on the radio and is interviewed about the piece afterward. She's stirred, not only by the chance to display her talent but to actually talk, to reveal herself as a human being.

"Isn't this a most difficult composition, Miss Myerson? The tempo is marked *allegro agitato*, and it begins with great speed."

"Yes, the fiery tempo combined with the number of notes make it very hard to play smoothly. It's mostly finger work, the coordination of the right and the left hand. Practice is what my mother and piano teacher have always stressed."

"Well, I'm sure our listeners are now aware of the virtuosity of our Miss New York City. We wish you great luck as you go on to compete in Atlantic City."

Back home, Bessie is assured by Sylvia that she sounded great on the radio. Sylvia, a speech therapist, has been training Bess to pronounce her consonants and deregionalize her accent, and it is paying off. But with the approach of the pageant, panic begins to seize Bessie. Her formative sense of being unworthy resurfaces. *There must be something wrong. The evil eye. Poo, poo, poo.* Feeding on her mother's suspicions of all things too good to be true, Bessie doesn't let herself feel joy. She denigrates her appearance, telling herself she's not so attractive as others say. She learns about the engagement of a fellow Camp Birchwood counselor. *Lucky girl,* Bessie thinks enviously, considering this crazy ride she is on. Everyone is promising her wealth and fame, but she's losing her tan, is getting thinner by the day, and is weary from the back-to-back photo shoots. Feeling low, she postpones an appointment with *PM Magazine.*

At the end of the month, with just days before her departure for Atlantic City, Bessie meets for a photo op with Mayor LaGuardia that Don Rich sets up. Bessie hasn't seen him since he delivered the commencement speech for her graduating class at M&A. The mayor asks her if the Miss America Pageant is merely another fanny-shaking contest, where she will be competing with a lot of empty-headed females showing their legs. She swallows hard, unsure of how to respond as she stands behind a desk next to LaGuardia, who comes up to her shoulders. One of the photographers asks the mayor to "please stand up."

"I am standing up, dammit!" he yells before turning to Bess. "Promise me you'll stick to your music. And write to tell me what school you plan to attend."

Bessie tries to smile for the photo, though she suddenly feels sick as the flash goes off.

Hunter College friends Lenny Miller and Margie Wallis keep Bessie company the next afternoon. Bessie's small bedroom is strewn with clothes.

"Wow, these are some very gorgeous gowns." Margie fingers the close-fitting bodice of one of the silk designer dresses.

"I can't figure out what to pack. Like it's a monumental decision or something." Bessie closes her eyes, willing everything to disappear.

"You don't seem yourself, Bess." Lenny folds a blouse and two sweaters and moves them so she can sit on the bed.

"That's an understatement." Bessie squeezes her temples. "My nerves are drawn taut as piano wires."

"Just go there and show them what you've got," advises Margie.

"It's just that I'm not beauty-queen material. This is not me. I'm just a poor girl from the Bronx who wants to make it in music."

"Where is all this coming from?" Lenny furrows her brows. "You win, and you get a chance to do that."

"It's just all this . . . stuff. Learning how to properly walk in high heels. Having a schedule with every hour filled. All this sudden attention. Not all of it is good." Bessie shares about the smutty calls and letters she's received and she recounts her brief encounter with the mayor who wonders about her music aspirations.

"This"—she gestures her arm across all the gowns and clothes—"is not my career, or where my life is going."

Lenny and Margie look at one another in silence as Bessie starts sobbing.

CHAPTER TWELVE

ARRIVING IN ATLANTIC CITY

Monday, September 3, 1945

Bella unexpectedly comes to see them off. The sight of her mother waving as their train pulls out of Grand Central Station produces a tightness in Bessie's throat. *Is that an emptiness in Mama's eyes?*

Sylvia lightly touches Bessie's cheek, drawing back her attention. Bessie notices Syl's hair is done in a sophisticated updo. "We've never seen the boardwalk or stayed in a hotel, Bess!"

Bessie nods, taking in her sister's enthusiasm. "Or had room service." Bessie imagines the famous resort town from all that she's heard and what she viewed in the eponymous movie. She salivates thinking about its saltwater taffy. "Atlantic City is where my Birchwood campers vacation, especially around Rosh Hashanah."

"I think of it as a summer playground for the likes of Frank Sinatra and Judy Garland. And the Easter parades . . . and big bands on the Steel Pier."

Bessie nods dreamily. It was about a year ago when she went to see the movie *Atlantic City* with friends. The flashy nightclub scenes with performances by Louis Armstrong and Dorothy Dandridge left her yearning for romance.

"We're going to have a wonderful time, Bess." Sylvia brushes away a strand of hair that falls into Bessie's face. "Whatever else happens, we'll have a terrific time."

———•————•———

From the moment they step out from the Atlantic City train terminal, Bessie becomes aware of the disabled soldiers—leaning on crutches, limping from store to store, nurses pushing them in wheelchairs. She grabs Sylvia's arm, leading her out to the boardwalk. The drumming of numerous footsteps upon the boards continues without interruption. The soldiers are everywhere.

And so are the vacationers with their children. Tourists ride down the six-mile boardwalk on rolling chairs. Everyone is friendly and welcoming. All around, people are grinning and joyful. To Bessie, her arrival feels more than a respite before the competition ahead. The sense of collective relief is palpable. With the war over now, it is as if they have all been released from a prolonged and hopeless confinement.

Bessie inhales the first blast of salty sea air. Breathing free. So pure and fresh. The weather is perfect, the sun's warmth comforting. The sisters lean on the railing, their faces toward the Atlantic, holding hands. Bessie keeps drawing in that waft of ocean breeze. She closes her eyes. *This is what heaven must be like.*

They walk to Pennsylvania Avenue and Boardwalk, where they enter a mid-nineteenth-century boarding house called the Seaside Hotel. This is where the contestants register for the pageant. Among the forty contestants, some represent states; others, like Bessie, represent cities, depending on the availability of local sponsors. Several are standing in an uneven line looking unhappily at one another. Bessie eyes one beautiful girl after another, some chatting and laughing, their mothers impeccably dressed, wearing stylish hats, and displaying perfect manicures.

A chestnut-haired girl approaches Bessie and holds out her hand, smiling. "Hi, I'm Frances Dorn. From Birmingham, Alabama."

"I'm Bessie . . . Bess Myerson. Representing New York City."

"I've always wanted to see New York. Now we're so close, I'm hoping we can make the trip once all this is over." Frances seems relaxed, revealing none of the tension Bessie is feeling. Her accent is heavier than Lenora Slaughter's but her manner much more delicate. "Who are you here with?"

"I'm with my older sister, Sylvia. What about you?"

Frances points past the registration desk. "I have two chaperones, Lily May Caldwell and Jimmy Hatcher. They're family friends from Birmingham." Lily appears distinguished, in her fifties. Jimmy looks charming, sophisticated, and friendly, widely smiling as he catches Bessie's gaze. "I'm a tap dancer. What's your talent?"

"I play the piano and the flute."

"I always wanted to play an instrument. I look forward to getting to know you and hearing you play, Bess Myerson. But now, I need to scoot to complete my registration and pick up that Catalina swimsuit. You know we can't call them bathing suits? The Catalina executive said, 'Bathing is for tubs.'"

With that, Frances gives Bessie a sweet smile and joins her chaperones.

• — • — •

At the registration table, an older woman hands Bessie a packet that she takes to a bench to peruse, away from the tumult of contestants, mothers, chaperones, and the ubiquitous Lenora Slaughter. Inside, she finds background-information forms to fill out and a little booklet with her daily and hourly schedule for the week.

Bessie raises her head at the sound of Lenora's high-pitched voice, the pageant director visible a moment later. She pats everyone she passes in her extravagantly cheerful manner as she hands out badges and ribbons to the contestants. When she reaches Bessie, she calls her "Darling," gives her a vigorous hug, hands her a ribbon reading "Miss New York City," and tells her to wear it from the right shoulder to the left hip. "Next, you'll go upstairs to be fitted with your Catalina swimsuit and get your picture taken. Tonight, we're having a nice meeting with all you girls to tell you what's what." Lenora's perpetual smile, even while she's talking to Bessie, feels insincere. Bessie flat-out doesn't trust her.

"Wear your identifying badges at all times, girls," Lenora squeals to the contestants in the Seaside lobby. "Then everyone knows this flood of beauty is courtesy of the Miss America Pageant!"

Bessie goes back to reading from her packet. "The entrants will be judged on four counts: appearance in a bathing suit"—Bessie smiles at the outlawed descriptive—"appearance in an evening gown, personality, and talent." The opening message in the information booklet from the president of the Pageant Board talks about the careful selection of the judges and their experience in appraising beauty and talent to assure every girl "an equal opportunity for the coveted title of Miss America." One statement jumps out to her: "True Americanism prompts us to win or lose graciously."

As Bessie scans the survey, pen in hand, she realizes this nod to "Americanism" is not only rhetoric. There are questions about her war work record, her favorite food, and the genealogical particulars of her family's background in the United States. Bessie chews on the tip of the pen, just as she glimpses June Jenkins, packet in hand, across the lobby. June's reddish-brown hair is hard to miss.

"Bess Myerson! Boy, am I glad to see a familiar face!" June's dimpled smile puts Bessie instantly at ease.

"As am I!" Bessie gives June a hug. "Did you see this form? I mean, how specific do we need to be?"

"I plan to embellish for sure. Leslie Hampton—she's Miss Arkansas—she told me she traced her American ancestry back to 1783. Polly Ellis, who's Miss California, said her forebears had come over on the *Mayflower*. Come *on!*"

"Glad I asked you. And that there's some, uh, flexibility in the answers." Bessie winks at June.

"Let's try to get together if we can ever find any free time, Bess. I hope we get assigned the same hotel."

Bessie gives June a quick squeeze before she returns to the darn questionnaire. Certain she is the only Jew and the only first-generation American in the entire pageant, she writes that her family encompasses three American generations, meaning her parents as the first generation (though inaccurate, since they weren't born here), her and her sisters as the second, and then her sister's kids as the third, congratulating herself for coming up with such absurdity. Regarding food choices, she recalls June saying that Mary Louis Weaver, Miss Atlantic City, listed mashed potatoes and gravy. It clearly wouldn't help her chances to admit she loves kasha knishes and schmaltz herring, so Bessie writes that her favorite food is Southern fried chicken. For the career question, she decides she shouldn't appear grandiose and say she wants to study orchestra conducting. She pauses momentarily, then puts pen back to paper: "Would like to continue with music (flute and piano); pursue my MA degree and perhaps go on for additional training. Would include dramatics courses while working for master's."

She rereads her answer and thinks that sounds pretty good, actually.

— • — • — • —

After Bessie returns her form to complete her registration, a matronly straight-backed woman with white hair, white gloves, and a brown perch hat introduces herself as Mrs. Charles Wheeler, Bessie's designated hostess. Bessie learned earlier that society ladies in town, members of the Quaker elite that had founded the resort, were assigned to each contestant. She couldn't help noticing Mrs. Wheeler's upper-crust accent.

"I'm here to get you settled in your hotel. Miss Myerson, you and Mrs. Grace will be staying at the Brighton. But first we've got to go upstairs and get you that swimsuit."

Bessie learns that all the girls have the same style swimsuit but in different colors. With her dark hair and camp tan, she knows white is the most flattering shade, even though the suits are shapeless tanks. They have no support, with a wraparound panel that accentuates the belly.

As the suits are handed out and fitted in one room, Sylvia and Mrs. Wheeler wait in another. The fitting room is quiet enough that, through the partition, Bessie overhears nervous chatter among chaperones.

"Have you seen Minnesota? I hear she's a real threat."

"What's her talent?"

"She's a musician. A good one."

"I think this year's is a better-looking crop than last."

"The 1943 girls were my favorite."

Meanwhile, the seamstress asks Bess for her height and weight and marks down measurements. So it's official: Bess Myerson, Miss New York City: height, 5' 10"; weight, 135; bust, 35½"; waist, 25"; hips, 35".

Bessie dresses and rejoins Sylvia and Mrs. Wheeler. The three walk a block along the boardwalk to a nice clapboard hotel. In the lobby, there's a large framed photo of redheaded Venus Ramey, Miss America of 1944, and smaller frames of June Jenkins as Miss New York State alongside Miss Maryland, Miss Pennsylvania, Miss Philadelphia, and Miss District of Columbia, all of whom, Bessie is told by the congenial man who greets them, have been assigned to the Brighton. Most of the girls are posed in swimsuits that will be used in the pageant program. At first, when she doesn't see her own photo, she has that sinking feeling of being left out; then she spots the less conventional portrait of herself in cap and gown just as the man sticks out his hand. "Alan Graf. I'm the owner-manager, Miss Myerson."

Bessie takes in the many suitcases stacked in the lobby, imagining all the pretty frocks and skirts and blouses and hats the other girls brought for the trip. Her clothes are packed in shopping bags. She begins brooding about how inadequately dressed she will be.

"Bessie, are you ready? Mr. Graf just asked if he can escort us to our room." Sylvia gives her a prodding look and nods toward the stairs. Mrs. Wheeler excuses herself, promising to return to walk Bessie to the evening meeting.

Graf gathers Bessie's bags and gestures for her and Sylvia to follow him. He turns the key to their second-floor room and opens the door for them to step inside. The white wicker furniture gives the space a prim and decorous feel. Bessie eyes the white starched sheets on the bed, a stark contrast to the floral chintz curtains billowing from the cool ocean breeze. She feels like she has fallen into the Atlantic City chapter of the Daughters of the American Revolution.

She is thrilled that June Jenkins is down the corridor. She quickly meets the extroverted and chestnut-haired Gloria Bair, Miss Philadelphia, her room next door. And within hours, she meets Miss Maryland, Miss Pennsylvania, and Miss District of Columbia. Before the day ends, Gloria has introduced Bessie to several contestants rooming in the nearby Claridge, including the pretty and petite Miss Minnesota, Arlene Anderson, who shares that she plays the marimbaphone and has studied music for many years. Besides being self-conscious standing next to the tiny brunette, Bessie suddenly realizes the talent part of the pageant will not be a shoo-in. Won't an exotic percussion instrument beat Bessie's more conventional repertoire for sheer entertainment's sake?

That night at the Warner Theatre, Pageant Board President Arthur Chenoweth—stout, elderly, and bald—acts as master of ceremonies at the meeting of all the contestants. He introduces Lenora Slaughter as the first speaker, describing her as a dear friend who has been working for the pageant for the last decade and bringing it nationwide acclaim. "Lenora single-handedly kept the pageant alive during the war years." Chenoweth casts an admiring gaze at Lenora, causing Bessie to glance around at her fellow contestants. Most are sitting attentively, stiff in their suits and hats, their hands folded in their laps.

Lenora stands up and scans the audience. "I look out at all you lovely ladies, and I see the hope and the dreams on your faces. And I know you are thinking you are one of forty talented, beautiful girls in this contest, and you have your eye on the prize: the title of Miss America. But you're already winners, all of you queens in your own right!" Applause begins slowly and then builds as does Lenora's wide grin, exposing her white teeth, shining in the bright lights. Gloria, sitting on Bessie's right, turns her head slightly, takes Bessie's hand, and squeezes it.

"And one of you, after five wonderful days together, will be crowned and will be the very first to receive the $5,000 scholarship prize." The applause arrives in a thunder. "Now, let me tell you a little story about that." She pauses, licks her lips, careful not to smudge her bright-red lipstick. "I wanted to go to college more than anything in the world, but I didn't have the money. I know the shine of a girl's hair isn't going to make her a success in life. And what is a fur coat going to do for you?" She pauses again and scans the faces in front of her. "This scholarship is about your education, girls. It's about opportunities!"

Cheers quiet down as a heavyset woman takes Lenora's place at the podium. She introduces herself as Mrs. Richard Steel, chairman of the Hostess Committee. "We're here for your protection and comfort. I know your schedules are tight and you have many places to be, so we will escort you from your hotel to the pageant activities and back again."

Bessie thinks about that just as June, on her left, whispers, "Guess they don't want us out of their sight."

Mrs. Steel continues to list rules of decorum the contestants will have to follow. "You are not to make dates with any man or even have dinner with your father if he's here because the public has no way of knowing whether or not that man is your relative. You are not to enter a cocktail lounge or night club."

Some murmurs can be heard throughout the hall.

"You are all potential Miss Americas. So we need to keep you safe."

Both June and Gloria turn toward Bessie at the same moment, the three sighing in unison. "They don't take any chances, do they?" June says.

"This is just like grade school," adds Gloria.

Next up is Kentucky-born Venus Ramey, who represented the District of Columbia to win the contest last year. During her reign, she entertained at service camps and sold war bonds. For her work, Venus Ramey's picture was painted on the side of fighter planes. "These planes made sixty-eight raids over war-torn Germany and never lost a man," Mrs. Steel emphasizes in her introduction. The fact that Miss America is now seen as a national ambassador and activist isn't lost on Bessie.

Venus is wearing a becoming floral suit of Everglaze, a product of Joseph Bancroft & Sons Co., one of the pageant sponsors. Flashing a smile from ear to ear, she tells the contestants to look cheerful and pleased from the instant they wake up to the moment they fall asleep. "Keep smiling. You'll feel happy, and others will too. That's what we need in the world now—happier people."

Bessie finds herself grinning as Mr. Bob Russell is introduced as the master of ceremonies of the pageant. He comes forward with that trademark hop in his step, like every nightclub emcee and singer she's seen in the movies. "Girls, this week, you're performers, you're actresses, you're models, you're singers and entertainers. Show this great city that you're happy American girls, happy to be in Atlantic City, the city of beautiful girls!"

Lenora, Mr. Chenoweth, Miss Ramsey, and Mrs. Steel, sitting just behind Russell, are all beaming. Bessie finds it all quite syrupy but doesn't want to be a naysayer, so she says nothing to her new friends. They all listen to the final instructions: to wear an evening gown, but not their best one, in the parade to take place tomorrow. The contestants, who all seem to Bessie to be painstakingly smiling, file out of the theater.

Bessie is exhausted when she returns to her room. Still, she fills Sylvia in on the entire meeting, leaving out nothing, her sister always the very best sounding board. Fatigue soon turns into hunger, so they order room service and giggle like schoolgirls when the knock on the door announces the arrival of their food. They goggle at the silver dome they lift to find the simple grilled cheese sandwiches they devour in less than five minutes.

Along with being the only Jewish contestant, Bessie determines she may be the only college graduate. She wonders, as her head hits the pillow that first night at the Brighton Hotel, if she is about to cross a line, break a barrier.

CHAPTER THIRTEEN

THE PAGEANT, DAY ONE

Tuesday, September 4, 1945

Bessie rolls out of bed and groans. "I've got nothing to wear!" Sylvia runs to the closet, pulling out several blouses and skirts, throwing them on the bed. "Oh, but you have such an abundance of choices, Miss New York City!" She offers her best imitation of Lenora Slaughter, adding a Southern drawl, her voice rising in pitch. "The royal-blue skirt is striking, and how lovely it would look with the chartreuse top, or the chartreuse skirt with the royal-blue top, or the royal-blue scarf around your raven hair!"

Bessie's nervous flutters subside, at least for as long as she's giggling.

"That's my girl. Now let's get breakfast. We do have to report to the City Press Bureau at Convention Hall to hear from Lenora. And you know Mrs. Wheeler will be eagerly awaiting to escort you." Sylvia picks up the phone to order room service.

"Syl, just coffee and toast for me. My stomach is turning somersaults."

"Come on, you have to eat more than that."

Over breakfast, Bessie feels her throat close from nerves and she picks at her food. Sylvia ends up eating both of their meals. She orders a beer, with plans to use it to set Bessie's hair and keep it under control for the photo shoot that will follow Lenora's second lecture.

Bessie can't help thinking ahead to being on display in a swimsuit. It feels dirty somehow. Is she selling out here? Isn't she supposed to be a musician, a soloist, attending a conservatory instead of parading around half-naked?

———— • — • — • — • ————

Lenora scours the room, likely making sure she has the full attention of every contestant. Bessie numbly listens to the pageant director hammer out much of what they've already heard about contest rules. A blonde girl in front of Bessie whispers that Lenora reminds her of Mother Superior.

"Do not speak to your neighbor while I am talking, Miss Florida. It brings out my nasty side."

Bessie can see Jeni Freeland's neck turn scarlet and feels sorry for her and every other girl Lenora singles out and embarrasses. The room becomes eerily quiet. "There will be no drinking, absolutely no fraternization with men, no falsies or other artificial padding. If you've lied about your age and you're under eighteen, you will be disqualified. Anybody who has been married is disqualified. If you think what you're doing is sinful, don't do it, as it will disqualify you!"

Lenora takes a deep breath and lets it all out as she inspects the room and pastes on her toothy smile. "You are all perfectly beautiful girls and extremely intelligent, and I daresay you will learn more from the experience of being in the glorious Miss America Pageant than from any other single thing you do in your entire lives.

"You are the living symbols of American womanhood! No matter how the voting goes, you must never, ever be discouraged.

The competition is not over until the very last vote is counted. So chin up!

"Now, it's time to change into your swimsuits, girls. Onward to the panorama photo shoot, the most recognized symbol of the Miss America Pageant!"

———•—•—•—•—•———

Bessie wears a white Catalina suit, her Miss New York City ribbon draped across her torso as she's been instructed. She eyes those many contestants shorter than she, with more rounded hips. She feels strange and out of place, certainly not the national standard of beauty.

Makeshift bleachers are set against the background of the ocean. The photographers begin arranging the girls on the two rows, forty insecure beauties lining up hip to hip and displaying the Catalina emblem. But the photographers keep moving the girls around, taking one from the back row and moving her down, switching another from mid-row to a few places over, the trading of contestants apparently based on height and suit color. One photographer disagrees with the other's choice and counters with a new movement among the contestants. It feels chaotic, unorganized. Bessie is placed on the higher bleacher in the center of the row between Miss North Carolina and Miss New York State, June Jenkins. The photographers prep for the photo, lugging their equipment along the line of girls, whose long hair blows in the ocean breeze, resulting in much brushing and tucking of hair behind ears.

"Keep smiling!"

"Don't move!"

Bessie looks around her, and it suddenly hits her that there is not one Negro face among them. Perhaps she is not supposed to be in this elite club either. All the contestants seem to be sucking in their bellies, smiles frozen on their faces, immobile. Bessie feels herself round her shoulders, trying not to tower over the other girls. As she smooths her hand over her head, she realizes the beer is not working. Her hair is curling and frizzing from the humidity.

"Move back, Miss New York City. You're too close to Miss Connecticut."

She grits her teeth beneath her frozen smile. She overhears Miss Ohio telling Miss Pennsylvania, "These photos are hung in pool halls and saloons." To keep from feeling demoralized, Bessie tries to remind herself of the scholarship money, that this year talent matters.

"Come on, ladies, pull your shoulders back and stick out that chest." The taller photographer is shouting over the splashing sound of the breakers. "Now, give me a little saucy look."

Tension erupts below the bleachers between Lenora and the two major photographers in Atlantic City, Fred Hess and a man from Central Studio. "My girls are not horseflesh! These were never to be salacious portraits."

There's a lot of back-and-forth, shouts about "thousands of dollars at stake." Bessie hears one of the photographers say that he only takes his orders from the sponsor. All the girls continue to stand like statues, the hot sun beating down on them, until Catalina's E. W. Stewart shows up and insists on keeping the panorama shot as is. "The tantalizing swimsuit pose stays." Stewart rages at Lenora. "If you have your way, soon they'll all be marching down the runway in caps and gowns!"

⋄—⋄—⋄—⋄

As the girls begin to disperse, a different man with a camera approaches Bessie and a handful of girls standing near her. He introduces himself as Anthony Camerano from Associated Press. "Just an informal shot for the wire service, ladies. If you could stand across the boardwalk right here, please."

He motions toward a spot where the cement columns of the overpass tower in the background. Bessie and seven contestants quickly follow. Camerano then begins to position them side by side, moving one girl or another in some order he has in his head. He pulls out Phyllis Mathis, Miss San Diego, and places her in the center, her dark swimsuit balancing the lighter shades on each side. Bessie, with her white suit, stands on Phyllis's right. Flanked at each end are Lee Wieland, Miss Chicago, and Frances Dorn, Miss Birmingham. The eight girls link their arms as if old friends, flashing their most winning smiles for the camera.

Back at the hotel, Bessie changes clothes and hurries to meet Sylvia so they can grab lunch. An elderly couple timidly approaches her in the lobby. "*Du bist a yid?*" the lady asks.

When Bessie answers yes, the lady becomes gleeful. The frail couple hug Bess as if she were family. They pat her on the back. They hug each other.

"We live in a Jewish neighborhood of Atlantic City and heard a rumor that a Jewish girl had entered the pageant for the first time. We came to the hotel to see if it was true."

"Well, it's true."

"You are as lovely as they say. So you've got to win."

"But it's just a beauty contest."

"And you're *our* beauty, my dear. You've got to win. For all of us."

Bessie is touched and somewhat bewildered. Five minutes earlier she was worrying about how her hair would stay neat during the Victory Parade, scheduled for later that afternoon on the boardwalk. Now, she thinks about what these strangers have said to her. She is no longer just a girl seeking a scholarship, but a symbol for Jews seeking good news, yearning for a victory after word has spread that millions of them perished at the hands of Nazis. As she considers this nightmare, a sense of duty stirs inside her. She feels vindicated for her decision not to change her name, not to disguise who she really is. It would have cut her off from her own people and the outpouring of affection now greeting her.

"Bess, we've got to go." Sylvia turns to the old couple, thanking them for their good wishes. "We're grateful for your support," she tells them, then gently leads Bess to the hotel dining room.

They find a table. A waiter soon pours water into their glasses and takes their lunch order. They eat in silence, Bessie pushing the food around her plate.

"How will they feel if I lose, Syl?"

"Don't worry, Bess. These people love you. They're our friends, your supporters."

"Syl, why aren't there any Negroes in this contest?" Bessie takes a sip of water, that knot in her gut churning. "What if I'm not supposed to be here either?"

Sylvia stares at her hands, now folded in her lap, before looking up to answer. "The world we live in now is far from perfect, honey. Negroes, Jews, even women have little value. We are all easily cast aside. But things can change. You can help that change." She reaches across the table to squeeze Bessie's hand. "Now eat something. You don't want to lose any more weight than you have already."

Later that afternoon, Bessie heads to the Breakers Hotel, escorted by Sylvia and Mrs. Wheeler. It is a long walk to the hotel, located all the way near one end of the boardwalk, where the Victory Parade begins. She's happy she heeded Sylvia's advice to wear her most comfortable flats.

This year's version of the annual event is dedicated to the victorious armed forces. Bessie joins the other contestants in the Breakers' ballroom, many still in their petticoats, satin gowns of every color strewn across the backs of chairs. She watches everyone frantically don their dresses, her attention drawn to a long skirt of red suede slit at one side and a large hoop skirt, its front decorated with the official flowers. She slips on her pale-green gown, courtesy of Samuel Knapp, Sylvia zipping it just as they are directed to assemble in alphabetical-by-state order for their four-and-a-half-mile promenade to the other end of the boardwalk.

It is a fine day for a parade: clear and sunny, the air brisk. Leading the procession strides reigning Miss America Venus Ramey. Bessie stands on one of a long chain of elaborate rolling-chair floats, each pushed by a couple of men, as hundreds of eager and excited spectators line the route, some standing six and eight deep, others in beach chairs, many carrying small American flags as they watch and cheer for their favorite. Just ahead rolls a float proclaiming the merits of Fralinger's saltwater taffy, winning shouts from the audience. Bessie stands and waves to the crowds, smiling widely, her black hair flowing in the wind, her tension gone thanks to her earlier encounter with the elderly Jewish couple. Her eyes fill as she passes wheelchair-bound veterans in front of England General. Except for those Negro soldiers just home from fighting a war to defend democracy, the only Black people she sees on the boardwalk are those working as servants or waitstaff. State police surround the crowds, clearly brought in to keep order.

From start to finish, the parade takes two hours. Bessie is both weary and exhilarated—and ever more determined to win this crown.

———◦—◦—◦—◦———

That evening, Bessie wears her flowy white dress and silver shoes. Sylvia stands back, her eyes sparkling. "How lovely you look, Bess! The contrast of the dress against your dark hair and complexion is perfect."

"Yoo-hoo!" Mrs. Wheeler knocks on their room door, early as usual. Bessie gives her sister a quick kiss and heads down the stairs, Mrs. Wheeler not far behind. Tonight is the Military Ball at Convention Hall, given in the girls' honor by the officers in charge of Army Air Force Redistribution Station 1. More than two thousand servicemen, many of them ex-POWs, and their guests are present. Each contestant is matched with a male escort for the evening. Mrs. Wheeler takes Bessie to the executive office of Colonel A. W. Snyder, who makes all the introductions. Bessie meets her Jewish date, Sergeant David Gerber from Brooklyn. She immediately notices his deep-set brown eyes, which remind her a little of her father's. And the way he smiles at her makes her think of Frenchie.

"From a prison camp to this," he tells her. "Don't wake me up."

As Bessie dances with David, her long dress flows with each step, the two a match in height. He is lean with broad shoulders, and she feels safe in his arms. She begins to imagine herself married, secure, happy. She feels relaxed and projects a warmth for David and the other soldiers, grateful for their service and sacrifice.

During the evening, each contestant takes a turn across the Convention Hall stage and receives a key to the city from Mayor Joseph Altman. It's a magical night for Bessie. At the end of the evening, the soldiers at the dance take a straw poll on their favorites to win the Miss America Pageant. They choose Phyllis Mathis of San Diego for third place; Miss Wisconsin, Ellen Christy, for second; and Bessie herself—*Bess Myerson!*—as the girl most likely to win the crown.

She arrives back at her Brighton Hotel room elated from all the admiration.

"Bess, I hate to break this to you," Sylvia says. "But the soldiers aren't the judges here."

Still caught in a hypnotic swoon, she lets Syl's remark slide. As she hits the pillow that night, the glow of a glorious evening carries her into dreamland.

CHAPTER FOURTEEN

OPENING NIGHT, TALENT COMPETITION

Wednesday, September 5, 1945

Bessie stands among the already weary contestants on the stage of the Warner Theatre, wilting in the afternoon heat. Situated in the front, she hears some of the girls behind her whispering among themselves.

Bob Russell, pageant emcee, faces them. "Please, ladies. I must have your full attention!" The usually convivial Russell wipes his forehead with a hanky he pulls out of his shirt pocket as he apologizes for the faulty cooling system and promises it will be fixed by the evening's opening festivities.

"Now, let me get you all caught up on how these next three nights will proceed. I'm going to divide you girls into three groups. Each night, one group competes for points on their appearance in evening gowns, another group in swimsuits, and the third group for their talent. You'll rotate on Thursday and again on Friday. The winners of the swimsuit and talent competitions are announced each night, but not the runners-up and not the winners or run-ners-up in the evening gown contest."

Russell pauses just as Bessie turns around to catch the many blank faces staring back at him. Her gaze returns in time to catch Russell nodding, as if acknowledging their befuddlement. "That's so no one knows who the semifinalists are until they are named on the last night of competition."

Bessie can't be alone among her fellow contestants as she struggles to grasp what he's saying. Why, she wonders, is the evening gown category the one whose results are kept secret? Does that have a higher value?

Acting as if everything is nicely settled, Russell proceeds to divide up the forty contestants into Group A, Group B, and Group C based on what section of the stage they're standing in. Bessie is relieved to be in the final group so she can perform tonight and lead with what she sees as her strength.

"Girls, there is a fourth category. Personality. You will be judged on personality at a round-robin of breakfasts with our esteemed judges." Bessie notices a layer of sweat building up on Russell's forehead as his words are met with additional silence. "You just have to meet and talk with them."

The girls knew about all four categories if they read the pamphlet. Bessie had. Every single word. But hearing this now as she imagines herself sitting down and conversing with the judges makes her stomach feel jumpy.

"By Saturday night, every contestant will have competed in each category. You'll be getting scores on all four. Those of you with the highest total number of points will compete in the semifinals."

Bessie is now completely confused and, without forethought, raises her hand. "Are you saying there are two whole rounds on Saturday night—semifinals and finals? I mean, what will the semifinalists be expected to do? You know, to become a finalist?" She suddenly worries about being presumptuous but sees that many of the girls are leaning inward, nodding in affirmation.

"Miss New York City, what an insightful question." Russell almost congratulates himself, as if he set her up so he could further explain the whole cumbersome process. "The chosen semifinalists will have to compete in all categories all over again that night. Then—and only then—will we move to name the finalists. Further questions?"

Miss Rhode Island, Mary Stevens, raises her hand. "If I'm in the C group, does that mean I compete in the talent competition tonight, evening gown tomorrow, and swimsuit on Friday? It's a little confusing, is all." Her bangs stick to her forehead. She uses a pageant program to fan herself.

"You needn't worry your pretty blonde head about the order, Miss Rhode Island. We'll be guiding you every step of the way." Russell moves to the left wing of the stage. "Now, ladies, I want you to line up alphabetically. You'll parade together from the wings onto the stage and then off it, down the long ramp. You'll do this to begin each night's program."

"But we'll be wearing different outfits, won't we, Bob?" When Bessie hears Mary address the emcee by his first name, an emphasis on the *b*'s, she covers her mouth so Russell won't see her smirk. Miss Rhode Island is not one who likes to be treated like a dummy. *Good for you, Mary Stevens!*

— — — ◦ — ◦ — —

Much of the day is spent rehearsing with Joe Frasetto, the pageant bandleader. His band has two violins, three saxophones, a trumpet, a piano, a bass, and a drum, providing full orchestration for any music the contestants have chosen. Frasetto is a pro, well known in Atlantic City through his frequent appearances at the swinging 500 Club.

Despite the large number of girls singing and doing musical routines, besides Bess only Arlene Anderson brings appropriate arrangements. While Bessie feels especially fortunate to have so much experience playing her piano and flute, she has no idea what will *entertain* the judges. The limited rehearsal time leaves her feeling unprepared, something most of the girls begin to express to Lenora as they plead for a second run-through.

As she mulls over her evening performance during the break, she is approached by a local photographer named Frank Havens. "Don't you want to see all the scenery and props backstage? It's where Miss America's throne is stored. Follow me."

Her curiosity piqued and eager for the distraction, she follows him.

"Come on, Bess. Sit in that chair. If you sit in that chair and I take your picture, I bet you will be Miss America."

She backs away, almost frightened of Havens's suggestion.

"Look, I like you. You're different from many of the gals here—down-to-earth. I'm rooting for you to win." Havens looks away from her direct gaze for a moment, then takes in a large gulp of air before he locks eyes with her. "But you need to watch yourself. There are people involved here who don't want a Jewish winner."

Bessie's lower lip quivers. "How do you know that?"

"Yesterday a pageant official came into the press office. He said that the swell of support for you had to be stopped. He insisted there had never been a Jewish winner and there never would be. I say you prove him wrong, Bess."

She tries to calm herself, to process the reality that she now knows surrounds her: that she is among people who see her as a tall Jewish interloper. As if steeling herself for what is to come, she agrees to pose for the photograph. But before she sits down on the throne, she very quietly says to herself, *Poo, poo, poo,* just like Mama taught her.

＊ ー ＊ ー ＊ ー ＊

Bessie only has ninety minutes between the end of rehearsals and opening night. She and Sylvia have taken copious notes on all of Lenora's speeches as well as what they've heard on the ground.

They spend their little time alone in the hotel room studying every last jot as if cramming for school exams.

"I want to collapse on my knees every time I stand next to Arlene Anderson during rehearsals. She's five three!"

"You *must* stand tall, Bess. Just like what your piano teacher told you."

Bessie remembers the afternoon Mrs. LaFollette made her practice her approach to the piano and how her teacher reacted when she slouched: *It's not the altitude, Bess; it's the attitude.*

"In some ways, I wish Mama could be here. Her toughness sort of got me here, you know, Syl?" Bessie recalls the discipline Mama always insisted on, her nonstop commands to practice her piano, even her insistence on Bess playing Olive Oyl, and with style, back in that grade school production. "On the other hand, it would be tough for me if she were here."

"I bet many of the girls who come to Atlantic City may have reached this point because of their mothers' ambitions. But they are different kinds of mothers." Sylvia gives Bess a reassuring smile.

"And I'm so different from their daughters. Just a poor Jewish girl from the Bronx. I don't have a chance, Syl; let's face it."

"Wrong! You are just the type who stands out above the rest." Sylvia takes Bessie's hands in her own. "You're poised, talented, and intelligent. And suddenly the world will be seeing someone who looks like you—tall and lean with dark, sometimes-frizzy hair—and who comes from a different culture and religion. The Bronx shtetl, for God's sake! And that's just fine. It is more than fine!"

⸺•⸺•⸺

Wearing a slenderizing dinner jacket and distinguished glasses framing his oval face, Bob Russell skips out onstage and announces the Parade of States is about to begin the opening night of the Miss America Pageant. Miss Arkansas, Leslie Hampton, leads the forty contestants onstage. She is followed by Miss Atlanta,

Miss Birmingham, Miss Boston, Miss California, each girl walking with the graceful techniques Russell taught them, smiling brilliantly, allowing their arms to relax instead of hang stiffly. Watching from offstage as she waits for her turn, Bessie reminds herself to stand tall and show confidence.

The girls line up in front of the judges, who sit in their enclosure that connects to the ramp. Russell introduces each judge, all in evening attire. Bessie knows each of their backstories, thanks to Sylvia's inquiries. There are the four artists/illustrators. Arthur William Brown is well known for his illustrations for three of Booth Tarkington's novels, including *The Magnificent Ambersons*. He is distinguished in a snappy jacket and ascot, familiar to most as "Brownie," currently serving as president of the Society of Illustrators. Artist Bradshaw Crandall's reputation stems from his ability to create immortality for any girl he renders, and his style is often copied. Bessie knows that Crandall appreciates originality and sees that as working to her advantage. Dean Cornwell's fame goes back to the 1920s for creating portraits and dramatic art. Finally, Vincent Trotta, considered a jolly and kind man by the contestants he mingles with, is an advertising art director for big film companies like Paramount Pictures. Of course, everyone knows Lenora Slaughter has badgered the group on the importance of special talents and disposition, taking issue with their focus on physical measurements and facial structure. Her constant message to judges is that during this first scholarship year, the winner must be more than beautiful. She must also be trusted to make a strong public impression, have real talent, and demonstrate intelligence. It seems that Lenora doesn't care who hears her directives.

There are three women judges this year. Each stands as their names are called: former contestant Lois Wilson, now a starlet in Hollywood; Prunella Wood, a fashion news writer for King Features; and Vyvyan Donner, one of the few women directing in Hollywood. Bessie is most impressed with Vyvyan, a tall, sweet-faced woman who has produced hundreds of short features covering world fashion for *Movietone News*. Still, Bessie worries about Vyvyan's interest in fashion and her own lack of experience modeling. She knows it is her talent that must impress the judges and has her eye on Conrad Thibault, a popular radio tenor working for Mike Todd Productions. She shudders when Harry Conover is introduced, recalling her rejection by him not even a year ago.

———•—•—•——

Bessie watches while Miss Indiana sings "Indian Love Call," then as Miss Connecticut belts out "I'm in the Mood for Love." Miss Arkansas enacts a torch song interpretation of "My Man," Miss Iowa tap dances, Miss Utah performs a ballet. Miss District of Columbia plays the part of Joan of Arc in the courtroom scene from George Bernard Shaw's *Saint Joan*. Miss Mississippi stages a stand-up comedy routine that produces few laughs. Miss San Diego does a hula dance.

When Frances Dorn is introduced, she appears center stage in a two-piece frilly glitter costume, wearing white high-heeled tap shoes and a gardenia in her hair. Music begins and, unlike what Bessie considers the mediocre talent displayed so far, Frances captures the crowd's enthusiasm, the rapid clicks of her heels and toes rhythmically striking the floor, the audience clapping their hands and tapping their own feet in tandem. She shuffles forward and back, alternating each foot, stomping and stamping, the speed and hops of her footwork slowing, then speeding up, the energy of her movement and the music palpable. The applause is deafening.

Bessie has butterflies, knowing she's following the best talent of the night. She looks out into the theater where Sylvia is sitting—her loving and loyal sister, so certain of her win. Sylvia pulls the top of her hair upward to remind Bess of Mrs. LaFollette's direction, and Bessie straightens, takes a deep breath, steps confidently onto center stage in her white gown, and settles herself onto the piano bench, her hands poised to begin at the orchestra's cue. After striking the powerful opening chords of Edvard Grieg's Piano Concerto in A Minor, her rapid finger work continues flawlessly. The orchestra's backup accentuates her soft undulation of the melody as Bessie inhabits the emotions of each note, each phrase, each musical pattern. She follows with Gershwin's familiar "Summertime" on the flute, her expressiveness producing a dreamy song reverberating and oscillating throughout the silent theater. The crowd is enthralled, their approval delivered with whistles and cheers. Her rapidly beating heart is full. They like her! Maybe Syl is right, and she has a chance after all.

While the judges submit their points and numbers are tabulated, Bob Russell sings the Miss America Pageant song. Bessie barely listens until she sees he is handed an envelope from the judges' box. Russell opens it, his eyes widening, and announces Miss Birmingham, Frances Dorn, the winner. Bessie's heart drops, the disappointment crushing. But, in the next split second, Bess hears her name. Hears Russell pronouncing her title, Miss New York City. Her heart skips a beat, and she feels her face flush.

". . . a tie in the talent competition!"

Eyes gleaming, she quickly displays her most winning smile.

Russell brings Frances and Bess to the front of the stage and asks them about their performances. Bessie remembers when she talked to Mrs. LaFollette about the concerto, and she decides to convey the emotion of the piece. "I adore the spirited lyricism of Grieg's melodies. There's an almost contagious rhythmic element in his work. It comes right from the heart, I think. His music is so natural, and very real, very honest." More applause follows her answer.

Meanwhile, also on the stage, Miss Tennessee, Lee Harriet Henson, takes top honors in the first night of the swimsuit contest. Chatter among the girls tells Bess they predict high judge ratings in the evening gown for Lee Wieland, Miss Chicago; Arlene Anderson, Miss Minnesota; and Miss Florida, Jeni Freeland. But it will remain conjecture until Saturday.

At the end of that evening, Sylvia appears more animated than Bess has ever seen her sister. "Rumors are flowing that you have it in the bag!"

Bessie shakes her head. "Syl, come on, that's just gossip. Something could happen to ruin my chances. I might break some rule inadvertently."

Sylvia tenses her brows and doesn't reply. Bessie tries to expunge the negative thought filling her head: that she will lose despite all the hopeful wishes of her sister, her Jewish fans, and her soldier friends. And despite the crowd of newsmen and photographers who seem to follow her everywhere.

"I overheard Lenora talking to the press earlier today . . . about treating all the girls the same. She's referring to me, and to my Jewish fans. She wants a Miss America she can sell, and she doesn't think she can sell a girl named Myerson. There are others, too, worried if I win. And that makes me want this crown more than anything I've ever wanted."

CHAPTER FIFTEEN

EVENING GOWN AND SWIMSUIT COMPETITION

Thursday and Friday, September 6 and 7, 1945

On Thursday morning, when Bessie leaves her room to head to the Warner Theatre for the swimsuit run-through, she finds adoring fans in the lobby.

"Miss Myerson, will you sign my napkin?"

"Of course! What's your name?" Bessie takes the pen from a dark-haired girl, no older than fourteen.

"Susie. Susie Stein. Thank you so much! I hope you win!" Susie flashes a gap-toothed smile before she skips off.

Another young girl, no taller than four feet, approaches as Bessie weaves her way through the crowd. "Can I give you a kiss for good luck, Miss Myerson? I so hope you become Miss America." Bessie bends down and offers her cheek.

After tying as talent winner and thanks to her young fans, she leaves her hotel cheerful and more positive than she's been since she arrived in Atlantic City.

In the theater dressing room, Bessie strips down to the white suit they gave her at registration, dropping her clothes across a nearby chair. She takes her turn walking down the runway under the watchful eye of Lenora Slaughter.

"Bess, come over here, please."

She dutifully walks over to Lenora, who leans close in, barely speaking above a whisper. "That swimsuit is too small for you."

Bessie looks down at herself, somewhat puzzled. "It's a twelve. That's my size."

"Well, it's riding up very immodestly in the back. I'll have Catalina send a size fourteen replacement over to your hotel. Now, let's continue with the rehearsal."

Bessie doesn't consider arguing. The last thing she wants to do is cause a problem or draw attention to herself, the newsman's warning still roiling in her mind. Unable to shake off her edginess as she rejoins her sister, she is grateful when Sylvia suggests they go to the beach for their few free hours. Bessie is eager to feel the warmth of the sun, the novelty of a real ocean a source of calm for her. Soldiers approach as the sisters lay their towels on the sand. Bessie nods politely but then turns away, her face catching the sun's rays, her eyes closed. She's not interested in giving the pageant naysayers a reason to disqualify her for fraternization.

Shortly after they return to the hotel room, as Sylvia is setting Bessie's hair, the Catalina representative delivers the size-four-teen suit. The man seems to look suspiciously at the glass of beer perched on the dresser. Sylvia grabs the beer and takes a big gulp.

"It's so hot here. Nothing better than a nice cold brew." Sylvia speaks fast, trying to catch her breath. "My sister, Bess—she's Miss New York City. She never touches the stuff."

After the man leaves, Bessie cries, "Sylvia, how could you

drink that awful stuff? You could have just dropped the comb in it, so he'd know you were using it as setting lotion."

"I panicked." Sylvia burps, and she quickly puts her hand across her mouth. "Geez, excuse me."

Bessie rolls her eyes at her sister before taking a good look at the new swimsuit, a nauseating color of pea soup. She tries it on; it looks like a sack on her tall, thin frame, and she begins to fret. "The size, the color . . . it makes me look sickly." She wrings her hands. "This is going to end my chances to be Miss America." For Bessie, it's back to Olive Oyl as she looks at herself in the mirror. String-bean thin with all her nervous stomach upsets over the last few weeks. Gangly. Ugly. She hates what she sees.

"Look, maybe we're overreacting. Let's get another opinion." Sylvia leads Bess to Gloria Bair's room next door and knocks.

Gloria's smile turns into an open-mouthed stare as she takes in the new swim garment. "*Where* did you get that suit? It looks *awful*!"

While Bessie explains her predicament, June Jenkins appears around the corridor, equally appalled by the baggy swimsuit. "What a repulsive shade of green! That's not your suit for tomorrow's contest, is it?"

Bessie and Sylvia look at each other, their opinions now validated. "Ladies, thanks for the input." Sylvia gives Bess a reassuring smile. "We'll figure something out, Bess. Let's focus on tonight. You've got the evening gown competition to deal with first."

That evening, Bessie feels confident in her Grecian-draped Knapp gown. She looks out from backstage and is surprised at the size of the audience, almost double from the previous night. She intently watches the talent contest, beginning with Miss Rhode Island and Miss Maine singing the blues. Then Miss Tennessee, Lee Henson, walks onstage. Bessie recalls she won the bathing suit division on Wednesday. She is charming, an audience favorite.

Lee takes one look at the audience and freezes. "Folks, I can't remember one word of the speech I'd planned to make tonight. Forgive me. How about I sing a song instead?"

The crowd, especially the soldiers, cheer as Lee brightly begins "I Didn't Know the Gun Was Loaded." The band follows along. The crowd erupts.

Next comes Miss California in a sombrero with a short, fringed skirt, singing a cowboy tune. She is followed by Miss Maryland appearing in a long gown as she launches into "Ain't Misbehavin'." In the middle of her performance, she disrobes and cavorts around the stage in a black sequined dancing brief with a top hat and cane. Bessie is shocked. Surely this couldn't be the sort of routine that Lenora would approve. Maybe Miss Maryland was bold enough to spring it as a surprise. And, perhaps, the girls don't have to follow Lenora's instructions to the letter.

She becomes further astounded when Miss California is named talent winner for that night. Bessie was sure that Lee Henson would win, having overcome a major blunder with such composure and with the audience behind her. Another teaching moment: the audience reaction has no influence on the judges. Knowing she's also an audience favorite, Bessie tries to shake off her worry with the evening gown competition about to begin.

A backstage supervisor interrupts her state of agitation, calling out for the girls to line up in the wings. "Be careful not to step on each other's dresses, ladies!"

When she hears her name, Bessie gracefully glides down the runway, her wide smile natural as she makes eye contact with audience members and judges alike. The ovation after her runway stroll is explosive.

In the privacy of their room, Bessie shares her insights with Sylvia. As she takes off her evening gown and hangs it in the closest, Sylvia stands in the middle of the room with the green swimsuit in one hand, the white one in the other. Suddenly, she squeals, "I've got it!"

She throws the green suit on the floor, peels off her clothes, and pulls the size-twelve white suit onto her own size-sixteen body. She strains, pulls, and wriggles, trying to squeeze into that suit.

"You'll rip the seams, Syl!"

But Sylvia gets the suit on. She grabs her nightgown and pulls it over her head, then collapses on the bed. "I'm going to stretch this thing out. You're going to be wearing this white swimsuit tomorrow, Bess."

The next morning, Sylvia takes off the suit and Bessie puts it on. It is a bit bigger. She wears it in a swimsuit parade at Thomas M. England General Hospital before the wounded GIs. She walks sideways, leg over leg, careful not to turn her back to the audience. Lenora is fortunately not in attendance.

From onstage, Bessie takes in the scene in front of her: men on stretchers, in wheelchairs. And so many amputees. Her chest tightens as she sees, firsthand, the sacrifices of war. Once the parade concludes, hospital staff ask the girls to visit the boys from their home states. Bessie listens incredulously as most of the girls refuse with the excuse that they have to rehearse or rest. She stays on with Jeni Freeland and June Jenkins. She can't leave these men, so sorrowful yet so courageous. These are the soldiers who saved her and her family from the Nazis, who gave up their arms and legs to stop Hitler.

But she is completely unprepared to handle the devastation in front of her. A man in a bed with the sheet dropped where his leg ends. Another reaching out his hook to shake her hand. She watches as a nurse carries a maimed boy down the hall on her back. Bessie tries to hold back tears, the lump in her throat almost choking her.

A staffer pokes her hard and tells her to straighten up. "Don't you dare cry. You turn around and smile at these men, cupcake."

She steels herself then, determined to do whatever she can in this role as a Miss America contestant to bring the soldiers some solace. She introduces herself to two seemingly cheerful, optimistic men about her age. Jimmy Wilson, a quadruple amputee from Florida, is the sole survivor of a B-24 crash that happened during a training mission last October in Vermont. By the time rescue workers found him in the snowy mountains three days later, he suffered severe frostbite of his hands and feet. Ernie Sardo, originally from Elmira, arrived at England General a couple months after Jimmy. He is a triple amputee, and Bess learns he was wounded in a German counterattack in Alsace-Lorraine when someone threw a grenade in his foxhole. Both men have lost more than their limbs. When they let their guard down, Bess can see that the horrors of war they don't talk about are etched deeply into their faces. As she sits at their bedsides, she tries to imagine how she could help overcome the hatred and bigotry of a war that caused such barbaric slaughter.

Just the previous night she was brooding about a swimsuit. Now, she contemplates what can be done so the sacrifices of Ernie and Jimmy won't have been meaningless.

———•—•—•—•——

Sylvia concludes that the white swimsuit is still too small and won't get past Lenora that evening. She puts it back on and wears it for the rest of the day until it is time for Bess to get ready. Syl says it still needs three-quarters of an inch more in length, so she removes the buttons on the straps, loosening them so that Bess can pull down the bottom of the suit, sews up the buttonholes, cuts off the unneeded excess strap material, and sews that directly to the suit.

It works—not a trace of Bessie's butt shows in the back. There is only one problem. Bessie seems to be sewn into the swimsuit, and she can't take it off. Carefully, she puts on the evening gown she'll be wearing for the Parade of States. At the theater, she does her runway walk, and just before the swimsuit competition, she hides backstage to remove the evening gown. She doesn't sit down, and she tries not to breathe very hard as she watches Arlene Anderson play the marimbaphone.

At the appointed time, Bessie takes as deep a breath as she can to get calm and proceeds onstage to compete in her white, stretched and stitched, size-twelve Catalina. There is a lot of cheering, but by now, Bessie knows that audience reaction, while it feels good, is meaningless.

Arlene Anderson wins the talent competition that night with her marimbaphone. When Bob Russell announces that Bess is the winner of the swimsuit division, she realizes she is the only contestant who tied in talent and won outright in swimsuit. If she was going to believe the press, she'd conclude that she had a strong showing in evening gown, which would mean that, on points alone, she could be one of the semifinalists. She feels faint, given her tight suit and inability to breathe deeply.

She also feels more than a little guilty since tonight is Erev Rosh Hashanah. The Miss America Pageant would never consider a Jewish high holy day as they scheduled their event. Bessie is certainly not going to bring this up to anyone, but it reminds her how she doesn't fit into their world. *Will I ever?* she wonders.

CHAPTER SIXTEEN

THE FINAL DAY!

Saturday, September 8, 1945

"Just think about it as a conversation, Bess. Nothing more." Sylvia paces back and forth in the small hotel room.

Bessie is terrified because she'll be having breakfast with the judges this morning for the personality evaluation.

"Tell them what you care about. Your music, your dreams. Your family. Just be honest."

"The family?" Bessie shrugs. "Oh, right. That would go really well, Syl."

"Okay. I'm just saying . . . be prepared to talk about a range of topics. It will be better if you consider what you might be asked and how you could answer." Sylvia begins straightening the bedspread, then turns back toward Bess. "By the way, Helen arrives this afternoon and will attend tonight!"

The thought of her sister watching her perform this evening calms Bessie for a moment, but she quickly remembers that she must stay focused on the audience she will be engaging with this morning. She wishes she could have breakfast with Helen instead.

Less than an hour later, Bessie gathers with the other contestants on the sundeck of the Claridge Hotel. Eight tables are set up, as well as a long buffet table.

"Fill your plate and take a seat at any table." Lenora's voice carries over the nervous chatter. "Leave one or two open spots for the judges. When the bell rings, the judges will move to another table and others will sit down in their places. You girls stay put."

Bessie's stomach is in knots as she surveys the breakfast spread. She takes a piece of toast and some strawberry marmalade. She spoons scrambled eggs onto her plate and considers the bacon. She doesn't eat bacon but doesn't want to be called out for avoiding it, so she places one strip on her plate. Then she heads for the table where Gloria Bair and June Jenkins are seated. Jeni Freeland and Arlene Anderson follow Bessie from the buffet.

Bradshaw Crandall and Vyvyan Donner join her table for the first round. A waiter comes by and asks what she'd like to drink. "Milk," she says, without thinking. She's a big milk drinker but suddenly worries that she might be talking to a judge with a white moustache over her upper lip. She must take tiny sips. So much to think about.

Most importantly, she needs to get the backstories of these judges straight. Bradshaw Crandall is the illustrator, the one whose drawings make girls famous. Sylvia read that he appreciates individuality and distinction among his models—if one is to believe the beauty columns. Movie director Vyvyan Donner's short documentaries on world fashion have influenced farm girls in Kansas and secretaries in Cleveland. She's done as much as any single person to internationalize the couture market. Bessie tries not to be obvious as she inspects the filmmaker's hairdo, admiring how she wears her upswept pile of tight curls on the top of her head.

"What would you say is your passion, ladies? You know . . . that something that gets you most excited." Vyvyan scans the

faces of the five contestants, who glance at one another uncomfortably as if trying to figure out who will answer first.

Bessie forces herself to speak up. "I'm pretty passionate
about music, Miss Donner. I applaud all that you've done in
the fashion world, and I'd like to have that kind of influence on
women about music. There are next to no female conductors and
few women members of any orchestra in this country."

As Vyvyan nods pensively, Bradshaw jumps in. "I like your
initiative, Miss Myerson. Confidence is what American girls need
more of."

Bessie feels far from confident but is glad that Mr. Crandall
thinks otherwise.

"But where does that passion come from, Miss Myerson?"
Vyvyan smiles kindly at Bess. "If you are to influence others, you
need to know the source of your enthusiasm."

Bessie thinks about the hundreds, perhaps thousands, of
pages of music she's played. How each note is linked to the next,
how the sounds form patterns and melodies and whole worlds.
"Composers and musicians use their art to tell stories. Music can
depict characters, faraway places, dramatic actions, emotions."
She pauses to consider her next words. "Music is as important
as any art form because it allows the expression of thoughts or
feelings when mere words are not enough."

"My passion is also in music, Miss Donner." Arlene Anderson,
the pretty, petite marimbaphone player, may be the only other
contestant with musical knowledge as extensive as Bessie's. "The
marimba can be a difficult instrument to learn how to play, and
while there isn't a wealth of classical repertoire, learning to play
one is well worth it. The sound that is produced by a marimba is
one of my favorite sounds in the world. Playing it is pure pleasure!"

Gloria shares her love of modeling and fashion. June Jenkins comments on Vyvyan's hair style, wondering if she could
manage that kind of updo. The conversation becomes entirely
girlish, leaving Bradshaw Crandall uncharacteristically quiet. He

tries to change the subject by asking about their future plans, but he is cut off by the ringing bell and another judge arriving to take his place at the table.

Bessie later describes Saturday's morning activity to Sylvia as "musical judges." That afternoon, Sylvia quotes parts of an article by Morley Cassidy in the *Philadelphia Bulletin* to Bessie: "'Forty potential Miss Americas were called on this morning to prove that they can . . . carry on a sprightly conversation . . . and drink a glass of orange juice without getting lipstick all over the glass. . . . The results will have a lot to do with . . . who will appear tonight, to compete for the crown that will be awarded at midnight.'

"And listen to this, Bess! 'The new Miss America will either be Miss New York City, Bess Myerson, of the Bronx, or somebody else.'"

The electricity is palpable on the final night with thousands crowded into the Warner Theatre, hundreds of them servicemen, cheering and whistling. The press section is packed. The US Coast Guard Band plays "The Star-Spangled Banner." A spotlight illuminates the American flag. A gold-and-silver curtain parts, revealing all forty contestants in their evening gowns. After the Parade of States, Bob Russell, dressed in tails, steps to the microphone. He tells the audience to hold their applause until the end as he announces the highest scores. One by one, each of the ten semifinalists stands as her name is called. Bessie is introduced right after Arlene Anderson, Miss Minnesota. She rises, her heart beating fast, trying to remember to look natural and smile.

Russell instructs the judges to view these girls with a fresh eye. The semifinalists parade before the judges, then withdraw to change into swimsuits. Bess enlists Arlene to help her manage her straps. For the next several hours, they must engage again in the swimsuit, evening gown, and talent competitions. Bess thinks Lee Henson, Miss Tennessee, will get the top score in swimsuit with talent a toss-up between Virginia Lee Van Sant, Miss Maryland, or Polly Ellis, Miss California. The tension escalates with each competition and each passing hour. A twelve-year-old piano prodigy from Atlantic City plays Debussy's *Clair de lune*. Russell introduces the leaders of the five sponsors of the first Miss America scholarship.

It is near midnight when he is handed the card with the final five names. He calls them out in rapid succession: "Miss Birmingham, Miss Florida, Miss Minnesota, Miss New York City, Miss San Diego!"

Bess finds herself being hugged by fellow contestants as the reality begins to sink in. But she has no time to get the jitters, since the agile emcee immediately brings each finalist to the front of the stage to answer three questions. When he asks Bess how she plans to use the scholarship, she replies, "To pay for graduate school."

"Do your future plans include marriage, a career, or both?"

Bess knows her answer must be nuanced; she can't seem only interested in her career. And, in honesty, she's not. "Mr. Russell, I'd like nothing more than to fall in love with a wonderful man and have a family. And if I can also bring music into people's lives, I would find that tremendously fulfilling."

The final question: "What did you get out of the pageant?"

"I'm grateful to the pageant for giving me the opportunity to meet so many extraordinary girls from all over the country. For a girl who grew up in the Bronx, it has been a wonderful experience."

The judges vote again. As the ballots are being counted, Russell gets the audience to sing along to Perry Como's "Till the End of Time."

His voice upstages that of the lively audience for the closing lyrics: "So take my heart in sweet surrender and tenderly say that I'm the one you love and live for, till the end of time."

Trying to keep the audience engaged while waiting for the balloting to be finished, Russell cracks one joke after another. Bess smiles like a statue, calm on the outside, her head filling with disjointed fragments of thoughts: . . . *actually, competing to become a beauty queen? . . . Mama didn't bring me up to parade around half-naked . . . what about my music ambitions? . . . the audience loved the Grieg piece . . . maybe I have a chance . . . but I'm so tall, I tower over petite Miss Minnesota . . . how can I think about anything this trite in a world filled with Nazi death camps and atomic bombs?*

Suddenly, the envelope naming the winner and runners-up is in Russell's hand. He opens it, looks down at the card; his eyes widen. The orchestra plays a drum roll. Bess holds her breath as he announces: "Fourth runner-up is Arlene Anderson, Miss Minnesota!"

Barely pausing, he calls out, "Third runner-up is Jeni Freeland of Florida!"

The crowd's cheers are louder, as is Russell's pronouncement: "Second runner-up is Frances Dorn, Miss Birmingham!"

Bess can't believe her ears. Only she and Phyllis Mathis remain. She grips Phyllis's hand, not knowing what else to do, her heart pounding. Time feels as frozen as her beaming expression.

Russell remains animated. "First runner-up is . . ." He pauses for dramatic effect, drawing out the tension charging the packed theater. Bess takes in a gulp of air. ". . . Miss San Diego, Phyllis Mathis!" Bess silently gasps as Russell continues, "*Bess Myerson is Miss America!*" His booming voice is quickly drowned out by screams and stamping feet.

In that instant, the shock of it hits her like a thunderbolt— Bessie Myerson, the daughter of Russian Jewish immigrants. She feels that special flush of gratification at hearing her name. If she hadn't stood up to Lenora, it would have been a sham, an imposter's name resounding in this grand theater. For a second, she flashes back on the war that just ended, the bomb that a few weeks earlier they dropped on Japan. The Nazi death camps liberated now, yet their images seared into memory.

She closes her eyes momentarily to erase the horror from her mind, then steps out for her entrance. She is aware of her long, lean body as she glides down the runway, aware of the white evening gown's milky fabric against her skin, its long sleeves and high neck. "Graceful," she hears someone describe her stature. "Elegant." Bess is now the most famous Jewish girl since Queen Esther in ancient Persia.

The applause is deafening as cries of "Mazel tov!" fill the space. Bessie searches and finds the familiar faces from her Bronx neighborhood, her sisters, her community. She sees individual faces, hears each cheering voice. Her heart swells as she spots Ernie Sardo and Jimmy Wilson in the front row. It's as if everyone in America were there that night.

"Beauty with brains, that's Miss America of 1945!" shouts Bob Russell as Bess steps forward, a jeweled scepter placed in one hand, a bunch of long-stemmed red roses in the other. A scarlet silk cape is draped around her shoulders, and Venus Ramey, Miss America of 1944, places the rhinestone crown on Bessie's head. In that moment, she feels everything she always desperately wanted her mother to express to her. Acceptance. Appreciation. Love.

Ernie and Jimmy are brought up with other wounded soldiers for a photo with Bess. She hugs them before she walks offstage, each person she passes embracing her—squeezing her arm, offering their good wishes. She is engulfed by photographers, newsreel men, and reporters. Lenora takes Bess by the arm and steers her through the crowd, the pageant director's controlled, pasted smile having disappeared but not her tight grip. "You are our first scholarship winner, Bess. The first college graduate to win the title. We want to make sure that makes the headlines."

And the first Jewish winner, Bess thinks to herself. All that inspirational rhetoric Lenora spouted over the past week feeds into Bessie's current emotions. At this moment, she believes that she is going to be a real queen presiding over the onset of postwar prosperity. She imagines the pageant office booking her into ad campaigns and endorsements with thousands of dollars accumulating in her savings so she can move her family into a spacious apartment in a building with an elevator, purchase a car for her father, have her mother fitted for new teeth, hire a housekeeper for Sylvia, buy a new violin for Helen, get that grand piano she wants and a new flute, and, as she told Bob Russell, go to graduate school to make her mark as a professional musician.

The next day, instead of embarking on a regal procession through the finest suites and boardrooms, Bess begins her reign with two appearances on the Steel Pier in Atlantic City. With the hundred-dollar fee in her pocket, she returns home expecting the earth to move.

⸻ ⸺ ⸻

Hanging out with Bessie at her apartment the next evening, Ruth Singer, Lenny Miller, and Margie Wallis beg for every detail. Bessie embellishes wherever she can. She describes the boardwalk, the intoxicating sea air, staying at the fancy Brighton Hotel with Syl, and ordering room service.

"No! You didn't!" Ruthie giggles. Lenny and Margie are goggle-eyed.

Bessie describes the upper-crust chaperones assigned to each contestant: "Mrs. Charles Wheeler was glued to my side." The Catalina swimsuit she is given: "Not a 'bathing suit.' The Catalina folks said bathing is for tubs." More laughter. The tale of the stretched Catalina and Sylvia's heroic deed. Bessie has great fun exaggerating Lenora Slaughter's mannerisms and Southern drawl and her time with the musical judges.

She is respectful in relaying the hotel lobby scene with the elderly Jewish couple, quoting their greeting to her: "*Du bist a yid?*" How much they wanted her to win, like it would be a duty to the Jewish people. "I felt so out of my element the whole time

I was there, until this couple came forward." She doesn't miss the irony that she won the pageant on the very day of the Jewish New Year.

A *New York Times* article comes out during her few days celebrating in the Bronx. Referring to their Sholem Aleichem housing co-op, a "childhood family friend" is quoted as saying: "Nobody [there] cared about looks. They cared about books and brains."

Bessie wonders what her next year will look like. She *is* the first college-educated Miss America, after all. But the competition is, at its core, a beauty pageant. And the world sees Bess Myerson as a beauty queen. That's the role she is now being asked to play, but isn't she just Bessie Myerson, the daughter of Louis and Bella, an aspiring musician, a Jewish girl from the Bronx? How will she navigate the disparity between who she is and how others see her?

CHAPTER SEVENTEEN

THE TOUR BEGINS WITH VAUDEVILLE

Early Fall 1945

During those first few days before her tour starts, Bessie stays in Manhattan at the Ambassador Hotel with dinners at the Pierre, all on the pageant's dime. She visits again with Mayor LaGuardia, who is now filled with pride that an M&A graduate has become the darling of New York and the country. She goes to a beauty parlor for the first time in her life. She gets a pair of black satin heels. She poses for more photographs and answers reporters' questions.

"Any boyfriends, Miss Myerson?"

"Sure, I have a few. But men have to be tall and enjoy music for me to go out with them."

"What's your favorite cocktail?"

"Milk."

"Ever say 'damn' or 'hell'?"

"No. I say, 'Gee whiz.'"

"Do you like Sinatra?"

"I can take him or leave him."

"Would you call yourself beautiful?"

"I'm kind of attractive. A little different-looking, I'd say. I'm not being glib, just honest with you."

She tolerates being asked if she wears a girdle and a brassiere. "Ya use pads with those?" one reporter shouts out. And she directly answers, "No, yes, no."

When asked what stood out for her at the Miss America Pageant, she quips, "When I won it."

The press loves her.

She can't help but feel tickled by how Mama and Papa are treated like celebrities at Sholem Aleichem. There are parties and toasts, cries of "Mazel tov, Bella! Mazel tov, Louis!" Other than Bessie herself, they are the most honored guests in the complex's cafeteria. They are interviewed by the newspapers, embarrassing Bessie. (Louis: "I wouldn't say Bess is bad-looking, but maybe if I was the judge, I would have chosen one of the other girls." Bella: "She's not one of those runaround girls; that's why we're proud of her.") Bessie hates reading how the press describes her as "a raven-haired, hazel-eyed Oriental beauty," quickly followed by her measurements: height, bust, waist, hips, thigh, all the way down to her calf and ankle, her neck and upper arm and wrist. What is she, some giant piece of meat?

Then there's the tug-of-war about who is managing her life now. She watches the fighting heat up among her brother-in-law Bill, John Pape, Don Rich of WJZ, Sam DuBoff of Birchwood Camp, and Harry Kalcheim of William Morris—the agent who had a written agreement, signed before the pageant winner's selection. Bill fights it out with Kalcheim, insisting on higher appearance fees, making his demands through Lenora Slaughter.

"I'm representing the pageant and the title," an annoyed Harry Kalcheim counters. "Bess Myerson is the body with the title attached and has to go where the title's agent dictates."

"Bess is a person, not a body," Bill retorts. "And she hasn't signed any personal deal with William Morris."

Bessie doesn't want to cross anyone and has no desire to take responsibility for the decision herself. Lenora convinces her that Harry Kalcheim will give her the attention she deserves, that he'll bring her success. Fearful as she remains of this new confusing world she is entering, the idea of being professionally managed appeals to her.

The night before she leaves, Papa tells her, "Now, Besseleh, don't forget who you are out there."

The tour begins on September 14 in Newark, New Jersey with four of the five finalists. The act is dubbed the "American Beauty Review," an alias for a slimy vaudeville tour but one that carries a huge salary—$1,000 a week minus living expenses and the 10 percent cut for the agency. The girls are told they'll be working hard for that paycheck, performing four shows a day.

They check into their assigned hotel with Arlene Anderson's parents in tow. Frances Dorn takes one look around the lobby and mumbles, "Bleak. Wonder what the rooms are like."

"At least you don't have much of a trek to the shows." Arlene's mother points out that the Adams Theatre is right next door.

Bess stands, speechless, with Frances, Jeni Freeland, and Arlene in front of a large poster with their names in block letters and flashy headlines: "Atlantic City Bathing Beauty Winners starring in person . . . They Sing . . . They Dance . . . They Entertain."

With no time to spare, they enter through the Adams stage door from an alley separating hotel and theater. As she passes overstuffed bins with trash spilling onto the pavement, the smell of spoiled food makes Bess gag.

"This stinks of urine." Arlene screws up her face in disgust as they enter their dressing room. Several unattended dogs walk up to the girls and sniff at their ankles. "Ugh! What are these dogs doing in here?"

"They have the same right as you do." A squat man with a greasy handlebar mustache enters the dressing room and calls out to his dogs. "Audiences love our animal acts here. Can't get enough of them doggies."

Bess watches the dogs wrestle on the floor in the corner, then spots poop smeared into the carpet.

"Geez, this backstage area is a mess. Do they ever clean here?" Jeni pinches her nose. "A far cry from the Warner Theatre, eh, ladies?"

The opening act features a comedian whose jokes insult bystanders, particularly those standing backstage. "Some of Miss America's girls you're about to see this evening have those Southern *draaawlllsss* when they talk." The audience whoops it up. "They aren't the sharpest tools in the shed, folks. Haw, haw." Bess can't believe her ears while Jeni Freeland and Frances Dorn remain cool, only their reddened faces betraying them.

The acts are mostly worn-out vaudevillians without talent or charm. Screeching chorus girls wearing falsies and too much makeup follow the gagster. Past-their-prime ventriloquists with crude-talking dummies are next. Trilling Irish tenors are joined in song by off-key drunks in the audience.

When Arlene Anderson sings and plays her marimbaphone, she is booed by the Irish fans. Frances performs her upbeat tap dances, and that seems to keep with the beery, raucous music hall audience's expectations. Bess then walks onstage in her high-necked Knapp gown to perform "The Ritual Fire Dance" on the piano. Its rapid finger movements and the tension in the piece escalate as do the denigrating comments from the guys in the front rows.

"What is this, some kind of highbrow concert? Who needs this broad in the long dress? Get her into that bathing suit."

Bess does her best to ignore them, injecting her agitation into the music itself. She pounds the final chords as much in anger as the *fortississimo* called for by the song's notations. She returns backstage to change into her swimsuit, a final performance expectation of the Miss America finalists, relieved that the suit has finally been properly altered. Waiting at the wings, she detects a musky smell as the theater owner rushes past her onto the stage.

His booming voice grabs the audience's attention. "And now, what you've all been waiting for!" He licks his lips and turns his head toward where Bess and the runners-up are standing. "Those luscious beauties you saw earlier will now return to the stage in their bathing costumes."

A slovenly man in the front-row group shouts, "Bring on those hot babes now!"

Bess cringes.

"Let's give a hand for our long-legged queen at five feet and ten inches, 135 pounds! And get these measurements, fellas: thirty-five and a half, twenty-five, thirty-five! Come on out, Bess Myerson, *our* Miss America!"

The men hoot as Bess strides onto center stage, her face and neck reddening, her smile tight and immobile. She wants to scream but instead forces herself to tune out the jeers and catcalls, joined in humiliation by her sister contestants for the evening's finale.

◆━━◆━◆━━◆

The girls are backstage in their dressing room after the show, muttering among themselves about the wretchedness of the evening, when two sleazy guys walk in. "Hey, there. We thought a couple of you cuties might join us for a beer." The shorter one begins to snicker. Bess tries to look away but can't help eying his sizable paunch and how it pulls against the shirt buttons at his midriff.

"Why don't you two simpletons scoot? This space is off-limits to you." Bess has never heard Arlene's mother sound off so decisively. The two slugs lumber out the door. She envies the girls who have their parents there to protect them.

The days blur together, the girls having only enough energy to go from onstage to the hotel and then back to the theater the next morning right after breakfast. Since Bess and Frances Dorn are both unchaperoned, they room together, staying up late and talking into the night.

"Franny, how did you feel during pageant week?" Bessie hesitates, then adds, "I was always so scared, especially of Lenora."

"We were all petrified, Bess. You came from the Bronx, but most of us came from smaller cities and more rural states." Frances bunches up the pillows before leaning back into them.

"Oh, I was sheltered, believe me. My mother kept us on a tight leash. We practiced our instruments and studied and had very little time to socialize." Bessie wonders now if she was afraid of her mother or maybe she was just afraid of her mother's dark moods.

"Do you have any other siblings besides Sylvia?"

"I have a younger sister, Helen." She pauses. "And there was a brother . . . before I was born. Joseph. I came after him, and my mother was probably still grieving his loss. Sometimes I think it's why Mama placed so much expectation on me, although she was tough on my sisters too." Bess considers all this, and it comes to her then. "I sort of became the dutiful daughter. A pleaser. I guess I always kept trying to make things right in our household.

"The community at the apartments where we lived . . . the residents were also protective of me and my sisters. I mean, they were all immigrants, and artists. And they were just happy to be in America."

"You are the first Jewish person I've ever got close to. I mean, there are Jewish shopkeepers in Birmingham. I know Jews live in Montgomery and Mobile as well, but I didn't have much . . . exposure to them. You're nothing like what I expected."

Bessie wonders what Franny expected of a Jew. Her eyes now adjusted to the dark, she can make out Franny's warm smile, one of acceptance, and she feels an ease in sharing more about

herself. "There were plenty of children to play with, always someone to take care of you if you hurt yourself. The first non-Jewish
person I got to know was my piano teacher, who lived in Manhattan, and I actually had never met anyone from the South until
I met Lenora. You're quite different from her, Franny."

"Lenora is not like anyone *any* of us have ever known. I
assure you that!"

"She's tough. I like that about her. I wish my father could have
a bit of that in him—I adore my Papa, but I can't depend on either
of my parents to help me along, the way Arlene's father does."

"Well, that kind of management will help all of us once
we finish our tour." Franny sighs. "I really want to get out of the
Deep South. To dance and even be a little famous. You know, to
see the world."

"I'm a little scared of being out on my own. Being independent, you know what I mean?"

"But you must want this Slime City gig to be over, don't
you?"

They both laugh at once, a shared moment of release. Bessie
is grateful to have someone to talk to, even someone as different
from her as Frances, yet also so similar.

"Of course!" she says. "This is a nightmare I want to end.
And I think it would be awfully nice to settle down and get
married, to be protected by a nice man and be safe."

"I suppose." Frances yawns, then Bessie does, and before
even a minute passes, she can hear her friend gently snoring.

◆—◆—◆—◆—◆

By October, the girls are carted from Newark to New York City,
then to Hartford, then Detroit. Loew's State is the only theater
left in Times Square still booking vaudeville acts, and it is no
better than the Adams. Bessie is grateful that at least Lenora
didn't share their tour schedule with her family. God forbid any
would see her in such a compromising situation. By the time

they get to Detroit, Bess has lost twelve pounds. Despite the growing friendship with Frances and the camaraderie the four girls develop, she is homesick and miserable. This experience is a far cry from Sholem Aleichem and the spotless concert stages where Dorothea LaFollette held Bessie's recitals—far from the pristine pageant world that Lenora directed, controlling their every move, only to abdicate all oversight and subject the girls to this garish and vulgar tour. Is this what she gets for winning the Miss America contest?

Bessie hears that the William Morris Agency plans to extend the tour after Detroit, and she knows she cannot go on. One afternoon between shows, she summons her courage and calls Harry Kalcheim, expecting the worst. "With all due respect, Mr. Kalcheim, I can't stand any more of this. The audience degrades us. They only want one thing—to see our bodies in swimsuits, not the performances. It's beneath all of us to do vaudeville. Please. Let me come home!"

"Don't worry," he tells her. "That was only a rumor. The tour is coming to an end. Call me when you return to New York, and we'll talk about your future in movies."

She isn't thinking of her future at this point. All she wants is to regain her dignity.

CHAPTER EIGHTEEN

VICTORY BONDS AND VETERANS

Late Fall 1945

Bessie mopes around the house upon her return, sleeping late, retiring to her room immediately after dinner. She's grateful that Helen leaves her alone most evenings by doing homework in the kitchen, only using their bedroom for sleeping. Bessie initially avoids conversation with her parents, unable to even make small talk. Her mother coaxes her to eat more; her father wears a permanent look of concern on his face. She tries to smile around them, makes idle conversation, even studies for a screen test Harry Kalcheim arranges that she knows will be a dead end. She is too tall for the role and has no talent for acting. She doesn't even care about being rejected.

Finding music that helps her escape, she plays the piano with total abandon. Over and over, she performs the evocative *Clair de lune*, sinking into its quiet, slightly melancholic melody. The piece soothes her, as if taking her on a much-needed solitary walk through a moonlit garden. Or she plays the simple and whirling "Spinning Song," her fingers mindlessly and mechanically flying over the keyboard. At times, she sits idly. For the first time in her life, these moments are not interrupted by her mother screaming for her to practice.

Mama is aware something is wrong, Bessie thinks. If only Mama knew that her reign has turned out to be a kind of indentured labor, that the "Miss America" title itself gives people the impression her daughter is some empty-headed bimbo. Bessie won't share the demeaning details of her last month with Mama or Papa. No doubt her mother would wag her finger and say, "I told you so," and her father would cuddle her and tell her it will all be okay. She is long past expecting her parents to be helpful or provide her with guidance.

She decides to reach out to her old camp director, who always treated her like a daughter. She recalls Sam as the only adult, other than Sylvia, expressing genuine happiness during the early competition for Miss New York City, even when she had many doubts. And she sees herself in safe hands given his work as a New York lawyer. She places a call to him in mid-October when her parents are at her Aunt Fanny's and speaks openly with him about her vaudeville experience.

"I can't believe the pageant sent you out to be disgraced, Bess, but I'm sorry you went along with it."

Her throat tightens. "I didn't have a choice, Sam. There was a contract."

"I suggest you disengage from any contract. It's time you think through what is being asked of you." There is a moment of silence on the line. "And you rise to the occasion. You do your best to be a force for good. And you stay close to the people who've known you throughout your life."

She recalls her father's warning not to forget who she is. Feeling guilty, she even bought him a new yellow station wagon with her vaudeville earnings when she returned. She believes she not only let herself down but that she's disappointed her family, even disgraced the Jewish people. That's what her father was telling her, wasn't it? That she's now representing her entire community.

While she is determined to do better, she has no idea what that looks like. She needs to be directed, to be told what to do. So Bess follows Sam's advice and asks to be released from her contract with William Morris, leaving Sam to take over her career. He finds her a new agent, Claire Wolff, tasked with gaining commercial endorsements. Bess hopes she'll receive lucrative offers, like promoting frozen dinners or that new Slinky toy everyone's talking about.

Invitations begin to flow in, but few carry a price tag. An appearance at the Soviet-American Friendship League luncheon. Guest of honor at Columbia University's Fall Festival Dance. Given all the public appearances, she spends money on hair and nail appointments, often takes cabs instead of subways. She tries to fit in a piano lesson from Mrs. LaFollette on any free day. Her expenses start to pile up, and before she knows it, she finds herself running out of money. Not sure where else to turn, Bess makes an appointment to see Lenora.

At the pageant director's suggestion, they meet at Tavern on the Green on Central Park West, a luxury eatery Bess can't afford right now. Lenora can't be missed in her flashy silk outfit and bright-red lipstick, the confident manner she strides into the restaurant. After she orders a tea sandwich and Bess a parfait, Lenora asks Bess to bring her up to date on the tour. Bess gives her an accounting of their four-week vaudeville experience, leaving out the most gruesome details.

"Well, you earned a bundle of money, Bess. And now it's over and you'll have better work."

"I'm beginning to have engagements, but they don't pay and I'm pinched for funds. Can you help me find paying assignments?"

"That's what agents are for." Lenora begins listing all the details she is already handling for next year's pageant.

Bessie realizes she is on her own as far as Lenora is concerned. She nervously wrings her napkin. "Then can I have an advance on the scholarship?"

"You know those funds can't be released until the end of your year's reign and once you've enrolled in a proper graduate program." Lenora raises her hand to get a waiter's attention before she turns back to Bess.

Bessie is too upset to respond, but her long face gives her away.

"Oh, Bess, you're doing so well. Why, a lady in a beauty parlor told me she heard you speak at that Jewish War Veterans event, and your words brought her to tears. You can't just judge everything on the money coming in. What you do should bring you happiness, bring others inspiration. Believe me, honey, you'll find success and fortune eventually."

Bessie wants to please Lenora. She wants to please Sam DuBoff. She wants to please her parents. She craves acceptance by everyone.

"You know you must accept all appearances requested by any of the five pageant sponsors. And promote their products graciously."

"Of course I'll do that, Lenora."

• — • — • — •

And Bess does so without complaint. The Joseph Bancroft & Sons marketing team use her in a tour of department stores. The Fitch Shampoo Company displays her image in advertising layouts in magazines. But the sponsors don't owe her anything for her time since they, indirectly, are paying her by supporting the scholarship.

In early November, the Joseph Bancroft group brings her to Wilmington, Delaware, for a large Victory Bond rally, part of a national fundraising effort to support veterans. Reporters are on hand, cameras clicking photos as Bess tours the fabric finishing plant and takes a motorcade through town. A few days later, she makes an appearance for the Victory Bond drive in Washington, even visits the Senate and the White House, shaking hands with Mrs. Truman. She meets with the wounded at Bethesda Naval Hospital and is given a certificate of merit for her work on the Victory Bond campaign. Throughout the fall of her reign, Bess travels, speaks at bond rallies, poses for pictures, and autographs until her fingers are too stiff to play her beloved piano. Women are even writing her for beauty advice. She begins to feel she's achieving something as media attention and crowd adulation envelope her.

But her confidence is short-lived after she makes a few missteps with the sponsors. Inadvertently, she gets on the wrong side of Fitch when she appears in a drugstore advertisement touting a competitor's shampoo. Then she angers the California-based Catalina Swimsuit Company by posing for a magazine layout in a bathing suit that is not a Catalina, set up by her new agent. A visit to Kentucky on behalf of Sandy Valley Grocery turns sour when the CEO reclines on the train seat and rests his head on Bessie's lap. Shocked, she jumps up and wails, "Please don't do that!" embarrassing them both. Bess feels not like a respected human being but a commodity.

She finds herself rejected by sponsors, misled by Lenora, and mishandled by her agent, without Sylvia there to prop her up. This must be all her own fault. Her mother's voice creeps into her head: "Do better. Work harder."

Yet, through all these incidents, she begins to grasp that any Miss America fights an uphill battle. *A beauty queen wanting respect?* Bessie's upbringing is incompatible with this role she now plays. Her Jewish social conscience—drummed into her by her family, her Sholem Aleichem community, the ideals of her high school—is screaming inside her. *Do something meaningful! You crave esteem? Earn it!*

Bessie's appearances at dozens of veterans' hospitals are a start. She visits with thousands of wounded soldiers, sitting at their bedsides, kidding around with them. At a Marine Corps air station, they whistle and cheer when she arrives, exhibiting decorum and making her feel noble, not cheap, as she had just two months earlier. She brings her flute to play tunes they request, and if an upright piano is on the ward, she performs a sonata or concerto as well. One veteran tells the press, "She put her Bess foot forward."

The injured servicemen inspire her. She can't fathom how they can be so hopeful after losing so much. She knows that men like Jimmy Wilson and Ernie Sardo feel secure in their hospital havens, where everyone is dedicated to their rehabilitation. She wonders if they fear being on the outside. She tells all the boys she meets at facilities across the country that they'll be fine, even though she doesn't believe that. She can't imagine what will become of these brave soldiers, how and if they will be able to one day conduct business, drive cars, marry, conceive children. So she keeps them company. She signs their casts.

After several months of posing and smiling in her role as Miss America, she wants to count more than anything. She is invited to attend an affair at the Waldorf-Astoria in New York to benefit the March of Dimes and the victims of infantile paralysis. She happily accepts, determined to have Jimmy and Ernie accompany her. Bess takes the train to Atlantic City to personally invite them. Entering the hospital lobby brings her back to that visit, a swimsuit parade, when she first met these two valiant fighters.

She enters the large room she thought had been the space where she paraded with her sister contestants just months earlier, but it is filled with chinning bars and pulley weights now. She watches several wheelchair-bound patients doing strengthening exercises under the supervision of an aide. In a far corner, a physician is teaching a young man to walk with a leg prosthesis. The ricochet of a ping-pong ball grabs her attention; two wheelchair-bound men in a fierce match smack the small object across the net.

A young Negro nurse approaches, her eyes suddenly widening in recognition. "Oh, you're Miss Myerson! How can I help you?"

"I'm looking for two of your patients—Jimmy Wilson and Ernie Sardo." Bess fingers the faux pearls on her necklace. "Things look different from when I was here last September."

"I'd be pleased to show you around, Miss Myerson. My name is Althea Dove. I'm a member of the Thirty-First Women Army Corps. Trained as a surgical nurse." Althea looks away for an instant, as if deciding on her next words. "Different from our segregated units in the army, at England General we all work together."

Bess raises her eyebrows as she takes this in, incredulous that the army separated Black and white soldiers. "Please call me Bess, Althea. I've toured so many veterans' hospitals but haven't seen anything like what is going on here."

Althea tells her that England General is the largest hospital in the United States specializing in amputations and neuro-surgery, that the entire staff is devoted to rehabilitation. Even patients confined to the bed are given physical therapy in their rooms. Althea acknowledges several nurses and aides as she leads Bess into the corridor.

"If you peek inside their rooms—the patients are now in occupational therapy—you can see they're the size of hotel suites." Althea explains that the hospital took over several hotels during the height of the war.

Bess finds herself looking around a large patient room with soft pastel window draperies, colorful wall pictures, and com-fortable chairs for visitors. "I'm learning all kinds of things this morning. The hospital might consider letting you serve as a tour guide—between your nursing shifts, of course."

Althea smiles. "Our top concern is the well-being and com-fort of our patients. We're here to assist these men as they return to some sense of normalcy. Let me show you our occupational therapy area, where a lot of the magic happens."

They enter a furnished area, with table heights and activities all accommodating wheelchair patients. Bess spots a makeshift library, filled with books and magazines. There are spaces where patients are working with ceramics, wood, metal, even sketching and painting.

"Paraplegics learn to do even more with their arms," Althea tells her. "Those with prosthetic arms can also learn to do functional activities, with practice."

Bess looks around in amazement, her presence unnoticed amid all the busyness going on.

Althea brings Bess to a smaller room filled with artificial limbs. Several aides appear to be receiving instruction. "This is our Limb Shop. Proper fitting requires much more attention, as each patient's needs are different. We can never have enough well-trained orthopedic mechanics. Now, let me take you to Jimmy and Ernie."

❖──◆──◆──❖

Ernie is in Jimmy's room when Bess enters, the two engrossed in a game of chess.

"If it isn't our Miss America! To what do we owe this surprise visit, Miss Myerson?"

Bess bends to give each of them a hug. "Sorry to interrupt. You two are looking well." She is pleased to see that their faces don't show the strain she detected months back and that both have gained some weight. "I have an invitation, and hope you'll accept."

She explains about the March of Dimes benefit. Not a beat goes by before Ernie whoops, "Yes siree!" Jimmy insists on driving to New York in a regular car, with his prosthetic hooks. Ernie says he's been in Jimmy's passenger seat before and looks forward to the trip. Bess thinks they are kidding until Althea confirms that the hospital has outfitted a car for use by both quadriplegics and paraplegics and that Jimmy has been trained as a driver.

For Bess, Jimmy and Ernie are her guiding light during that dark winter. To her, they stand in for all the veterans she meets. She believes that if these soldiers can recover from so much suffering and loss, the whole world can recover—from war, from hate, from every horrible affliction.

CHAPTER NINETEEN

TRAVELING THE SOUTH

Late 1945

As Bess continues her tour of veterans' hospitals through the fall, she notices many improvements in the facilities she visits. Some are new; others have been paired with nearby medical schools. Staffing changes—including an increase in doctors, nurses, and even social workers—boost morale. Bess learns that many of the changes are a result of a new medical director of the US Veterans Administration.

After Thanksgiving, she arrives at yet another medical facility in Tennessee, where a thin middle-aged attending doctor approaches her. "Miss Myerson, could you pay a special visit to a young man on my ward? He's badly wounded and may never get out of here."

Bess doesn't hesitate and follows the physician to the patient's room. A stout woman in her fifties stands in front of the door blocking her from entering. "My boy doesn't need to see you. I don't want you near him. It was you Jews who got us into this war . . . because of the damn Jews, my boy was maimed. We would have been better off if Hitler had killed every last one of you people. Don't you come near my boy!"

Bess stands frozen, speechless, trying to take in the hateful words. No one in her short life has spoken to her like this. No one has ever sounded off such antisemitic venom against her. Her own mother is sharply critical, but that's different. Bessie knows Bella's harsh tongue comes from a place of love and loss. This woman standing in her way is also a mother in pain, Bessie thinks, grieving for her wounded, dying son and angry enough to want to blame someone.

All these thoughts rush into her head at once, and Bess begins to cry. She weeps because of the insult. She weeps because of this attack on her as a Jew. She weeps for this poor boy, for all the poor injured boys. She weeps for this bereft mother watching her own son dying. She weeps and blames herself for weeping because her personal pain at being insulted is so much less than this woman's grief for what happened to her son. Bess carries all this feeling deep inside her. And yet she wants—*she needs*—to pour it out and do something. Anything. Not just stand there helplessly weeping.

⟡

Bessie continues searching to find herself, each day filled with expectations, each day experiencing disappointments. As the end of the year approaches, she is still discovering the depth of hostilities against the Jewish people and the resentment toward all Jews—from the European refugees directly affected by the war to the American Jews. And she tries to come to terms with the sheer magnitude of loss—of the lives of hundreds of thousands of soldiers, of the lives of millions of Jews. *What kind of God would allow this wholesale slaughter of innocents?*

The images of Jews that she sees in newspaper reports take on a horrifying form—that of a starved body: gaunt, hollowed, abused. While she is attacked as a Jew by those seeking someone to blame for the death or suffering of loved ones, she also starts to understand why her win as Miss America is so crucial—offering a different view of the Jewish body: tall, graceful, beautiful.

———————

The continuation of the Miss America tour takes Bess into the South to Kentucky, North Carolina, Mississippi, Louisiana, Alabama. She sees signs over restrooms that she never saw in New York: "White Only" and "Colored." Or maybe she just didn't see them in her Bronx neighborhood. She walks onstage to greet the crowds in theaters where white people sit in the orchestra and Negroes are consigned to the balcony. She recalls Althea's description of the women's army units, also segregated.

Other than a pageant chaperone—really an office staffer sent with her to ease her travel and keep her on schedule—Bess is on her own. There is none of the camaraderie with her fellow finalists like she had during the vaudeville tour, not that she wants to relive that experience. One night, she calls home just to hear her parents' familiar voices. Instead of bringing her comfort, the call leaves Bessie in a state of panic when they tell her about the desecration of synagogues in her own city. *What is going on in this country? Are hatred and bitterness becoming deeply entrenched in the American heart? When you don't know someone,* she thinks, *you don't look like them, you don't speak like them, you don't know their culture, you don't eat the same things, it's too easy to just label them, to exclude them, to hate them, to make them scapegoats.*

———————

One evening in Kentucky, Bess is invited to a local country club to make a short speech and play the piano. She's driven to a breathtaking antebellum mansion, complete with carefully landscaped gardens, uniformed servants, and crystal chandeliers. She is escorted up a winding staircase to a spacious bedroom with a canopied four-poster bed, eyelet-trimmed throw pillows on silk-upholstered chairs. She can smell the earthy wood scent of the fireplace. A Negro woman comes in and uses a bellows to blow air into the fire while Bess carefully dons the magnificent ball gown she packed for the occasion. She stands tall in front of a mirror admiring the gown's romantic design, feeling like a Southern belle in these surroundings.

When she starts down the staircase, she overhears the hostess informing her pageant escort there has been a terrible mistake. "You didn't tell us she was Jewish. This is a restricted country club. We don't have Negroes, and we do not have Jews."

Bess feels these words in her chest, as if someone has struck her there. She turns and climbs back up the stairs, lets the dress drop off her body, removes her pageant crown, and puts it on top of the gown that the staffer quickly folds and packs back up. She walks over to where she left her clothes and dresses in silence. Her escort drives her to the railway station that night and arranges for a ticket. Bess waits for the train bound for New York to get her home, where she feels safe and secure. She doesn't know when the next one is due to arrive, although the chaperone may have told her. All she knows is that she is desperate to leave that town as quickly as she can. She stands, waiting on the platform for at least an hour, sobbing uncontrollably. Relieved as she spots a train arriving, she runs toward it and up the steps of the nearest passenger car that opens its doors. Blinded by tears, she clumsily finds her way to a seat as the train slowly begins to lurch forward.

She drifts in and out for the first hour of travel, calmer and able to think more clearly as the distance between her and Kentucky grows. She considers that she is somehow not a desirable Miss America, that her ethnic origins place her on the outside. This is not a new revelation, just one that she now feels at a deeper, more visceral level. She always knew she was different. Lenora tried to warn her, pushed her to change her ethnic name hoping to avoid problems, but Bess now realizes she has become a problem for Lenora, for the pageant, and for the sponsors. They wanted her because she is educated and well-spoken. She fits this new image for Miss America that Lenora was selling.

Bess stares out her window and into the darkness at the passing shapes. It is evident that many parts of America don't value intelligent women. And being a Jewish Miss America in 1945 is a conundrum. Though Hitler is dead and the Nazis defeated, their antisemitic, racist, and sexist propaganda still spreads hatred and distrust. In her travels around the country, she has seen all these prejudices firsthand. She recognizes the irony: a war supposedly fought to end racism, yet bigotry is surging.

She flashes back to her high school civics class, the morning her teacher held up a copy of the *New York Times* with the headline "JEWS ARE ORDERED TO LEAVE MUNICH." A violent act, *Kristallnacht*, brought terror and destruction against the Jews of Germany and Austria. A religion and a people were persecuted, exiled from their homes. While her banishment this evening is just from a non-Jewish country club, the message conveyed in well-bred hostility, Bess sees the same hatred, the same superiority.

Despite all this, Bess still wants to believe that great good can be achieved through the Miss America Pageant, that she can be a voice for understanding, for empathy. That thought gives her comfort, even though she doesn't yet know what form this impulse might take. The notes of *Clair de lune* enter her mind, soothing in their melody. Her lids become heavy, she closes her eyes and, finally, falls into a deep sleep.

CHAPTER TWENTY

THE BROTHERHOOD
CAMPAIGN

Early 1946

Helen, at last, has a beau: Harold Flender. The two were introduced by a mutual friend finishing studies with Helen at Hunter College. A budding writer, Harold has just graduated from City College and is applying to Columbia for graduate school. Bess finds Harold entertaining to be around as he begins to test his comedy skits on her. But she also observes him to be intelligent and socially aware.

Just after the new year, Helen, Harold, and Bess are sitting around the kitchen table at the Myersons' apartment. Bess shares her frustration about her demeaning encounters as Miss America and the ugliness she's seen and experienced—the antisemitism, the segregation. She recounts her "No Jews or Negroes" country club story, long-faced in the telling.

"The uptick of bigotry toward all minorities is a sad reality." Harold strokes his trim beard, a deep furrow appearing in his brow.

Helen looks at Bess in disbelief. "I didn't realize you went through such hurtful incidents, Bessie. I thought it was all glamour and fun."

"Most of the press articles Helen showed me did make it seem like you were the belle of the hospital circuit." Harold gestures to Helen, who is nodding.

"Hardly." Bess cringes as she tells them what that one mother screamed at her. Her story is met with silence and troubled expressions from Helen and Harold. "I am fully aware why many of the commercial offers didn't come through for me. My slightly Jewish name doesn't go down well with the local customer, you know?" She shrugs. "It feels like there's no way to fight back, nothing I can do but remain sweet and dignified. But inside I'm so angry."

Harold refills his glass with water at the sink and sits back down. "I have an idea for you, Bess. My cousin is married to a bigwig at the Anti-Defamation League. Do you know much about their work?"

"Not really." Bess sits forward. "Tell me about them."

Harold places his hands firmly on the table's edge and pauses, as if searching for where to begin. He explains that before the war, there were hundreds of thousands of people in America who hated Jews—members in the Christian Front, the Ku Klux Klan, the German American Bund. Many of these organizations hated Negroes as well. "With the onset of war, these groups went underground and became silent because what had been pro-Nazi but legal suddenly became treason."

The divisions of these groups, Harold explains, put Negroes in one community, Jews in another, Catholics in another as the war ended. The ADL *had* been concentrating on finding and exposing the antisemites and pro-Nazis, but it became evident that discrimination and hatred persisted unabated. "So agencies like the NAACP and the Urban League sat down with the ADL, and they all agreed it's time for a massive educational drive to repair the damage." Harold sits back in the chair, his eyes locked on Bess.

Bess's eyes widen. "You're saying that preventing prejudice is ADL's focus now?"

"Better than that." Harold smiles. "It believes that educating young people to understand tolerance, empathy, and acceptance of those who are different from them could have a far-reaching impact. That it could help put an end to hatred and the violence it breeds."

"Can you introduce me to your cousin? I want to help. What's his name?"

"Arnold Forster. I'll call him tomorrow."

<hr />

Not even a week later, Harold brings Bess to ADL's midtown headquarters. Stepping into the foyer outside Arnold Forster's office, Bess takes a deep breath and smooths the jacket of her most professional midnight-blue wool suit. A secretary opens Forster's office door to let them inside. Harold makes introductions; Arnold holds out his hand in greeting. He is lean and stands tall, just like most men when they come face-to-face with someone of Bess's height. His eyes directly meet hers. "I'm honored, Miss Myerson."

"Bess."

"Bess, then. And call me Arnold." He walks around his stately mahogany desk and motions to the leather armchairs facing him. "Please. Sit."

She lowers herself into the chair, aware of the firmness of the cushions, and assesses the situation. Arnold is impeccably dressed, his face clean-shaven. Bess figures him to be in his mid-thirties, although the tuft of hair between his temples, while neatly combed straight back, is thinning. She glances around the spacious office, appointed in dark woods with soft lighting coming from several Tiffany lamps on side tables. When she turns back toward him, she sees Arnold has been observing her as well.

He leans forward over his desk. "Miss Myerson . . . Bess, Harold has shared with me some of your, ah, more uncomfortable experiences during the Miss America tour. Was this prejudice unexpected for you?"

Bess doesn't expect his direct question, at least not so quickly, and she takes a moment to consider her answer. "Unexpected? Not entirely." She hesitates for a split second. "I began to hear rumblings in Atlantic City. A photographer tipped me off that some powerful people didn't want a Jewish winner." Bess keeps her voice steady even though she's uncomfortable reliving these intimidating encounters with a stranger. She stares at her hands as she continues. "But actually, it really started when I was competing for Miss New York City. The pageant director suggested that I change my name to something that sounded less Jewish." She raises her head and meets his gaze. "I refused."

Arnold stares at her intently. Several moments of silence pass before he responds. "You have more courage than I." He leans back in his chair, a pained look crossing his face. "I was born Arnold Fastenberg. I earned money for my undergraduate education and for law school by working as an actor. While performing at the Provincetown Playhouse, the director suggested I anglicize my last name. So Fastenberg became Forster."

Bess tries not to show her shock, suddenly realizing that her determination to keep her name was extremely unorthodox— something Lenora Slaughter couldn't have expected, certainly not from a twenty-one-year-old beauty contestant.

"Maybe that experience is why I have become so passionate about my work at ADL. I had to change my name to keep working so I could pay for and complete my education. Your encounters speak for themselves." Arnold's lips are pursed. "There are so many indignities we are asked to accept." He sighs before continuing. "I officially joined ADL in 1940. My focus has been to combat the myriad forms of antisemitism in our country.

"We must build bridges that have been torn down by Hitler. We plan to create an educational campaign to change the institutions of all forms of prejudice. Just like you didn't get certain endorsement work because you were Jewish, we live with Jewish quotas and discrimination in education, housing, banking. Everywhere."

Arnold pauses, his eyes on Bess. She notices they are light brown, deep set. His chiseled face has an intensity and self-confidence.

"Harold says you may be interested in working with us. You are intelligent, consciously Jewish." He nods at Bess, offering his approval. "You have the skills and ability to seize the platform, so to speak."

Bess does not have to prove anything to Arnold Forster. She doesn't have to convince him that she is smart as well as pretty. She feels she can finally do something worthwhile. "I want to join your campaign. I feel I am home now."

Arnold's mouth stretches ever so slightly into a smile. "Bess Myerson, you can be that common touch of humanity that we have been looking for. You can help us make a real difference."

<hr />

The ADL develops a tour through fifteen cities where Bess can reach out to young people, promoting values of tolerance and empathy for people from all religious, ethnic, and racial backgrounds. She embraces her new responsibility with enthusiasm, thrilled to finally be able to display substance and be a positive role model for American girls. ADL pays for her travel, helps write her speeches, and arranges for a travel bureau to coordinate appearances at high schools and colleges. Her speeches focus on the theme "You Can't Be Beautiful and Hate."

In February, Bess begins her speaking tour in Chicago. Several ADL staffers there throw a deli luncheon in her honor. A public relations consultant for the Chicago mayor's Commission on Human Rights introduces herself as the group begins to disperse. "I'm Martha Glazer. The commission is sponsoring your appearances in the Chicago area, Miss Myerson. I can see that all the men here are overwhelmed seeing a real Miss America. While I'm thrilled to meet you, I have to say that standing next to you, I can feel every inch I lack."

Bess laughs as she realizes how awkward short women can feel, as she always has because of being so tall. "Yes, I have that effect on most people. And please call me Bess. I'm grateful to the commission for underwriting my appearances."

"We're hoping your talks can prevent some of the racial unrest we've seen in this area, troubles that developed when the war began."

"What kinds of issues are you seeing?"

"It's what exists everywhere, Bess. White students demanding Negro students be removed from the school. Bigotry starts with the parents, which is why teaching tolerance and brotherhood must begin in kindergarten. If you're ready, we can head out for your first appearance."

———•———

Bess faces a large assembly of students that afternoon. She is introduced, receives applause, and approaches the podium. She looks out at the crowd of young people, waiting for the normal rustling and whispering and movement to cease. And then she begins.

"Miss America represents all America. It makes no difference who she is or who her parents are. Side by side, Catholic, Protestant, and Jew stand together. And we would have it no other way.

"For prejudice is a dangerous thing. It makes you hate—and once you start hating, you don't stop."

Bess assesses the faces before her. They are focused and attentive. She stands straighter, speaks louder.

"You can't hide it. Ever. It shows in your eyes. It warps your expression. It affects your character, your personality.

"And all those things are important in Atlantic City, or anywhere else where real Americans take your measure and pass judgment.

"In veterans' hospitals I have seen white and Negro, Jew and Gentile, Yank and Dixie sharing the same ward, sharing their thoughts and hopes and plans as they shared hardship and struggle on the battlefield. If you have any prejudice against any race or religion, they would tell you—beg you—to rise above it."

She takes a breath and holds back for a split second. She wants her closing to be forceful so the students can feel her message.

"For there is no happiness in hate. No one ever succeeded by it. Nothing good was ever built by it. No nation was ever permanently unified by it.

"And if we want a strong, united America pushing on toward its unlimited horizons, there can be no place for prejudice in our nation . . . or in our hearts.

"You can't be beautiful and hate . . . *We* can't! Aren't we 'America the Beautiful'?"

The students give Bess a standing ovation. Some cheer. She repeats the same speech to a second assembly at Von Steuben. There are other high school assemblies, an interfaith youth dance, a Junior Association of Commerce luncheon, and an address to the Chicago City Council. Martha books Bess for interviews on several radio programs before she leaves Chicago.

"Be kind to people different from you—the strangers who might speak with foreign accents, for example," she tells a high school audience in Minneapolis. "In Atlantic City, there were girls from big towns and little towns. Nobody asked if your parents spoke with an accent. Nobody called you, 'Hey Jewish girl. Hey Catholic girl.' Not there. We competed and won on our merit."

After stopping in Milwaukee, she returns to the East Coast. In mid-March, under a banner reading "Freedom from Religious or Racial Prejudice," Bess stands before sixty admiring editors of Greater Boston high school newspapers, sponsored by the

Institute for American Democracy. She urges all young people to learn to live together, cooperatively and in friendship, regardless of racial and religious differences.

"Hatred of another person because of his creed or race is a poison that corrodes the soul," she tells the wide-eyed teenagers. "True beauty is marred and diminished by angry, unreasoning prejudices, which eat away at the heart. If our fighting men lived, fought, and died together to make America safe, we are untrue to them if we harbor thoughts unworthy of Americans!"

From there, she travels close to home to address groups in Hartford and New York. She speaks at high schools located in troubled areas, and she wins an enthusiastic reception. Wire stories of her tolerance messages are carried from coast to coast. Commentators repeat her slogan "You Can't Be Beautiful and Hate" on national radio networks. Comic magazines dramatize her life story. Feature stories appear in the national magazines *Seventeen*, *Salute*, and *Redbook*.

Crowds gather and children swarm around her in the streets with a look of wonder and adoration. At one engagement, two neighborhood children hang back to talk to her.

"Miss Myerson, could you tell us, are you Jewish?"

"Yes, I am."

"I knew it! I knew it!" the other child squeals. "Oh, my mother is going to be absolutely just so excited when I tell her it's true, you're really one of us!"

—·—·—·—

She makes nine appearances in two days in Buffalo—including the youth assembly of the Urban League, the Girl Reserves of the YWCA, and the Young People's Club at Temple B'nai Zion. Then she heads to Philadelphia, where she is to appear in a moderated conversation with Dolores Fairfax, a sophomore at Temple University whom Bess is told is the first Miss Sepia America. *Are we supposed to advocate tolerance from the standpoint of beauty contests?* she wonders. *Pure hypocrisy!* Bess is all too aware of the whiteness of her Miss America Pageant, ashamed that she only now realizes that Negro girls did not qualify. Her nationally recognized competition is as segregated and racist as the army and so much else in America.

Worrisome thoughts fill her mind as she is driven to the Quaker City Lodge of B'nai B'rith in North Philadelphia. What kind of classification is "sepia"? A reddish-brown color in photographs? Like when she would get a bit burned on Tar Beach? Or is it a brown pigment, the tanned look she had when she competed to win her crown? Bess is outraged yet feels some trepidation about how she can acceptably tackle what is a potentially contentious topic. She takes deep breaths to get herself in the right frame of mind to address a large public gathering.

Bess approaches the front of the assembly hall, where a table with a microphone has been placed. She introduces herself to Dolores and finds the young woman poised and friendly. The two are greeted by an ADL representative, Addie Klein, who tells them she will serve as moderator, asking her own questions and taking queries from the audience. A loudspeaker announces that the program is about to begin and for people to find their seats. Bess pulls out a chair to sit and collect her thoughts. As she faces the crowd, she notices the audience is comprised of mostly college students and some older adults, both white and Negro.

Addie's initial questions address the history and elements of the respective beauty contests. Bess shares that the Miss America Pageant began in 1921 in Atlantic City as the Inter-City Beauty contest. "I understand it was designed to encourage visitors to stay in the resort past Labor Day, the traditional end of the season." Bess notes that the first pageant was held in September of that year, with eight finalists from cities in the Northeast competing for the title. And she shares that the title changed to Miss America the following year.

"Two sisters established Miss Sepia last year, so I was the first winner, as you said in your introduction, Addie." Dolores rolls her eyes upward, as if trying to recall something. "I think there were Miss Sepia contests in Canada—the Windsor area—for more than a decade. Negroes from Detroit participated." Dolores smiles as she speaks, her voice low and mellifluous. "I'm twenty now, but I was nineteen when I won. The contest is open to single Negro girls between seventeen and twenty-four who are high school seniors or graduates."

"Can you tell us about your experience during the contest, ladies?" Addie turns toward Bess. "Miss Myerson?"

Bess realizes Addie is keeping the discussion at its most concrete level and shares a glowing appraisal of her five-day experience in the competition, the way the different elements of talent, swimsuit, evening gown, and personality were evaluated. "There were forty of us from around the country. We all felt the tension of competition since there was a $5,000 scholarship at stake for the winner. But we helped one another and became friends."

She listens closely to Dolores' description of Miss Sepia America. "We also competed in evening gowns, swimwear, and talent. In addition to the honor of being crowned Miss Sepia, winners also received prizes in the form of cash, a trophy, and flowers."

"What talent did each of you compete in?" Addie asks.

"I love to dance, so I did some modern dance for my talent." Dolores turns to Bess as though the two are having their own conversation. "My dad is a musician and songwriter and my friends thought I'd learn to play an instrument, but I never did."

Bess smiles. "Music is my talent—piano and flute."

Addie clears her throat. "We are so fortunate to have two national beauty queens, role models, white and Negro, who can address the topic of bigotry and the need for tolerance in our country."

"I'd like to comment on this, if I could." Bess tucks some loose strands of hair behind her ears. "I've been on a tour now for a few months talking about tolerance, about the fact you can't be beautiful and hate, about the fact that Miss America represents all America." She takes in a gulp of air. "But it doesn't."

A wave of murmurs spreads across the room. Bess is determined to charge on. "I was the only Jewish contestant in the Miss America contest, and I'm not sure my being Jewish was something the organization wanted to promote." Bess feels a flush creeping up her neck. "Even though I am considered to have white skin, I was not like the others. I am considered ethnic in a world still filled with antisemitism. And I'm troubled that the classification of color or race is any part of the vocabulary of beauty pageants."

Again, audible gasps from the audience. Addie's face tenses, and she begins to rearrange some papers in front of her before she looks up. "How about if we take some questions from the audience now."

A Negro woman in her twenties raises her hand and stands up. "I'm curious, Miss Fairfax, how did you feel about Miss Myerson's comments?"

"I appreciate her frankness. Women of color have been barred from entering mainstream beauty pageants, and that is why a Miss Sepia contest was created. I'm hoping things might begin to change, thanks to this brotherhood campaign." Dolores turns to Bess. "Teaching tolerance and acceptance is what we need now."

—————

Returning home, Bess receives a message from the pageant's Stamford offices to call Lenora immediately. The director sounds snappy on the phone, pushing for a meeting the next day in New York. She tells Bess to meet her at the Russian Tea Room on Fifty-Seventh Street near Seventh Avenue at two o'clock.

Bess arrives a few minutes early and is escorted to a tufted red leather banquette, the table covered with a fine white cloth. She takes in the elegant decor: the walls a deep forest green covered with gold-leaf-framed oils, pastels, and sketches; gold-trimmed wall sconces providing perfect lighting; a luxurious, red-accented carpet. The restaurant is bustling with women in elegant dresses and matching hats, men wearing tailored three-piece suits. As she bides her time, she watches waiters bring out an array of scones with clotted cream and jam, sweet pastries, and cakes.

She spots Lenora hurrying through the revolving glass doors. Bess raises her hand to get Lenora's attention.

After a perfunctory greeting, Lenora quickly insists they order. It is obvious to Bess that Lenora has something on her mind. The woman looks like she's about to burst.

"You've squandered the good name of the Miss America Pageant, making these highly publicized appearances at political events."

"I can't believe what I'm hearing, Lenora. I've done everything you've asked of me." Bess pauses as the waiter arrives with hot tea and several finger sandwiches, then resumed. "I willingly toured the sleazy vaudeville theaters where we were introduced by our measurements. I did everything the sponsors asked of me, promoted their products, except for the one whose executive made an ugly pass. I supported the Victory Bond campaigns, toured many veterans' hospitals, met with thousands of wounded soldiers." Bess tries to control her voice as she realizes she sounds almost shrill. But she can't hide her anger. Lenora should be proud of what she's done. "What I am doing now cannot be called 'political events'!"

"What you are doing and saying now has not been cleared through me. Did you see this headline from the *Philadelphia Inquirer*?" Lenora pulls out a newspaper article. "Miss America Calls Out Bigotry of Beauty Pageants." "What in the world do you think you are doing?"

Bess is caught off guard. She hadn't thought that her recent event would be reported, hadn't considered how Lenora and her pageant allies would react.

Lenora's eyes are ablaze, and she clutches her fists as she continues to rant. "You've fallen into the clutches of the Jewish Communist garment manufacturers of New York City. You're betraying the people who gave the scholarship by allowing yourself to become a tool of the racial minorities."

"How can you say that? Betrayed them? You sent me to local pageants where I've talked up the scholarship program." Bess refuses to back down. "I brought the pageant more and better publicity than it has ever received before. If speaking the truth—and there is indeed bigotry in the Miss America process—if speaking the truth is wrong, then I accept responsibility for that error." Bess glares at Lenora. "So you now see me as a renegade, a political activist?"

Lenora remains tight-lipped and silent for a few moments before she responds. "I realize there could be some value to what you're doing. But the pressure that I'm under is enormous."

Bess knows those originally against her are convinced that their dire predictions have come true, that she is someone who must be caught and stopped. She realizes she's put Lenora in an untenable spot but can't back down now.

In April, Bess receives letters calling her a "nigger lover," telling her she has a lot of nerve to use her Miss America title "for that crap," suggesting the pageant take away her title. Other letters are from people thanking her for speaking out for racial and religious tolerance. Some even encourage her to continue her good work: "You are speaking as a true Miss America. Keep it up, and speak out damn loud."

Bess learns to speak more diplomatically and finds ways to compliment the Miss America Pageant for providing an opportunity for women, for encouraging scholarship and education. Privately, she continues to feel that the pageant could have used her voice and found a good cause for her to speak out about but didn't. The ADL has given her that platform and, through it, she has found her voice and her purpose. Her focus on injustice is freeing and is the right thing to do.

Do I want people to cheer for me as some empty symbol or for something I have done that's worthwhile? she asks herself. By now, it's a rhetorical question.

CHAPTER TWENTY-ONE

CARNEGIE HALL

May 1946

B ess sits on the piano bench at Dorothea LaFollette's studio, eager to work on the piece for her upcoming solo performance, now just one week away.

The invitation arrived last month. When Bess saw the Carnegie Hall letterhead, her heart skipped a beat. She tore through the envelope, her eyes immediately falling to the sender's name, actually to the title: Director of Booking. She quickly scanned the typewritten words and then shrieked, "Mama! Papa! I've been invited to play at Carnegie Hall!"

"What!? When? How did you find out?"

Bessie should have known that her mother would want every single fact. And that meant she had to read her the letter.

Bella's eyes widened that fateful afternoon as she listened to Bess recount the details: that she'd be playing as a soloist with the entire New York Philharmonic in a "pop" concert; that the conductor was Alfonso D'Artega; that the performance was scheduled for May 31. "I'm going to Aunt Fanny's apartment to share this marvelous news right now. The whole family must be there!"

That left Bess free to call her beloved piano teacher, her index finger shaking with each pull of the phone's dial. Dorothea let out an uncharacteristic squeal before she composed herself. "I *knew* it! It was just a matter of time! Now your exquisite talent will be heard on the world's finest stage!"

During their first practice session just a day later, they decided on "Full Moon and Empty Arms," a piece adapted from the third movement of Rachmaninoff's Piano Concerto no. 2 and one that fit well with the "pop" theme of the evening. The Carnegie Hall booking director allowed Bess to choose a piece, subject to their approval, which they gave immediately when she called them that day from Dorothea's apartment.

As Bess now sits down in Dorothea's salon to work on the piece, her teacher, as always, waits for Bess to get comfortable, sitting quietly next to her. Today, with the excitement building as the solo appearance nears, she has more to say. "This could be the turning point in your career we've been waiting for."

Bess remains silent. In three months, her reign is over. She doesn't think she's good enough for a career as a soloist despite Dorothea's encouragement, or even if it's what she wants. If she hadn't been Miss America, she knows she never would have had the chance to play at Carnegie Hall, although she is honored by the invitation and determined to make the most of this moment. It is why, when she's not taking lessons with Dorothea, Bess practices constantly at home, needing no prompts from Mama.

Dorothea stands and moves behind the bench, leaving Bess to situate herself comfortably in front of the keyboard. "I do think 'Full Moon and Empty Arms' is such a perfect piece to show off your talent. How about playing it straight through so I can assess your progress?"

Hitting the initial notes, Bess immediately feels the vibrancy of the piece. She plays it fast and lively, stirred by the melody. She is flushed when she finishes even though this adaption is only four minutes.

"Remember when I first played Rachmaninoff's concerto— the whole thing? It just wore me out. Its hand span is so challenging." She stretches her fingers beyond an octave on the keyboard and feels the strain. "I'm glad I'm not playing the first movement with all those wide-spread piano chords."

"Well, your long fingers and larger hands give you an advantage." Dorothea pencils some notations on the sheet music. "You nail the playful and sportive style of *allegro scherzando*. Just be ready at the start. The oboe and violas will introduce your entrance and the orchestration is soaring, so you'll need to maintain volume to be heard."

Bess plays the piece again, with more force and emotion.

Dorothea is pleased. "Mastery will come after you play it over and over, so it's imprinted in your head and your fingers. Keep up the practice, and we can work on this again at your next lesson."

Bess closes the sheet music and puts the score aside.

"I do think we need to prepare you for an encore. Is there a piece we've worked on over the years that comes to mind?" Dorothea tilts her head and raises her eyebrows.

Bess loves Dorothea's constant affirmation. Her teacher has been her lifeboat since childhood. "I'd like to play a pure classical piece for the encore. Maybe something by Chopin . . . remember when I played *Military Polonaise* for the M&A tryout?" Bess thinks through a list of her favorite compositions. "Maybe I'll play *Fantaisie-Impromptu*." Bess can hear the melodic range of emotive tones in her head. "I love that piece. The way the notes pile up. The speed, the intensity, and the precision it requires, almost as if one must conquer it, you know?"

⋄—⋄—⋄—⋄

The morning of the concert, Bess checks into the Park Central Hotel across from Carnegie Hall, a gorgeous classical-style building within a city block of Central Park. She's grateful to the pageant for arranging this convenience and luxury.

As a uniformed bellhop takes her small bag and escorts her to the elevator, Bess's mind fills with all the prominent musicians, actors, and notables who have stayed here—Mae West and Eleanor Roosevelt among them. When she arrives at her room, she turns the key in the lock and pushes the door open, taking in its spaciousness and elegance with its separate sitting area, dark wood paneling, iron chandeliers, and velvet drapery. She plops onto the king-size bed, reveling in its comfort—but just for a minute because she has a noon rehearsal at Carnegie Hall. After she puts away her belongings and hangs up her concert gown, she eagerly heads across the street, nearly an hour early.

She is wonderstruck by the scene before her. Stagehands are busy positioning chairs and music stands. Several men roll out the glossy Steinway & Sons grand piano to where a piano tuner waits to inspect each string. Her heart flutters when she sees a stack of concert programs. On its cover is a sketch of the brick-and-brownstone Italian Renaissance–style building stretching across an entire block of Seventh Avenue.

She lifts a playbill from the pile and rifles through to the page with the evening's schedule of selections and artists. Her eyes immediately lock on her name. Her pulse quickens. "Myerson, Bess" is listed under the heading "Soloists." Along with Bess is Lucille Manners, a soprano, who will sing numbers by Massenet, Tosti, Liszt, and Romberg. Following the first intermission, Rex Stewart, a cornet soloist formerly with Duke Ellington, will play "The Little Goose" with his instrumental sextet, along with improvisations under the title of "Jug Blues" and, later, with the seventy members of the Philharmonic Symphony Orchestra, the perennial favorite, "Boy Meets Horn." Following the second intermission is the orchestral feature of the evening, the first performance anywhere of D'Artega's "American Panorama," a symphonic tone poem of the Grand Canyon, with narrator Jim Ameche doing a reading.

The rehearsal is much like those she's experienced for the talent portion of the Miss America contest. But this time, as she sits on the Carnegie Hall stage at a Steinway grand piano with the New York Philharmonic behind her, it feels heady. She almost doesn't hear D'Artega asking her if she is ready to begin. She runs through her piece, then looks up and sees he's smiling. Now, her nervousness abated, she can better direct her attention to those on the stage with her. She assesses the conductor to be in his mid-thirties at most, detecting only a slight accent as he gently offers small suggestions to her, then to the entire string section. She stays to watch him lead all the other performances, most soloists playing their most challenging snippets and sometimes just the beginning and closing sections.

It is two thirty when she heads across the street to her hotel. She plans a nap because it will be a late night, the program not opening until eight thirty. She lays on the bed staring at the ceiling for nearly an hour, playing the keys and chords over and over in her head until she finally closes her eyes. For a light dinner, she calls room service, reminiscent of her days with Sylvia in Atlantic City.

Backstage, pillars of instrument cases are stacked along the walls while some orchestra members quietly drill their scales. Others amble onto the stage, settle into their chairs, adjust the sheet music on their music stands. Finally, as the lights dim and the hall falls silent inside, D'Artega walks past Bess in tails, his black hair slicked back. He smiles at her, his slim mustache curling upward, then enters the stage to loud applause.

She closes her eyes as the orchestra begins playing the opening piece, *Fantasia on Themes*, the playful and jazzy rendition of several of Gershwin's songs from *Porgy and Bess*. Hearing the melody of "Summertime" brings her back to the talent competition of Miss America. She is dazzled by the majestic and acoustically perfect hall, just like all the audiences have been for six decades.

She looks out at the assembled concertgoers from her darkened spot backstage, the mere size of the audience intimidating. She knows *her* people are out there. Mama made sure of that. But she focuses on the well-dressed men in gabardine suits, white shirts, and dark ties; the women wearing colorful suits and dresses. She imagines the smell of their cologne and perfume. She scans all five curvilinear levels of the grand space that must seat several thousand in those vibrant red velvet chairs.

So that she doesn't become completely unhinged, she backs up a few steps until it is time for her entrance.

• — • — •＋• — • — •

With her long-legged grace, Bess walks across the stage, her silk chiffon evening gown draping her lean body as she feels the heat of the lights above. A little voice in Bessie's head tries to tell her, *You don't belong here*, but she pushes it away as she looks out—proffering that wide-mouthed smile, those perfect white teeth—and bows to the crowd amid their applause. She shakes hands with Conductor D'Artega and then with the concertmaster, situates herself at the piano, moves the bench so it feels just right, places her feet near the pedals, and takes in a deep breath to calm herself. A hush falls over the enormous crowd. She looks over at the conductor and nods to him that she is ready. He raises his hands, and the orchestra members ready their instruments. He quickly looks toward the violas and oboe, then with his right hand indicates the beat of the music.

Bessie's performance could be described in many ways: vibrant, elegant, probing, lucid, exhilarating. Every musician knows Rachmaninoff could span an extraordinary twelve piano keys with each hand, and some of that is required here. But the reviews are yet to be written.

Once again, Bess hears applause from the large audience, and along with the "Bravos!" come the cries of "Mazel tov!" As she stands alongside D'Artega, bowing and smiling, she loses herself in this dream, this glorious and joyful trance that quiets and slows the world around her. He nods her on for an encore when the thunderous cheers refuse to abate. Bess places her hand on her heart in appreciation, bows again, then situates herself back in front of the giant black instrument for the Chopin.

The piece feels to her like hope rising from ashes. There's the frantic opening. The middle section that seems slower, almost like grieving, the rapid early theme returning, but then acceptance, as if she's crossed a long bridge. The notes end quietly and peacefully.

She turns to face the auditorium, letting the weight of the ovation wash over her. People are standing, applauding louder and louder. She receives it with her whole body, feeling her cheeks redden as the reverberating sound overtakes her. A young girl reaches up from the orchestra pit and hands Bess a bouquet of long-stemmed red roses.

This time, her mother is there to witness the acclamation.

———————

After two intermissions and the final orchestral numbers featuring work by Liszt, Romberg, and Reddick, the audience cheers, stands in ovation, and continues clapping as the orchestra members exit the stage. For Bess, backstage is a buzz of celebration with hugs, happy tears, and champagne among family and friends. Mama and Papa are the first to come on the scene, with Helen, Sylvia, Bill, and Bess's nieces in tow. Dorothea is one step behind, and barely minutes pass when Bess overhears Dorothea telling Mama how wonderful Bess's performance was and Mama replying, without skipping a beat, "I don't know why. The girl never practices."

Bess stands in the backstage area where musicians stream by with their instruments, giving her a nod or a smile; then she walks down the stage steps just in front of the first row to mingle with her Sholem Aleichem family, led by Aunt Fanny with cousin Hal. So many of her friends from elementary school through high school and college also hightailed to the front of the hall to grab her for a hug: Ruthie Singer, Harvey Katz, Murray Panitz, Lenny Miller, and Margie Wallis. Bess is surprised and honored to see her Music and Arts principal, Benjamin Steigman, and Mayor LaGuardia, who tells her that the evening has taken him back to his childhood when he performed on his cornet. Both pose with her for a photograph. Lenora Slaughter always seems to show up at occasions where she can blow the Miss America horn. Bess is particularly delighted to see John Pape. And Arnold Forster. She laughs with Malcolm Fried, reminiscing about her first real performance—of Olive Oyl. She imagines the snapshot of herself as the gangly damsel that she still has, tucked in the back of her wallet. Maybe she holds on to it to remind herself of how far she's come.

The group heads over to the Russian Tea Room, this time a more pleasant experience for Bess. Lenora's attitude toward her grew calmer, more professional, and respectful as the publicity around the Carnegie Hall concert helped the image of the pageant. Just days earlier, Bess received a letter from Lenora:

> *I am proud as can be of your scheduled appearance as the guest star of the Philharmonic Orchestra at Carnegie Hall this week. You certainly make the top spots, and everyone associated with the Pageant will agree with me that the reigning Miss America is about the finest and most accomplished person in the world. Good luck to you.*
>
> *With kindest regards, I am*
> *most cordially yours . . .*

Lenora released Bess's scholarship money when the Carnegie Hall concert was scheduled. Bess wastes no time buying a black baby grand Steinway, a Haynes flute, the complete *Grove's Dictionary of Music and Musicians*, dozens of orchestral scores and symphonic records, and a Victrola for her father. Instead of enrolling in Juilliard, the Curtis Institute, or anywhere else to get her master's degree—what she'd talked about during the pageant—she enrolls in a mix of graduate courses in music, elocution, and television at Columbia. And she remains, as always, ambivalent and indecisive about her future.

•———•——•——•——•———•

As the evening's revelry continues around her at the Tea Room—with the concert now in the rearview mirror, the congratulations finished, the newspaper interviews complete, her family gone hours earlier—Bess retreats inward, away from the swirl of the celebration. Deep down, she knows she will never be a concert artist despite Dorothea's dreams for her. She is beginning to accept, and own, her accomplishments—especially how she is using her voice to fight for social justice—although part of her still seeks approval from others, still is hungry for love and acceptance. To everyone else, she is the most beautiful girl alive. Yet some part of her remains, always, Olive Oyl.

While she's shown some moxie and independence, she's self-aware enough to know that she doesn't like being alone. Many of her friends are getting married, some already pregnant. The message she hears all around her is that women need to give up their jobs for the returning veterans, and for the sake of country and personal happiness, they should tend to household and family. The idea of a cozy home and of being cared for by an all-providing husband who keeps her protected is tempting.

Her mind drifts to the handsome navy officer she met just weeks earlier when she was in Atlantic City at Lenora's request, signing autographs and taking photos with manufacturers at a toy convention. Allan Wayne had just returned from four years in the Pacific and was spending time with his father, who was renting exhibit space. Letting her lids grow heavy, she pictures him as if he's standing before her: his dark wavy hair, deep-set brown eyes, and alluring smile. How he is even taller than she is. He introduced himself to her, immediately telling her he heard about her winning when he was still overseas. That, as a Jew himself, he was so proud that a Jewish girl had captured the crown. She holds on to the image of him in his crisp captain's uniform and reflects for a moment on how comfortable he made her feel. A safe harbor.

Bess excuses herself from the gathering, her purse and red roses in hand, and walks out of the Russian Tea Room across Seventh Avenue. From the lobby of her hotel, she rides the elevator to her room on the twenty-fifth floor. Sleepily, she looks out the window, imagining the trees and expanse of Central Park just beyond her view. Hearing the honking of cars, she presses closer, her forehead touching the glass. She makes out the headlights along the street and the tiny people on the sidewalk down below, the city still teeming with life despite the late hour.

How strangely her young life has turned out to be: a beauty queen who spent every day studying so she could get the highest grade in her classes, practicing and honing her musical repertoire; a piano soloist at Carnegie Hall because she won a pageant that judged her appearance in a swimsuit and an evening gown. How utterly inconceivable that a poor Jewish girl from the Bronx was chosen to be Miss America as the world tries to heal from the wounds of the most terrible bigotry.

She lifts her focus from the thoroughfare as a flash of light in the night sky draws her eye. It is brilliant, powerful, a distant star twinkling and glowing. She is now fully awake.

EPILOGUE

*Character is destiny. And the one thing that is important
to me above all is my character, my reputation.*
—Bess Myerson

During Bess Myerson's time with the Anti-Defamation
League's Brotherhood Campaign, a newspaper article
predicted that she would probably be remembered longer
than most of her Miss America predecessors. That statement
turned out to be prescient, as she went on to spend much of her
life in the public eye, making extraordinary achievements for a
woman in mid-twentieth-century America and continuing her
important work with the ADL advocating for social justice. In
many ways, the tolerance campaign opened doors for her, first
in television, then in politics, where she became one of the most
powerful women in New York City government. It was only in
her personal life that ill-considered, and at times reckless, choices
threatened to compromise her hard-earned reputation.

Soon after her reign concluded, she did the traditional act
and got married. It was what she'd always yearned for, what was
expected for women at that time, and the only way that Bess
could avoid returning to her family's cramped apartment in the

Bronx since no woman in her community left home to get her own apartment and live independently. After meeting US Navy captain Allan Wayne, she took him home to meet her parents in the summer of 1946. They eloped that fall. A more formal wedding thrown by Allan's parents at the Waldorf Astoria followed in December.

Spending most of her first year of marriage at home and teaching piano, she began to feel that something was missing from her life. She gave birth to her only child, Barbara, in late 1947. As her daughter approached her third birthday, Bess started working on a musical quiz show in the new medium of television, something she'd been interested in pursuing since taking graduate courses at Columbia. The quiz show led to a weekly interview program for housewives. Allan was supportive of Bess's work outside the home, a bold choice at that time, as long as her priority remained her role as wife and mother.

She kept a busy schedule, still committed to the ADL's campaign and to raising money at dinners for Israel bonds. At one of these fundraising dinners, her personality and presence impressed a television producer named Walt Framer. He offered her a job on a game show called *The Big Payoff*, first broadcast at the end of 1951, that went on to become one of TV's most successful giveaway programs. Throughout the show's eight-year network run, Myerson was "the Lady in Mink"—modeling the grand-prize mink coat, introducing guests, and announcing prizes. She returned as host of the Miss America pageant in 1954 and filled that role for the next fourteen years, sometimes with distinguished cohosts like Walter Cronkite.

It was shortly after Bess's initial appearances hosting the pageant that Allan started drinking and Bess's marriage to him began to crumble. A bitter custody battle for their nine-year-old daughter ensued, and the couple finally divorced in 1958.

The very public divorce took its toll on Bess. She was thirty-four, a single mother, and financially insecure, *The Big Payoff* her only steady paycheck. She regularly subbed for Dave Garroway as host of NBC's *Today Show*—groundbreaking for a woman at that time—and, after *The Big Payoff* was canceled, she announced the commercials on *The Jackie Gleason Show* and *Philco Playhouse*. After appearing on the popular weekly prime-time show *I've Got a Secret* with host Garry Moore, in 1958 she replaced Jayne Meadows as a panelist and remained on the program until it went off the air nine years later. For many years, Myerson hosted television coverage of the Macy's Thanksgiving Day Parade and the Tournament of Roses Parade.

In 1962, Myerson remarried wealthy finance and tax attorney Arnold Grant. An acrimonious relationship from the outset, the couple split in 1967, wedding again a year later. Meanwhile, Allan Wayne died, so Grant adopted Bess's daughter, who'd changed her name to Barra.

During the 1960s and into the next decade, Myerson served on several presidential commissions on violence, mental health, workplace issues, and hunger—work that spoke to her lifelong desire to make a difference in the world.

In 1969, she received a call from the office of New York Mayor John Lindsay about a job in his administration. Within a few weeks, she was named the first commissioner of New York City's Department of Consumer Affairs. Telling the press that her experience for this position came from watching her mother bargain with shopkeepers, she plunged energetically into the work and was noted by others as an extraordinarily effective public servant and an astute executive, hiring a legal staff who helped her establish tougher consumer-protection laws. She became the most visible city official apart from the mayor during the years she served under him. Through that period, New York City had what was considered the most far-reaching consumer-protection legislation in the country, with more than $5 million returned to defrauded customers over her tenure. In 1971, she made the cover of *Life* magazine as "A Consumer's Best Friend," having set up a hotline and a Consumer Action Team that conducted daily surprise raids at businesses in high-complaint areas.

Soon after, Myerson and Arnold Grant divorced for the second and final time.

By 1973, she chose to slow down. She resigned from Consumer Affairs to focus on her financial security, accepting a lucrative job as a consumer consultant to Citibank, later taking a similar post at Bristol Myers. But in 1974, she was diagnosed with ovarian cancer. While keeping the illness private, she gradually reentered the social and political worlds. In 1977, she served as campaign chair for Ed Koch's successful run for New York City mayor.

Building on her reputation under the Lindsay administration, she published a guide, *The Complete Consumer Book*, in 1979. After losing the Democratic nomination for the United States Senate in 1980 and suffering a mild stroke the next year, she coauthored a book based on diets developed by New York City's Bureau of Nutrition in 1982 that became a *New York Times* bestseller called *The I Love New York Diet*.

Myerson was again appointed to a city post, this time as the commissioner of Cultural Affairs, which she served from 1983 to 1987 under Mayor Koch. There she doubled the budget to better support the city's museums and other cultural institutions.

After two troubled marriages, Myerson's personal life was subject to close public scrutiny. But her most controversial relationship involved a much younger wealthy sewer contractor named Andy Capasso, whom she'd met while campaigning for the Senate nomination. She was accused of bribery and conspiracy to influence his divorce case, and an investigation led to her indictment by a federal grand jury on charges including conspiracy, mail fraud, and obstruction of justice. She was acquitted of all charges after a highly visible three-month trial in 1988, fodder for much tabloid coverage. The affair with Capasso and its subsequent controversy ended her long career in public service.

In later years, she largely avoided the limelight. She occasionally gave lectures and pursued charity work, mainly for Jewish causes, and she remained loyal to the mission of the ADL, where she had served as national commissioner and endowed a $100,000 scholarship fund. She continued to act as a spokesperson for Israel Bonds, was honored by United Jewish Appeal, and was a founder of the Museum of Jewish Heritage in New York, housing the Bess Myerson Film and Video Collection.

In 2002, Bess Myerson moved to Florida and later to California, where she remained until her death in 2014 at the age of ninety.

AUTHOR'S NOTE

After completing my World War II novel-in-stories, *A Ritchie Boy*, I came across an article regarding Bess Myerson, a talented Jewish beauty who became Miss America in 1945. While well aware of that distinction, what astonished me was the *timing* of her triumph, given the degree of antisemitism in this country during the 1930s and '40s. Myerson's victory took place *six days* after the official end of the Second World War, just weeks after the United States dropped bombs on Japan. I was familiar with the general outlines of her later life, especially her prominence in New York City politics in the 1980s when I lived in the city. But my curiosity led me to read several biographies about Myerson. After what I learned, I decided to fictionally focus on her formative years—the moral and psychological growth of this consequential woman. Following a brief prologue set in 1945 Atlantic City, my narrative begins when the preteen Bessie reaches her adult height of nearly six feet in 1936. I take the reader through a decade to the end of her yearlong reign as Miss America.

Bessie is a work of fiction. I chose to inhabit the emotional essence of Bess Myerson as she grew into a young woman, bring new insight to historical events, and remain faithful to the facts of her life. Some of the characters I've included in this novel, besides Bess Myerson herself, are inspired by actual people but used fictionally, while others are imagined. However, the history within these pages is true. I have remained as close as I could to the actual events that made up Bess Myerson's early life. Sometimes I briefly quote her actual words if I found them quoted in published works, or I create dialogue based on conversations reported indirectly. Elsewhere, I have imagined what might have or could have been said and created certain scenarios that might have taken place based on the true events in her life and the time in which they happened. The backdrop of isolationism, antisemitism, racism, and sexism were the context of Bess Myerson's world in the 1930s and '40s. My novel reflects that reality.

One example of mixing fact with fiction appears late in the novel when Bess meets with Miss Sepia America, Dolores Fairfax. While Bess Myerson indeed appeared on a panel with Dolores in Philadelphia in early 1946, I never found the details of that encounter. This was the perfect chance to imagine what could have happened. And I did, creating a significant scene where Bess calls out the bigotry within the Miss America pageant. I naturally had to follow that with an imagined confrontation Bess has with pageant director Lenora Slaughter.

I am indebted to several sources for the facts, the chronology, and circumstantial details surrounding Bess Myerson's childhood and her rise to become Miss America.

In reconstructing Bess's life, most helpful was the 1987 biography by Susan Dworkin, *Miss America, 1945: Bess Myerson and the Year That Changed Our Lives.* I read two other biographies, both released in 1990, that included Myerson's early years but focused more on later controversies of her adult life: *Queen Bess: An Unauthorized Biography of Bess Myerson* by Jennifer Preston and *When She Was Bad: The Story of Bess, Hortense, Sukhreet & Nancy* by Shana Alexander.

Enormously helpful for my understanding of New York City during the war years and other details of history was *Victory City: A History of New York and New Yorkers During World War II* (2019) by John Strausbaugh. Margot Mifflin's 2020 book, *Looking for Miss America: A Pageant's 100-Year Quest to Define Womanhood*, provided insight into the historic elements of this beauty contest. I was thrilled to discover an entire book about the genesis of the High School of Music and Art, written by its first principal, Benjamin Steigman, *Accent on Talent: New York's High School of Music and Art* (1964). Similarly, I found a book to help me capture Bess's college years: *Hunter College* by Joan M. Williams (2000). Corroborating much of my research was Lillian Ross's wonderful October 15, 1949, article in *The New Yorker*, "Here She Comes, Miss America, 1949," along with many other articles written through the decades up until Myerson's death in 2014. I am most appreciative of the Anti-Defamation League for providing me with archival material, including ADL bulletins from 1946 and its 1946 annual report, which was great background about Bess Myerson's role as the voice for ADL's Brotherhood Campaign.

When I am writing about real people Bess had a relationship with, I have used their names, such as her relatives; her piano teacher Dorothea LaFollette; some of her friends like Murray Panitz, Margie Wallis, and Lenny Miller; as well as those tied to the Miss America Pageant, from emcee Bob Russell to Lenora Slaughter to the contestants who are named. I have fictionalized scenes and interactions among these real and imagined characters.

On occasion, I had to alter certain dates, and I'll try to clarify my reasons here. First, the *Bronx Press-Review*, a local borough-wide newspaper covering local news, politics, and community events, wasn't established until 1940, but I have Louis Myerson reading it in 1936 because I wanted to establish the Bronx setting.

At the High School of Music and Art, the first class of students was admitted on February 1, 1936 (125 art students and

125 music students). One might presume subsequent admissions fell that way. Bessie actually was admitted to the school in early 1937 and graduated in January rather than June of 1941, as I have written. I departed from that time to align with what is more typical of today, having her end her elementary school year in early June and begin high school in early September. I also took liberties with some of the facts about M&A. For example, string orchestra is typically introduced in the second year, not the first. Thus, senior orchestra might be assigned at the end of the second year, not the first, with students joining in the junior year rather than a year earlier.

Since I couldn't confirm that Bess struck up a friendship with illustrator and later cofounder of *Mad Magazine*, Harvey Kurtzman, although he attended M&A when she did, I didn't use Harvey's real name but modeled Harvey Katz after Harvey Kurtzman. In my manuscript, Will Eisen was inspired by another student who attended M&A: Wolfie William Eisenberg, who later became known as Will Elder and went on to become a well-known American illustrator and comic book artist and helped Harvey Kurtzman launch *Mad Magazine*.

For confused sports readers of Chapter 7: In 1941, New York hosted both baseball and football teams called the Giants. The baseball Giants competed in Major League Baseball (MLB) as a member club of the National League (NL). Founded in 1883 as the New York Gothams, and renamed three years later as the New York Giants, the team eventually moved to San Francisco in 1958. The football Giants are part of the National Football League. They were founded in 1925 and legally named "New York Football Giants" to distinguish themselves from the baseball team of the same name. They were one of the first teams in the NFL, which formed in 1920. For further confusion, the Brooklyn Dodgers were an American football team that played in the NFL from 1930 to 1943, and they played in 1944 as the Brooklyn Tigers.

In Chapter 11, I introduce a Seventh Avenue fashion designer who I call Samuel Knapp. His real name is Samuel Kass, but I thought it would be confusing to use it, given his last name is the same as mine. Most often, I used the real name of people if the situation I dramatize happened, and this one did.

Finally, when I found actual letters or speeches, like the letters Lenora Slaughter sent to all Miss America contestants or speeches Bess gave as part of ADL's Brotherhood Campaign, I used their exact wording, although I slightly edited some of Bessie's speeches during the ADL campaign. For example, "Aren't we 'America the Beautiful'?" was not in her original text.

Just days after the close of World War II, the insecure, scholarly, and musically gifted daughter of Russian Jewish immigrants from the Bronx rises to a place where she represents an ideal against all odds. She grows up in an antisemitic America, a country filled with all kinds of bigotry, all too similar to our country today. Yet Bessie reaches beyond her insular beginnings, as an underdog who triumphs. My hope is that Bess Myerson's rise to become Miss America reminds you that talent, hard work, and fair play *can* be rewarded, that everyone has a shot. Most importantly, I hope you see a young girl thirsting to go beyond her beauty and talent, to find purpose and to make a difference in her world. As a young woman, Bess Myerson used her gifts to take action and help others as a voice for the ADL's Brotherhood Campaign to fight hate. Through its blending of fact and fiction, and through the context of this unique moment in American history, *Bessie* might inspire us all to use our voices to fight hate.

ACKNOWLEDGMENTS

Thanks are due to many.

First to my friend and writing mentor, Ellen Lesser, for her steadfast guidance through the years and for her strong encouragement that I pursue my desire to bring the young Bess Myerson to life on the page.

Heartfelt thanks to the extraordinary staff at my Columbus-area bookstore, Gramercy Books. I am so grateful for all that you do to enthusiastically connect our community of readers with the books they love. And I am honored by, and grateful for, the bookstores and libraries who have chosen to place my books on their shelves.

Thank you to the staff at She Writes Press and the team who helped me bring *Bessie* to the world; theirs is a partnership I cherish. Special gratitude to publisher Brooke Warner who is a role model and inspiration for me and so many writers, and to Lauren Wise who did so much to ensure a smooth editorial and production process. Also, to Barrett Briske, Julie Metz, Caitlin Hamilton Summie, Rick Summie, Lucinda Dyer, Paula Sherman, Libby Jordan, Alex Baker, Terri Dusseau, Lisa Hinson, Rich Yepsen.

I'm grateful for my first readers and those who took the time to offer helpful feedback: Davi Blake, John Gaylord, Ruth Guzner, Pamela Klinger-Horn, Alex Kass-Friedman, Julia Keller, Ann Kirschner, Estelle Rodgers, Alec Wightman.

For guidance in my research, thanks go to Deputy National Director Ken Jacobson and Senior Librarian and Archivist Miriam Spectre at the Anti-Defamation League, and to Angela O'Neal, manager of the Local History & Genealogy section at Columbus Metropolitan Library.

I am indebted to all the writers I know who have given me advice throughout my journey as an author, and to those big-hearted souls who read this manuscript and offered their endorsement. I'm also filled with gratitude to readers everywhere. Finding truth through story is our hope for a kinder world.

My love and gratefulness to my family, and family of friends, whose support I treasure every day, especially my husband, Frank, my first reader and biggest advocate.

Finally, to the inspiration of Bess Myerson, a woman who used her beauty and talents to fight for tolerance and social justice.

MUSIC FEATURED IN *BESSIE*

Warner Theatre
Atlantic City
- Edvard Grieg, Piano Concerto in A Minor
- George Gershwin, "Summertime" (Arr. for flute)

Chapter One
Olive Oyl
- Johann Sebastian Bach, *The Well-Tempered Clavier*

Chapter Two
Tar Beach
- Ludwig van Beethoven, "Fur Elise"
- Johann Sebastian Bach, Minuet in G Major
- Eric Satie, *Gymnopedie* No. 1
- Wolfgang Amadeus Mozart, *Don Giovanni*, K. 127: "Deh! Vieni Alla Finestra"
- Wolfgang Amadeus Mozart, *Die Zauberflote*, "Der Vogelfanger Bin Ich Ja"

Chapter Three
ESCAPE THROUGH MUSIC
- Ludwig van Beethoven, "Fur Elise"
- Johann Sebastian Bach, Minuet in D Minor
- Wolfgang Amadeus Mozart, Piano Sonata No. 11 in A Major, Alla Turca Third movement
- Frederic Chopin, Prelude Op. 28 No. 20 in C Minor
- Frederic Chopin, *Military Polonaise*
- Wolfgang Amadeus Mozart, Concerto No. 23 in A Major: II. *Adagio*
- Wolfgang Amadeus Mozart, *The Marriage of Figaro*

Chapter Four
A SPECIAL HIGH SCHOOL
- Frederic Chopin, *Military Polonaise*

Chapter Five
SOPHOMORE YEAR
- George Gershwin, Piano Concert in F Major (I. *Allegro*; II. *Adagio*; III. *Allegro agitato)*
- George Gershwin, "Summertime" (Arr. for flute)
- Ludwig van Beethoven, Piano Sonata No. 8 in C Minor, Op 13: *Pathetique*
- George Gershwin, *Rhapsody in Blue*

Chapter Six
A GIRL CAN DO; A GIRL CAN BE
- Wolfgang Amadeus Mozart, Quartet in F Major for Oboe, Violin, Viola, and Cello
- Edvard Grieg, Piano Concerto in A Minor
- Ludwig van Beethoven, Symphony No. 5 in C Minor, Op. 67: I. *Allegro*
- Franz Schubert, Symphony No. 8 in B Minor, "Unfinished" Symphony

Chapter Seven
THE WAR BEGINS; HUNTER COLLEGE AND THE 68 CLUB
- Edvard Grieg, Piano Concerto in A Minor
- George Gershwin: Piano Concerto in F; *An American in Paris;* "Summertime"

Chapter Eight
SUMMER CAMP AND WAVES
- Harold Arlen and Ted Koehler, "Stormy Weather"
- Kansas Joe McCoy, "Why Don't You Do Right?"
- June Allyson, Victoria Schools, Nancy Walker, "The Three B's"
- Glenn Miller, "Chattanooga Choo Choo;" "A String of Pearls"
- Joseph Copeland Garland: "In The Mood"

Chapter Ten
MISS NEW YORK CITY
- Edvard Grieg, Piano Concerto in A Minor
- George Gershwin, "Summertime" (Arr. for flute)

Chapter Eleven
MEDIA WHIRLWIND; PANIC SETS IN
- Frederick Chopin: *Fantaisie-Impromptu*

Chapter Fourteen
OPENING NIGHT, TALENT COMPETITION
- Otto Harbach and Oscar Hammerstein, "Indian Love Call"
- Dorothy Fields and Jimmy McHugh, "I'm in the Mood for Love"
- Channing Pollock (English lyrics), "My Man"
- Edvard Grieg, Piano Concerto in A Minor
- George Gershwin, "Summertime" (Arr. for flute)

Chapter Fifteen
EVENING GOWN AND SWIMSUIT COMPETITION
- Hank Fort and Herb Leighton, "I Didn't Know the Gun was Loaded"
- Fats Waller and Harry Brooks, "Ain't Misbehavin'"

Chapter Sixteen
THE FINAL DAY!
- Francis Scott Key, "The Star-Spangled Banner"
- Debussy, *Clair de lune*
- Buddy Kaye and Ted Mossman, "'Till the End of Time"

Chapter Seventeen
THE TOUR BEGINS WITH VAUDEVILLE
- Manuel de Falla, "The Ritual Fire Dance"

Chapter Eighteen
VICTORY BONDS AND VETERANS
- Debussy, *Clair de lune*
- Albert Ellmenreich, "Spinning Song"

Chapter Nineteen
TRAVELING THE SOUTH
- Debussy, *Clair de lune*

Chapter Twenty-One
CARNEGIE HALL
- "Full Moon and Empty Arms" (arranged from the third movement of Rachmaninoff's Piano Concerto No. 2)
- Frederic Chopin, *Military Polonaise*
- Frederick Chopin: *Fantaisie-Impromptu*
- Rex Stewart: "The Little Goose;" "Jug Blues;" "Boy Meets Horn"
- Alfonso D'Artega, "American Panorama"
- George Gershwin, *Fantasia on Themes*, "Summertime"

Note: Bess Myerson performed "Summertime" on the flute, along with her Grieg piano concerto, in both the Miss New York City and Miss America talent competitions. This piece is an aria that was composed in 1934 by George Gershwin for the 1935 opera, *Porgy and Bess.* It soon became popular and much recorded. Gershwin's highly evocative writing brilliantly mixes elements of jazz and the song styles of Blacks in the southeast United States from the early twentieth century. This connects to Bessie's later work against racism.

READER'S GUIDE

1. Why do you think Bessie was so insecure, always seeking approval and acceptance?
2. How do you think Bessie's family life affected who she became?
3. What was the impact of the community of Sholem Aleichem on forming Bessie's character?
4. What did the role of music play in Bessie's life? What did Bessie love so much about performing?
5. What role did Dorothea LaFollette play in Bessie's life?
6. What do you think was the impact of attending the High School of Music and Art on Bessie's growth and development?
7. How do you think the war itself impacted Bessie's college life?
8. Do you think Bessie would have competed in Miss America had there not been a $5,000 scholarship?
9. What relationships do you think had the strongest impact on Bessie?
10. What role did Sylvia play in Bessie's life?
11. Talk about the relationship Bess had with Lenora Slaughter.
12. How do you think a Jewish girl like Bess Myerson overcame the bigotry of her time to rise above it and be held in such esteem?

13. Why do you think it was hard for Bessie to accept her own beauty?
14. Do you think accomplished and beautiful women today have difficulty being seen for, and given credit for, their accomplishments?

ABOUT THE AUTHOR

L inda Kass is the author of two historical novels, *Tasa's Song* and *A Ritchie Boy*. She began her career as a magazine journalist and correspondent for regional and national publications. She is the founder and owner of Gramercy Books, an independent bookstore in Columbus, Ohio.

Author photo © Lorn Spolter

SELECTED TITLES FROM SHE WRITES PRESS

She Writes Press is an independent publishing company founded to serve women writers everywhere. Visit us at www.shewritespress.com.

Little Woman in Blue: A Novel of May Alcott by Jeannine Atkins. $16.95, 978-1-63152-987-0. Based May Alcott's letters and diaries, as well as memoirs written by her neighbors, Little Woman in Blue puts May at the center of the story she might have told about sisterhood and rivalry in her extraordinary family.

A Ritchie Boy by Linda Kass. $16.95, 978-1-63152-739-5. The inspiring World War II tale of Eli Stoff, a Jewish Austrian immigrant who triumphs over adversity and becomes a US Army intelligence officer, told as a cohesive linked collection of stories narrated by a variety of characters. Based on true events.

Among the Beautiful Beasts: A Novel by Lori McMullen. $16.95, 978-1-64742-106-9. The untold story of the early life of Marjory Stoneman Douglas, a tireless activist for the Florida Everglades in the early 1900s—and a woman ultimately forced to decide whether to commit to a life of subjugation or leap into the wild unknown.

Hysterical: Anna Freud's Story by Rebecca Coffey. $18.95, 978-1-93831-442-1. An irreverent, fictionalized exploration of the seemingly contradictory life of Anna Freud—told from her point of view.

An Address in Amsterdam by Mary Dingee Fillmore. $16.95, 978-1-63152-133-1. After facing relentless danger and escalating raids for 18 months, Rachel Klein—a well-behaved young Jewish woman who transformed herself into a courier for the underground when the Nazis invaded her country—persuades her parents to hide with her in a dank basement, where much is revealed.

Stitching a Life: An Immigration Story by Mary Helen Fein. $16.95, 978-1-63152-677-0. After sixteen-year-old Helen, a Jewish girl from Russia, comes alone across the Atlantic to the Lower East Side of New York in the year 1900, she devotes herself to bringing the rest of her family to safety and opportunity in the new world—and finds love along the way.